MY *Life* IS MINE

First Printed in a hardback edition
under the title
To Save a Life

SHIRLEY SEALY

Covenant Communications, Inc.
American Fork, Utah

Printed in the United States of America
First Printing: July 1989
94 95 96 97   10 9 8 7 6 5 4 3

Library of Congress Catalog Card Number:89–091740
First printed in hardover edition by Butterfy Press, 1980
under the title *To Save a Life*
ISBN 1–55503–129–3

Cover photo by Steve Feld

Thanks to: Loni Mae Sealy Hatch for her research papers
Covenant for publishing this printing
My readers who constantly keep me writing.

"With empathy we recognize hurts in the lives of others and bend to lend our love—and thus perfect unrecognized faults in ourselves".
Shirley Sealy

Chapter One

Signee Short was as individual as her name. She was the youngest of ten children born to a Mormon family. Some had supposed the Shorts had simply run out of names and just started putting letters together, but whatever the origin of her name, no one could deny that by the time Signee returned from college to teach English-Drama in the only high school at Green Village, Signee Short was already something of a legend.

Twice in her young years, Signee had been expected to take her marrige vows; and twice she had changed her mind with no apparent reason or good explanation, which left room for a lot of talk in a small town. But the gossip that followed her decisions had soon died down, for Signee was well liked and came from a strong, religious family of integrity. To top the reputation of her family, Signee herself had achieved a record in scholastic ability and social activity that was an example to all who cared to research. But Signee was watched and wondered about....

"Come on, Siggie," protested big Deek Pendalton, using the nickname of the favorite young teacher of Green Village High, "not on game day, there's a tradition about that." He smiled and

1

pointed his finger at her. "And you should know that."

"And Deeky..." Signee Short changed his name as he had hers, "the way you play, you won't have to lean on tradition to win. However, I do feel you need discipline, if today is any example. Now, open your books and get ready for your test before I add sections four and five." The cute, short teacher spoke to big Deek but made her remarks applicable to the entire English class.

"Siggie, I think you're serious. I can't believe you, knowing you're a sports fan. Why, back a few years Green Village couldn't have gone to State if you hadn't been head cheerleader."

"I have nothing against sports. We need good athletes, but along with sports we also need...."

"A little more culture and some good drama," echoed the class, obviously well-schooled in the phrase.

"I'm glad you understand my point of view." Signee smiled. "And someday, when I get my Little Theater, you'll understand why I am so intense about drama ... along with English, of course."

"Of course. We can count on Siggie," said Deek, moving his head back and forth to emphasize his words as he mimicked her. "Can't we, guys?"

His question was met with exuberant ad-libs from every desk in the room. Miss Short brought her hand down on her desk with a bang.

"That will do," she said, trying to be stern. It wasn't easy for Signee to teach English and drama in her own home town, especially when she looked as young as the students she was teaching and when many of them remembered her before she became a teacher. "Now, will you please open your books to the test page. We can at least review."

"Right! We can at least review," said Deek in an exaggerated serious voice, as he opened his book and sat up high on the back of his desk chair.

"Deek Pendalton, you are being obnoxious, you know that?" Her voice was stern, but there was a smile creeping around the corners of her mouth.

"I do know that," he nodded, still mimicking her words, careful not to smile this time.

"If we just didn't need you in the game so badly today, I would be tempted to make you take the test alone."

"Oh...." he moaned with all the drama he was quite capable of, "not alone, not that ... anything but that."

"Must I remind you that you have to finish your work by the end of next week if I am not to hand out some very poor grades? I have the authority...."

"She sure does," said Deek, standing up and waving his arms as if making a presidential speech. "Why, in this room our Siggie has more authority than the principal...."

"All right, Deek ... you've had your fun. Now sit down and open your book."

"Yes, you bet ... I sure will, Miss Siggie ..." Deek sat down, and the class followed his lead. They sat at attention, pencils in hand, waiting for another signal from Captain Deek. He was captain of the football team, and it seemed to carry over into other departments as well.

"All right," said Signee, closing her own book and walking in front of her desk. "I can see we aren't going to be serious today. And I will forgive you for a very disrupted class if you win the game today." She finished talking with the smile her students had learned to recognize as a signal that she was pal and not teacher for the moment. Deek promptly threw his book in the air and caught it. "Minta ... " he beckoned to the cute dark girl who sat across the aisle, "three cheers for Siggie."

Minta promptly went into her cheering act, and Deek and some of the other football players moved forward to pick up the small teacher, hoisting her to stand on her desk as the others crowded around. She knew it was useless to protest, so she joined in the fun for a moment. Then she raised her arms for silence.

"I have just been informed that today in your pep assembly you will have a special speaker ... Eric Langdon. Mr. Langdon is an alumnus of this school, and he was a member of the state championship team the year I graduated. Be nice to him, will you? He's a friend of mine." Another yell went up and she finished with, "You are all free to go now."

Another cheer, and the class started toward the door. Deek gave Signee his hand, and she jumped off the desk. He leaned his face close to Signee and spoke as if they were sharing a secret.

"I hear our speaker is more than just a friend ... an old boyfriend, huh?"

Signee felt her face warm to a sunburn temperature as she tried to answer Deek assuredly. "Eric Langdon and I were very good friends, and I am also a friend of his wife." Signee straightened the bow of her blouse.

Deek winked at her. "So I've heard. She caught him on the rebound, didn't she?"

"She did not!" Signee was suddenly furious, her face burning.

"Ah ... I have touched a tender spot."

"You have not."

"Careful, Siggie, I take psychology, you know ... when you protest too loudly ... ?"

"Deek Pendalton, you are a smarty and you think you are well informed, but nothing could be further from the truth. If you spread any rumors that might hurt my friends, I'll...."

"Siggie ... Siggie ... take it easy." Deek reached out to pat her shoulder. "Would I do anything to hurt a friend of my friend...?" He straightened up, smiling, but the glint in his eyes suggested they had a common secret. "Siggie, no kidding. I'm your friend."

"Deek...."

"No problem, Siggie," he said, lifting her up on the desk again, her short legs dangling above the floor, "and I can tell you something else. Whoever he is, this Eric Langdon and I have a lot in common."

Before Signee could rebuff anything Deek said, he had turned and was leaving. Signee watched as he filed in behind the students crowding through the door. Then she saw Minta Morgan, who seemed to have been lingering by her desk until Deek left, make her way to crowd in behind him.

"Minta!" called Signee, just as Minta was about to bump purposely into Deek. "Minta, may I see you just a moment before you leave?"

"Sure," answered Minta, knowing the request had been too loud to ignore, since everybody had also heard and turned when she turned. Even Deek turned around and gave her a look of "oh, you again...." But Minta smiled up at him as she backed

4

away in the direction of Miss Signee Short.

"I'm here," said Minta, obviously annoyed at the interruption. "What can I do for you, Miss Short?"

"Minta, I have considered your request to be allowed to make up your test."

"Funny you should find the time for me at this particular moment."

"Wasn't this a good moment?"

"Perfect from your point of view, I suppose."

"Would you like to explain what you mean?"

Minta glanced at the doorway where Deek and the others had disappeared; then, deciding they were alone, she faced Signee.

"Why is it, Siggie, that every time you see me anywhere near Deek Pendalton, you find some excuse to want to talk to me right then? Oh, this isn't the first time it has happened; shall I give you a list? I have mentally recorded...."

"You could be right, Minta..." said Signee, aware that Minta was startled at her admission. "I have tried to help you."

"Help me?" Minta's voice raised to a shouty pitch.

"Minta, you are a very pretty, very alive girl ... but you are forward with boys." Signee felt Minta's mouth drop open and knew she was leaving herself open to criticism, especially since Minta's father was the principal of Green Village High School. But she went on anyway. "I know you like Deek, Minta, but can't you see that he's annoyed when you always 'just happen' to be where he is?"

"I don't know what you are talking about."

"I'm sure you do." Signee was speaking kindly but truthfully. "Just now, you waited until Deek was through talking to me, and then you followed him."

"I was leaving the room, and he just happened to be in front of me."

"Do you really want me to believe that? I have seen...."

"I don't care what you think you've seen. And who are you to give advice, anyway? What do you know about men? A school teacher! I don't see any boyfriends hanging around you. If you're trying to live your school days over again, don't do it on my time."

"All right, Minta. I wanted to help, but I can't if you won't let me. It may make you feel better to insult me with what you think you know than to listen to what you don't want to hear. I'm sorry. From now on....."

"From now on, stay out of my life until you get your own life unkinked." Minta turned and walked away fast, then at the door she stopped and looked back. "You never did say what you wanted me to do about my test. But I guess that's all off now. Well, go ahead and flunk me. You know I have to pass your test to get my credit, and you can really hurt me ... so go ahead."

"I have no intention of hurting you in any way." Signee's voice had a tired sound. "If you are interested in making up your work, I have a lot of papers to correct on that test. I was going to ask you to come and correct papers; you could read the material as you correct, then we could make up another test from the same material covered. If you are interested in that plan, be at my home tomorrow morning."

"The day after the dance?"

"Suit yourself; that's when I work on my test papers."

"I'll be there," said Minta grudgingly.

Minta was gone, and Signee was glad; she was still feeling the warm color in her face from Deek's reference to Eric Langdon. If any of those stories made the rounds and Eric's wife, Alta, heard them, ... but there wasn't time to think about that; Signee only had time to lock her desk and get into the gym for pep assembly. Alta had called her just before school started to ask if they could meet in their regular old corner, the spot above where the pep club and the men's association roped off seats.

As Signee entered the gym she looked across the hall, and Alta Wendall Langdon was there. Eric was on the other side of the gym, talking to the cheerleaders and the coach. Signee lifted her hand and waved to Eric as she cut across the floor to meet Alta. Even with the band playing and all the noise of the student body, Signee heard Alta call her name as the two friends rushed to meet each other.

"Alta, you look wonderful."

"Oh, Sig, do I?"

"Of course. You're even prettier than I remember."

"Thanks, Sig. I was afraid I might be old and married-looking."

"How could you be? Married makes you beautiful."

"You were always my ego builder, but I haven't heard a word

from you since my wedding."

"Let's sit somewhere away from this band, so I can hear you."

"Sig, have you seen Eric?"

"Just a second across the floor. Is he a good husband?"

"Sig, he's the best ... just like you said."

"Come on, Alta, high up in the center. We used to be able to talk there."

"Lead the way, but not too far away, or I can't hear my husband."

"Me too ... hear your husband ... things haven't changed much here."

"I don't remember the band playing this loud."

"Just the same ... you are happy, aren't you Alta?" Sitting down, they were able to lean closer to hear each other. Signee thought there was too long a hesitation, so she asked the question again:

"You are happy, aren't you, Alta?"

"Of course I am ... only...."

"Only what? Alta, is something the matter? Are you all right?"

"I'm all right; at least I feel all right, but ... oh Sig ... maybe Eric should have married you after all."

"Alta!"

"I mean it, Sig. You were always so good together."

"But he married you."

"Yes, because of Jimmy. But if he'd known...."

There was a loud roll of the drums and the student body president was announcing Eric Langdon, former Green Village High athlete, member of the team the year Green Village took the state championship.

"And now," the student body president was saying, "I introduce you to Eric Langdon...."

"Alta," insisted Signee, "what are you talking about, if Eric had known what?"

"Oh, Sig, I was just thinking back and remembering, and ... it's a long story. I'll tell you after the game ... I promise. But right now I've got to listen to my husband ... don't you want to hear him again, Sig?"

"Ye-yes I do. But don't you dare go without telling me what's bothering you."

7

"I won't, Sig. I promise. Look Sig, there's my husband. Isn't he handsome? And he's just as wonderful as he used to be ... even more. Listen, Sig, listen...."

They sat there together, Alta and Signee, as they had done so many times in the past to listen to football greats. Only then Eric was one of the team, not a guest celebrity; and he was Signee's boyfriend, not Alta's husband. Memories ... the gym was full of memories today. The band, the noise, the cheering ... just the same, and yet so different. The last time Eric had given a pep speech was before their state game. He'd been the last speaker after all the guest speakers, and he'd inspired the whole school with his sincerity and his tears. Signee had led the cheers that followed that speech through her own tears. But now she had to stop thinking backward; Eric was talking, and she wanted to hear what he said. Eric raised his hands and the crowd was quiet. Signee took a deep breath and waited with the rest of the student body. Eric wasn't her property now, and she didn't feel a part of his efforts as she had once; but she was caught up in what he said anyway.

"As it was in the past, it can be today. Green Village High has the material, the spirit, and the drive. You are classified as the team to beat this year, and you don't have to be beaten if you don't want to be beaten. It's a matter of...." His voice trailed off as Alta leaned over to whisper to Signee.

"He hasn't changed much, has he, Sig?"

"Not a bit, if I'm any judge."

"Oh, you're a judge all right. There was a time when I thought..."

"Sh...." The kids behind them strained to hear and resented their whispering. Signee apologized and was quiet. Eric went on.

"A long time ago, when I was in the same position you ball players are in today, a wise man filled my mind with the concept that anything you can visualize you can achieve; and as a team we set goals to...."

"Eric still has the old magic," said Signee, leaning close to Alta's ear again. "He's even improved. Has he had a lot of practice speaking to crowds?"

"He works with people and he's a counselor in the bishopric of our ward. He loves people, you know; always has."

"Yes, he always has..."

Eric related old school stories to capture his audience and skillfully brought them into focus in the immediate "now" of football, leading their minds through a vision of victory with methods of story-telling enthusiasm to "psych" the players and student body to fight and win. Then, as he finished, Signee once again saw herself out of the past, into the present as Minta rushed forward with the other cheerleaders to shout his name and lead the school song which Signee had led so often. As the cheering came to an end, she saw Minta search for Deek, run to meet him, and jump up to throw her arms around him in her excitement. Then she saw Deek take her arms off and put her on the floor as he turned to join the boys.

"Rules around here must have changed," said Alta, and Signee knew that she too had seen Minta throw herself at Deek.

"Rules haven't changed, Alta. It's just that some people still break them."

"I guess there are some in every class. But in our day, remember, no one dared speak to a football player on game day; they were strictly team property from the team meeting the night before until after the game. I see they still dress up."

"Right. Our sometimes rather frowzy big men really look sharp on game day. That's a good rule I hope the coach never changes."

"Right. I love to see them dressed up."

"What?" The screams and the band were getting to them, and Signee couldn't hear Alta.

"I didn't say anything important."

"What?"

The friends were being separated now, and as Signee moved around the girls who had come between them she reached for Alta's hand.

"Let's get out of here where we can talk, Alta. Where are you going to meet Eric?"

"Same old place we used to meet," she shouted over the sound of the drums.

"The poster room on the other side of the field house?"

"Right ... let's go."

Together they made their way through the doors and the bulging halls, past students who called out to Signee ... and her answers were cheerful with school spirit. Finally, with a little crowding, they made their way through the double doors of the poster room. Alta pushed the left side open cautiously.

"Don't wor y, Alta, it doesn't spring back the way it used to. That's one thing we've had fixed."

"Remember the time Eric came through just as the door swung back, and it knocked him down?"

"He had a black eye for a week, but no one believed him when he said a door hit him in the face."

The girls laughed as Alta sat down on the art table and Signee opened the window to let the sunshine in. Then, turning, she looked at her friend.

"Alta, I'm glad you said you'd meet Eric here; we'll have a few minutes to catch up on what's been happening in your life since we last saw each other."

"I've a million questions to ask, Signee."

"Start asking. But first, is there anything wrong with your life?"

"Why do you say that? I'm married to the coveted Eric Langdon; isn't that proof of happiness?"

"It could be, but I thought I heard a note of ... something ... you said something just before we had to stop talking. Alta, is there anything wrong?"

"I'm happy. We've had some problems getting started in Eric's business ... he's on his own, you know. He's a good bookkeeper, public accountant, and he's finally started his own building. In the spring he'll be ready to hire some other CPAs to work for him. The struggle isn't over, but it is better. For a while we lived on nothing."

"He didn't like the firm he was with?"

"Yes. But you know Eric; he's always been creative."

"I remember when he was student body president and insisted we put in a race track ... just like the university. Nothing but the best for Eric. And he made it happen."

"That's right. He's the same way in business; he's full of ideas. When he couldn't get his boss to see the value of his ideas, he decided he'd quit trying to help them out and do it all for himself."

"Then everything is working out now?"

"Everything but me." Alta got up and started to walk around

the room. Suddenly she stopped and looked at Signee. "Oh, Signee ... maybe I'm wrong for Eric..."

"That's what you said before. Now, what you are talking about?"

"Signee ... Oh Sig.... I can't have a baby." She turned and walked toward the window. A silence followed while Alta looked out, wiping her eyes, and Signee tried to think of what to say. Then Alta went on. "Oh, Sig, I shouldn't talk about it because now I'm crying again ... and Eric will be coming in here any minute. I don't want him to know I'm crying, Sig."

"Are you sure you can't have a baby?"

"Would I say such a thing if I wasn't sure?" Alta's voice was harsh.

"Of course not, that was a crazy question, forget I asked ... but there must be something...."

"Oh, Sig.... we haven't given up hope. That's all Eric lives on is hope. He wants a son so badly. Once I thought I was pregnant, and he went out and bought a baby football outfit...."

"You have to think positive. You'll have children; don't worry."

"Oh, Sig ... you don't know Eric very well, do you?"

"I thought I did ... once."

"Eric doesn't say anything." Alta went on as if she hadn't heard Signee. "That's the trouble. Before I found out I couldn't get pregnant, we used to talk about our children. Eric designed a room for the baby. Now he doesn't talk about it at all anymore. Oh, Sig, it hurts too much for him to talk. But the worst part is that I feel so inadequate, like I've let him down. Oh, Sig ... you should have married Eric. You could have given him children."

"Now, we don't know that, do we, Alta?"

"No, but you were so right for each other ... if it hadn't been for me and Jimmy...."

"But there *was* you and Jimmy, and we all made our choices. So don't start looking back and using that for an excuse."

"An excuse ... " Alta turned and anger flared from her eyes. Signee had never seen her angry before.

"Wait a minute, Alta, don't get touchy ... you've never been touchy before."

"Well, I am now. Don't you see, I feel like I'm not a real woman, I feel like I've displeased Heavenly Father and he's punishing me .. I feel...."

"Stop it, Alta ... you can't be all of those things, it's all in your mind. Now dry your tears and get hold of yourself before Eric gets here." Signee threw Alta a box of tissues off the desk where she sat.

"Oh, Sig ... if I could just stop feeling so guilty."

"Guilty? What is this, Alta, the seventeenth century, when kings zapped off the heads of their wives if they didn't give them a son and heir?"

"Eric wouldn't care even if it was a girl, as long as ... but I can't."

"You haven't had enough time to be sure of that, Alta. Where's your faith?"

"Faith? Oh Signee, my faith is standing on the window ready to fly off."

"I don't believe that, Alta ... a girl who could wait for the man she wanted for two years while he filled a mission and then stick by him through college? No, there's got to be a better reason. You've always had faith."

"Maybe I was just here when he came home and he didn't want to marry me at all. If I knew for sure he didn't still love you and married me on the rebound...."

"Alta, stop that! You don't feel like that and you know it. If you want sympathy ... don't come to me ... you've got everything you ever wanted out of life and...."

"Everything but a baby."

"Do you want me to sit down and feel sorry for you? I won't ... you've got to care about yourself and have confidence in yourself. Nobody can give you that; you have to believe in yourself."

"Sig, when I married Eric I was sure I was the best wife he could ever have because I loved him so much and cared about him more than anything in the world. But now, now that I can't give him a son, a child, I don't believe that anymore. Maybe I ruined his life by marrying him. Maybe I'll be his only failure."

"Has Eric said that?"

"Eric? Of course not."

"Then you stop saying it too. You've got to believe he loves you and act like you know it."

12

"Do you think he will love me even if we don't have any children?"

"Of course he will. He married you for better or worse and for time and all eternity, didn't he?"

"Yes."

"This is for time, and we'll let eternity take care of itself. And give time a chance. Besides, there's always adoption. Have you thought about that?"

"Have we thought about it?" Alta almost yelled. "We've tried. Do you know what you have to go through to adopt a baby nowadays? It's almost easier to tell the doctor you don't believe him when he says that you can't have a baby, and then have your own in spite of him ... that's how hard adoption is."

Signee looked shocked. "I can't believe it."

"You'd better believe it. In our adoption agency, when we first applied there were sixty couples in the waiting room when we went to have an interview. In the same amount of time they placed 950 babies; the next year, when we applied, they were only able to get 110 babies ... you know, after abortion was made legal."

"Oh, Alta, I had no idea. And you've really tried to adopt."

"Of course, as soon as the doctor told me I couldn't have a child. Why we've been interviewed, prepared a financial statement, been examined for good health and good teeth, had our house inspected for cleanliness, had our neighborhood reviewed....it's hard and very expensive to adopt a baby."

"I had no idea. What does the doctor say?"

"That I'll never have a baby. I might get pregnant, perhaps, but I'll never carry one through. Of course he leaves room for miracles, but he doesn't have much faith in them."

"You'll get a baby, I know you will."

Tears came to Alta's eyes. "Thank you Sig, if you believe it will help me. You've always been a source of faith for me." She wiped her eyes and blew her nose. "Sig, once we almost got a baby."

"How?"

"Through our agency ... but there was a mistake on our papers, and we didn't get the baby."

"You will, you have to believe that."

"But the birthrate is so low and abortion so high ...

sometimes I feel like it's a sin just to want a baby as much as we want one."

Signee laughed. "Well, I don't think you'll find a sin in that. But I worry about the other ... abortion. I can see how a girl would be frightened and think about an abortion, but how could she really go through with it?"

"Sig, you are really naive, aren't you? I've always thought of you as wise."

"I don't mean I don't believe you, it's just hard to think about ... a baby ... You keep trying for the miracle and adoption, Alta."

"I know ... we will. You know, I think this is harder on Eric than it is on me ... he came from a big family and he's used to children."

"Speaking of Eric, where is that husband of yours?"

But even as Sig asked, the double doors swung open and a familiar voice filled the room with masculine vibrations.

"Did I hear my name? Front and center, that's me." As he spoke he held out his arms with a bright smile on his face. "Sig, you're beautiful; you haven't changed a bit." Then, without waiting, he took the remaining steps between and grabbed her in his arms. "You're a sight ... isn't she, Alta?" He asked the question looking over Signee's shoulder at his wife.

"She's a sight I needed badly today."

"Me too." He put Signee down and went on talking. "What about dinner and talk ... all together?"

"I'd like to, but ... " she started to say and was interrupted by a voice on the school intercom.

"Miss Short, can you come to the office? There is a room full of girls who need your signature on their check-out slips."

"You see ... my public," said Sig, and started toward the door. "And I may have to take some of them home if they've missed the bus. Never be a cheerleading advisor if you want time with your own friends." She turned back to look at Alta and Eric. "But I love every one of them ... they run me to death, but I love them. But I'll see you at the victory dance tonight, right?"

"If it is a victory."

"It better be, Eric, or we'll get another speaker for the next game."

"I imagine you'll do that anyway. We'll see you at the dance."

14

"Good, we can talk and then there's tomorrow. I have a few things in the morning, but about noon I am free .. call me, huh?"

"Same number?"

"Sure, Eric ... same number."

"Sig," said Alta, with the complimentary look Signee remembered so well, "you do have such an interesting life, just like you used to, always having fun. Isn't it a little like being back in high school all over again ... living your school days again in the lives of these kids?"

"Not exactly, Alta, but you're the second person today who's mentioned that fact. I don't think I like the idea."

Chapter Two

Minta Morgan stood in front of the open door when Signee answered the bell the next morning.

"Well, good morning, Minta. You look bright and shiny after the victory dance and the attention of a number of the football players."

"Thank you," said Minta without expression as she stepped inside. "But I'm neither bright nor shiny, and I didn't like the players who gave me the benefit of their attention."

"Well, your mood doesn't seem to fit your looks, or maybe I just always say things wrong when I'm around you. Shall I rephrase the sentence?"

"Don't bother; I probably wouldn't believe you anyway. I probably wouldn't believe anybody today. Can we get started?"

"Of course. Follow me, huh?"

Without further conversation, they moved into the study.

"This is a big house," commented Minta as she moved through the hall to the study, aware that there were other rooms.

"Really too big for me. The house of my childhood."

"Where's your family?"

"Father is on leave this year to write a book. He'll be back to teach at the University again next year, so I'm taking care of the place. Sometimes I wish I was back in my little apartment at school. I shared it with three other girls, and we didn't have a lot of housekeeping."

"I think it would be great to live alone."

"Are you having parent troubles? I thought Minta was the girl with everything."

"With nothing is more like it. Do you like this village we live in? I don't know why they call it a village; it's just the outer edge of a city."

"I guess we're trying to keep some of the old ways. We like our imaginary boundaries and try to keep our country style."

"The boundaries aren't so imaginary. You'd think there was a twelve-foot wall around us, and heckle is the word for anybody that goes with those on the other side."

"What's the matter, Minta? Have you gone through all the boys on this side of the lines?"

"The ones I wanted to go with I have been with. I could care less about any of them but one."

"You're talking about Deek, of course."

"Sure I'm talking about Deek. He promised to take me to that dance if we won the game, and he didn't even dance with me."

"That doesn't sound like Deek. He usually keeps his word. I thought you had a date; you certainly didn't miss any of the dances last night."

"I had a date. I always have to have one in reserve when I think Deek might ask me, because he never does. Anyway, he knew I'd break my date for him."

"Maybe he didn't want you to do that."

"But I wanted to...."

"Look, Minta," Signee sat down in the chair opposite Minta and looked up at her, "don't you see that...." She stopped, got up and walked away a little, then turned back. "You do things your way, Minta ... it's not going to be a lecture today. I was out of line yesterday when I tried to...."

"No you weren't. The truth is, I am very touchy about Deek. Well, wouldn't you be?" Minta began to pace back and forth. "There doesn't seem to be anything that works with him. Every other guy I've ever wanted I can get, and yet he won't ask me.

Why? What's his angle?"

"Probably no angle at all."

"You mean he doesn't care about girls? I'll never believe that. Why, every time he looks at me...."

"I didn't say he doesn't care. He probably cares too much. He's probably staying away because he doesn't want to get involved, not before his mission."

"Do you really think Deek will go on a mission?"

"Do you think he won't? Look at the signs."

"What signs?"

"Look at his background and his goals."

"You sound like you know him pretty well."

"I do. We both grew up in this town; his older brother was just a year ahead of me in school. Like you said, this is a small area and we know about each other."

"All right, if you know him so well, why will he go on a mission?"

"He comes from a good Mormon family; they believe in the prophet, and the prophet has said that Mormon boys go on a mission ... make themselves worthy and go. I just know that Deek will go on a mission."

"Not if I have my way, he won't."

"You mean?"

"I mean Deek is the only thing in this whole place that I care about. I would die if he went away for two years. My brothers didn't go, and they're doing all right."

"What is 'doing all right' to you?"

"They are married and have children."

"Are they active in the church?"

"No, but they're good people."

"But that wouldn't be enough for Deek. He has a family that loves and trusts him. Haven't you noticed the way his family comes to everything he's involved in? Deek will never be happy without pleasing his family and putting his church first."

"If I marry him I'll be his family, and he can please me."

"Oh, Minta. You can't change what Deek is, and you wouldn't like him if you did. Believe me, Minta, the girl that cares about Deek is going to have to love the Gospel. That boy has a very attuned spirit."

"Attuned spirit ... and you think I haven't?"

"I didn't say that."

"Thinking is just as much as saying ... but don't you worry about me. If I can just get one chance at Deek. ..." Minta's eyes filled with softness; there was a dreamy look on her face and Signee couldn't help thinking how pretty she was. Then Minta blinked her eyes ever so slightly. "Deek will know I'm alive before he's through with me. He already likes me, I know he does."

"Be careful, Minta," said Signee softly, trying not to disturb her mood. "You're not playing games now. This is real life, and you could be hurt as well as Deek."

"Just leave Deek to me."

Signee shook her head, "Oh Minta, be careful. Don't set your goals on emotional experiences."

"You said no lectures."

"So I did."

"I came to work. Where do you want me to start?"

Without saying anything more, Signee opened the desk, took out a stack of papers and handed Minta a red pencil and an answer sheet.

"Most of the answers are here. There are a few at the end of the test where they are allowed an opinion; you may have to ask a few questions when you come to those." Signee turned to leave as Minta sat down at the desk, but before she settled herself she caught Signee with a question.

"Teacher, have I shocked you?"

"I don't think I know what you mean."

"I mean, in your day girls probably weren't so bold as to set out to get a guy any way they could."

"Some of them did. What you are saying is that you intend to get Deek at any price, right?"

"Right."

"Then I say I hope he's too smart for you. I think he is. But I feel sorry that you are trying so hard to make me think you are a cheap girl. I don't think you are. For one thing, you wouldn't want a guy like Deek if you weren't good inside. I know you're moody and switch from being sweet to sarcastic quite easily, but I really think you want to be worthy of someone like Deek. I even think you could be, if you are willing to learn to put your life in order."

"Put my life in order? You mean do things your way?"

"Not exactly. We'll talk about it sometime . . . when you think you care enough." Signee turned to go but went on talking. "Minta, be careful how you correct those papers. Some of your friends are borderline on their grades, also."

Signee left the room and Minta didn't try to call her back. Signee busied herself in the kitchen, finishing cleaning up after the snack that had followed the game. While she worked, she thought about her own life a few short years before. Minta and Deek were so like Signee and Eric, only the roles were reversed. It was Eric who had somehow planned to have Signee; she'd known that instinctively, and what a hard time she'd had convincing Eric that they should wait and not get emotionally involved. Would she have been more like Minta if she had to do it all again? She'd thought about that a lot on some of the lonely evenings she'd spent since Eric married Alta. Reaching for the soap, she filled the sink with water and suds. As she dipped her hands into the soft water, her mind whizzed back to another time and another day, not unlike yesterday.

It was homecoming, and she was going to the dance with Eric. Hadn't she and Eric gone together to most of the dances during football season? They were always together. He was the toughest guy on the team, and she was the funnest girl. They'd laughed their way through their whole junior year, and then they were seniors and living every moment as if they were aware that this was their last carefree season. How could they have known that? Was it a natural instinct? Eric was a good guy but not too involved in church, except when he went to be near Signee. It had been after the homecoming dance, in this same kitchen. The other kids had gone home after their late dinner prepared by Signee's mother, and Eric had stayed to help with the last clean-up.

"I'll do the washing job," said Eric, picking Signee up and setting her aside as easily as he lifted a glass of water, then putting his hands elbow-deep into the suds, spilling water and suds all over the floor.

"Look what you've done!" laughed Signee. "Suds all over mother's wax job. Just wait until I tell her that her fair-haired boy did the whole thing."

"I'll deny it. Your mother and I are favorite friends, we

understand each other. I'll tell her it's all your fault."

"But that's a lie."

"She'll believe me," teased Eric, flipping some finger suds in Signee's direction. "Your mother believes anything I say."

"Until she catches you in a lie."

"Now what does that mean?"

"That mother thinks you're pretty neat. But she won't tolerate lies, even from you."

"Then I'll have to decorate the truth."

"Like what?"

"Like ... darling mother-in-law-to-be ... I cannot tell a lie. I did not chop down your cherry tree, but I splashed water on your wax."

Signee had laughed and reached for a towel to wipe up the suds. "And you're sure you are going to call her your mother-in-law-to-be?"

"She knows we're going to be married someday."

"After your mission, Elder Langdon."

"Right, that's what I said. After my mission. Now hand me the rest of those pans, if you want this job done right."

"Plates first," Signee had said, handing him a stack just as he turned around ... and the next thing they both knew the plates were in a thousand pieces all over the floor.

"Mother's china!" Signee had yelled; and the next minute they were both on the floor trying to save what they could. "It's a good thing it is only second best, and a few pieces were already chipped."

"We'd better hurry to town tomorrow and get her some more to make replacements before she finds out."

"Irreplaceable, Brother Eric. This stuff is too old...."

"Yipe, now what do we do ... ?"

"Better use your charm."

"My charm isn't effective."

"How do you know? Have you tried?"

"Yes, I've been trying it out on you for almost three years, and nothing...."

"Oh, I wouldn't say that. I'm vulnerable, and you've been very effective."

"I have?" With one hand Eric had reached out and grabbed Signee's arm and pulled her down on the floor in front of him.

He bent his head close to hers. She had faked a scream and tried to push him away.

"Vulnerable, huh? Then why...."

"No, no, Eric ... you're taking advantage of a defenseless woman."

"About as defenseless as a tiger. Why don't you hold still?"

"Because if I do, you would...."

"Would...." he had held her head tight in the crook of his arm. She couldn't move. His face was coming closer. She kicked and squealed; and then, just inches before he might have kissed her, he stopped smiling and his voice was serious. Something in his eyes made her stop fighting, too. "Oh, Sig," he said soberly, "when are we going to get serious?" His arms had relaxed as they looked at each other, and Signee quickly rolled over and moved away. When he reached for her again she was on her feet, and the chase began. He caught her in the front room the third time around the couch. He pulled her close to him.

"No Eric ... no ... " When he could see she was serious, he let her go.

"Why not? Sig, aren't we ever going to get together?"

"After your mission."

"What if I don't go on a mission?"

"But Eric, of *course* you'll go on your mission! Do you want our children to know their father didn't go on a mission?"

"Do you think it will be hard on them?"

"Why, how can they face the disgrace?" She had been teasing but there was a degree of seriousness. Eric knew very well how Signee felt about the church and going on a mission.

It had been later that night, when they were sitting side by side on the couch looking at the pictures they'd taken at the beginning of the week, when he had slipped his arm around her. Suddenly they were both affected by what had always been just a common movement.

"I wonder if I turned the stove off after we heated the hot dogs ...." She got up. Eric took hold of her arm.

"Don't go away. We've got to talk."

"What about, Eric?"

"You know what about. You are as flighty as a butterfly; I can't catch you."

"That's good, huh?"

"What do you mean, good?"

"I mean I'm making it easier for you to leave me."

"Don't do me any favors." He sat back on the couch, folding his hands in his lap.

"Don't be mad, Eric. We haven't long to be together, so let's not spoil it. Let's just have fun."

"Sig, we've had fun for three years, on and off between dates with other people, and I've never touched you. Don't you think it's about time we find out how we feel about each other?"

"I know how I feel about you."

"How, Sig?"

"I know I want you on the other side of the room."

He slid over, coming toward her, and she slipped to the next chair. "You don't want me to hold you and kiss you?"

"I do," she said, putting up her hands to remind him not to move closer again. "That's just the problem."

"Kissing, a problem? For whom?"

"For me. Too much and not enough."

"Sig, come here."

She shook her head. "No."

"Then I'll come to you."

She got up and pointed her finger at him, threatening. "If you even try, I'll never go with you again."

"Sig, you don't mean that."

"Yes I do." She was serious, and he had to recognize that.

"Sig, we're so much alike in so many ways . . . you will marry me, won't you?"

"Is that what you want? Are you sure?"

"I'm so sure . . . I'd planned on graduation . . . a ring for your graduation."

"Don't do that, Eric."

"Why, Sig? You love me, don't you?"

She nodded, then shook her head. "I love you, but no ring. It isn't healthy to tie ourselves together until we know how your mission affects us both."

"And you're going to insist on the mission, aren't you?"

"Don't you want to go?"

"If it means that much to you, yes."

"Doesn't it mean that much to you?"

"You want me to be honest?"

"Yes."

"I'm not as gone on church as you are. I'm gone on you. You attend, so I attend ... I like playing basketball and the guys are great, but I truly think it's more important to marry you than go on a mission for the church."

"You go on a mission for you ... for me ... not the church. The church will get along without us, but we can't get along without the church. What kind of a family would we be if we don't live up to what we believe?"

"You believe."

"You, too ... don't you believe?"

"I guess I do, Sig, but I want to be with you."

"But we need the Gospel to be happy."

"I know ... and I guess I'll go, if only because you ask me to."

"But that isn't good enough. You've got to want to go yourself."

"I do ... but you're the reason ... look ... I'll go just to make sure that issue isn't between us. I'll go and do all that's expected of me, and I'll try to believe. But I want you here when I get back."

"I'm not going anywhere."

"Promise?"

"I can't promise any more than you can, but I don't love anybody else. How's that?"

"All right ... Come on ... let's hold hands nice and tight ... I want to feel you close."

They'd laughed and the chase was on again, this time out into the snow. She'd come in wet and cold, but happy inside. Remembering now, Signee wondered if she'd been wrong to send Eric away. She'd been so sure then. But now, now that she was lonely, remembering how Eric had come home and married Alta....But she'd done what she knew was right at the time, and she hadn't been sorry.

"Miss Short ... " called Minta from the study where she was correcting papers.

"I'm right here, Minta," said Signee, coming into view from the kitchen. "What's the matter?"

"Are you really my friend?"

Signee nodded.

"Well, if you're my friend, how about getting me a date with

Deek for the next dance? You ought to be able to swing that...
with him liking you so much."

"If Deek likes me, it is because I like him ... the feeling is
mutual. I also care about him, Minta, and I'm not so sure you are
good for him."

"Three cheers for Miss Siggie...." returned Minta, her voice
edgy.

"Yes, three cheers for me...."

"Some friend. With a friend like you, who needs an enemy?"

"Look, Minta," and Signee's voice showed irritation along
with determination, "you may not believe it, but I am your
friend. I care about you; and maybe I don't know all about being
a friend, but I'm going to try."

"How do you try to be a friend? Either you are or you aren't,
that's the way I've always been taught."

"How much have you been taught, Minta? I know you're not
close to your parents, but I'd like to get to know you, and I will
be your friend someway.... I'll be your friend and Deek's
friend, Eric's friend and Alta's friend..." Her voice stopped, but
her thought went on... "Always a friend, never a bride."

Chapter Three

A full weekend, and there hadn't been much time for Signee and Alta to visit and talk about the old days. They'd said bits here and there at the dance, and it had been fun to dance with Eric again, everyone kidding and smiling; but there wasn't time for serious talk. Maybe that was better, Signee was thinking. And then the telephone rang early Monday morning. Signee reached for the extension beside her bed.

"Signee, this is Alta. I'm calling to thank you for a fun weekend."

"Alta, you sound like you're saying goodbye."

"We're leaving just after noon. Eric's in town right now, but when he's finished we'll be on our way."

"And I thought we might have time for a set of tennis."

"Oh, Sig ... how about this morning?"

"About an hour? I could pick you up."

"Great. I don't suppose I can beat you ... but I have been practicing with Eric."

"And I haven't been practicing at all."

"Great ... we'll give it a go, as Eric would say."

"I'll honk, all right?"

"All right."

An hour later, Signee parked her small car in the school parking lot, and with rackets in hand the two friends ran across the asphalt race track separating the tennis courts from the parking lot. As they began warming up, Signee experienced the old carefree feeling she'd always felt with Alta in the past. Alta had always been a true friend, a loyal friend. Looking at her across the net now, Signee remembered the first time she'd seen Alta. A new girl in school her sophomore year, Siggie had almost run into Alta as she came through the double doors from the gym that morning.

"Oh, I'm sorry," Signee had said as Alta backed away and Signee went past her. Then suddenly, she'd stopped and talked. "You're new in town, aren't you?"

Alta had nodded, her eyes wide as if she might be frightened.

"Would you like to have lunch with me today?" Alta had nodded. "All right, I'll meet you by the lunch room for the second lunch. Is that your lunch period?" Alta had nodded again. "All right, we'll meet then." Alta had nodded again and Signee had gone on her way, wondering why she'd bothered. Usually busy, Signee hadn't always taken time—in fact very few times, except when it was her duty as a cheerleader. But it was Signee's junior year, and they'd had a drive on in Seminary to make new friends.

"We've always been friends, haven't we, Signee?" said Alta, as if reading her thoughts as they stopped for a breather before they started scoring.

"Always. Alta, you came into my life just as I'd found out I couldn't trust girls. You didn't fit into the pattern."

"What pattern?"

"The pattern of girls who didn't know how to be a friend, especially when there was a boy involved. You were always loyal, Alta."

"I wonder if I would have been if Eric hadn't asked me to marry him."

"Of course you would. How many times did you sit around dreaming about Eric while he was dating me?"

Alta's face clouded. "Oh, Signee, I didn't...."

Signee laughed and put her arm around Alta as they sat down on the bench beside the courts. "Of course you didn't. You didn't even let me know how much you loved Eric until you knew my life was full of Jimmy."

"I'm sorry about Jimmy, Sig."

"I know, Alta. But it was all for the best. I guess I was never really in love with Jimmy . . . I just loved him . . . like a brother. I still do love him, but I'm very glad I didn't marry him."

"You were upset for a long time, weren't you?"

"Yes, I guess I was. Whenever anything hurts the people I love, I'm always upset. But I've learned there isn't a lot I can do about that. People make their choices and have to live with them."

"But it seems so ironic. Sig, you were the girl who had plenty of boyfriends; you could have had any boy you wanted. I always wondered how you did it. I was so shy."

"That was my plan. I didn't want to be classified as anybody's girl. I wanted to be free and not tied down. I worked at it . . . making friends and liking several boys at once. It wasn't easy. In those days all you had to do was walk down the hall several times with the same boy, and the whole school had you going steady."

"Is it any different now?"

"No, hasn't changed a bit."

"How did you keep so many of them happy?"

"I didn't make-out with any of them. Holding hands was a big deal with me. I don't think my friends believed that. In fact, some of the boys used to lie about what we did together. But lies don't hang on. . . ."

"How did you know enough to do that? I always wondered."

"I guess it was my mother who gave me the idea. She was engaged to my father when he went on his mission, and she said that ring came between them for a long time. They almost didn't marry each other because of that ring. She was engaged to a man she hadn't seen for two years, and she just didn't know what was expected of her . . . how to act . . . he was like a stranger, and yet she was wearing that ring. I decided that wouldn't happen to me. I found out watching other girls that if you started kissing a guy, you started liking him so much you either had to get married or break up and never speak to each other again. Somebody always got hurt . . . so I made up my mind that wouldn't happen to me either, so . . . well, I couldn't kiss one and not another, so I didn't kiss anybody ... but I concentrated on having fun."

"It worked, too. I watched you. I always wanted to be like you, Sig, but I wasn't. I never will be."

"I didn't know that, Alta. I thought you were content to just be a one-man girl and a loyal friend. That was dumb of me, huh?"

"No. I guess that's what I wanted. I just wanted to have as much fun as you did. But I always loved Eric, even when I knew I couldn't ever have him ... or thought I couldn't ... and the other boys that might have asked me out ... I'd always run away and be scared they might ... I was always frightened of boys, I guess. I think the reason I liked being with Eric was because he loved you and I knew he wasn't interested in me, and we talked about you ... we had you in common. Eric was the one boy you couldn't keep from being called his girl. Everybody knew Eric was your boyfriend."

"That was because we were always thrown together, because he played football and I did the cheering. Just like Minta and Deek."

"The two we watched at the pep assembly?"

"Yes, Alta. I'd like to help Minta. She's so like me in many ways, but she's dumb about boys."

"Chases them?"

"She chases only one. The others chase her, or used to until she started going with Deek and making a pest of herself when she isn't going with him."

"Sig, I got the idea she was kinda spoiled ... used to having her own way. Was I wrong?"

"You are right. She throws a tantrum really easily and doesn't seem to care who sees it. But I think she can learn, and I think she really wants to be different. She just hasn't had anyone to help her."

"If anyone can help her, you can, Sig. You helped me. I don't think Eric would ever have married me if you hadn't shown me how to dress and taught me how to write to a missionary. In fact, I'm not sure you weren't away on purpose when Eric came home, just so he and I would have time together. I wonder if I'll ever be sure Eric really loved me or just learned to love me because he couldn't have you?"

30

"Alta, don't be dumb. .... I'm sorry, but that's the only word for it. Eric proposed to you, not me. He fell in love with you. Maybe my not being there made it happen faster, but he'd have found out anyway."

"But you know you could have had him."

"I don't know that at all. And, I have never been sorry."

"Never? Really?"

Sig tightened her arm around her friend. "Of course not, silly."

"Not even now, Sig, now that you're not married and ..." Alta stopped, her face clouding up, afraid that what she was about to say might hurt Sig.

Signee laughed out loud. "Of course not ... not even now that I'm not married and an old maid. I've been lonely a lot of times, and if Eric had been around and not happily married, I'd probably have tried to make something of our old romance again ... but that wouldn't make it right. Why is it that I have to keep reassuring people of that?"

"Maybe because there's still so much feeling between you. Eric still talks about you a lot."

"Why not? He's part of my life and always will be, just as you are. Now let's stop all this crazy talk and get on with our game. Come on." Sig pulled Alta up off the bench. "I'm gong to beat you ... no matter how out of practice I am."

"You're on ... Eric has been training me."

"All right ... let's get on with the battle. I'm still out to win and a very poor loser."

Together they ran on to the court, and the match that followed was hard-fought. Signee won, but only by a small margin; and when they stopped to rest, Alta ran for the drinking fountain and Signee followed her.

"Wait a minute ... " Alta hesitated before putting her face down to take a drink. "I don't want you pushing my face in the water the way you used to."

"Don't worry, breaking your tooth that time cured me of that. Your dentist was very angry at me."

"You are so right." Alta took a drink, then cupped her hands and Sig turned the water on so she could fill her hands enough to cover her face. "That feels good."

"Probably the only unladylike thing I was able to teach you."

Sig followed her example, and then the two of them walked back to the bench together.

"You are such a lady, Alta; that's why you'll make a good mother."

"Oh, Sig, do you really think so? You've always had a sense about me ... if you say it, I'll believe it. If I could have a baby or adopt one, I would feel like a real woman again."

"Better turn that speech around ... feel like a woman, and you'll have a baby or adopt one."

"I'll try ... I really will, Sig. I dream about my baby every night. I see her with dark hair and a dimple in her chin like Eric's. Eric wants a boy first, but I always see a girl first."

"Hang on to your dream and maybe you'll have twins or adopt twins; let's not rule anything out. Wanting children is a righteous desire. You'll be blessed for a righteous desire."

"Oh, Sig, you're too much."

"But I believe in dreams...."

"Yes, you always did, didn't you? What about your theater dream? Do you still believe you'll have it, or have you given that one up?"

"Never. I'm going to make that dream come true. I guess I used to be partly kidding, but that dream has become a part of my life. Alta, do you realize how beneficial a neighborhood summer theater could be to the school, church, community and ... individual lives? Look at Minta ... if I had a theater now, I'd put her to work and train her in the art of how to handle her life while I made her a star. If kids have enough to do, they don't go overboard for things they shouldn't be doing."

"You haven't given up. You know what, Sig? I'm going to ask Eric if he'll help you. Eric is full of ideas of how to get building done and raise money for benefits. He's a real genius at raising money for projects."

"You're right, Alta...I'd forgotten, but remember when Eric decided this school needed an asphalt track instead of gravel?"

"I do."

"Well, there's the track; and it was the money Eric and his men's association raised that built it."

"See ... and why not have him help you?"

"Alta, you're right. Come on, one more game..."

"All right, one more and then I'd better look for a shower."

"We'll go to my place."

A little after noon, Alta was singing in Signee's shower when the doorbell rang and Eric stood outside Signee's door.

"Have I got a delinquent wife waiting for me here?"

"How did you find us? I thought I'd keep her a while."

"You weren't hard to track down. Alta was always with you when you were available."

"It's good to have her here again. Come in and sit down, Eric. I'll tell her. She's just finishing the purification process."

Eric came in as normally as if he'd never been away and sat down on the same couch he'd sat on so often in the past. Sig went to tell Alta her husband had arrived, poured a glass of orange juice from the fridge, and handed it to Eric while she sat opposite him on the big chair that was her father's favorite.

"Things haven't changed much around here, have they?"

"Not much, Eric. Except the family is away and that makes this place pretty big."

"Why don't you bring in some of your lonely hearts?"

"My lonely hearts?"

"You were always solving everybody's problems. Surely you have a few lonely hearts around."

"You're making fun of me, Eric."

"No, I'm not. I kinda admire the way you always try to help everybody. But sometimes you neglect yourself."

"I'm all right..."

"Are you, Sig?" Eric was suddenly serious. "Are you really?"

"Sure. I'm fine."

"Why didn't you marry Jimmy? Or is that a leading question?"

"A leading question, but I don't mind telling you. He found out he didn't need me ... or maybe it's more truthful to say he had previous commitments that didn't include me."

"He let you go? I don't believe it."

"Let's just say it was mutual agreement, all right? Now, let's talk about you and Alta."

"What do you want to know?"

"She says you are a very successful...."

"Eric ... " Alta's voice coming from the corner of the hall, where she stood wrapped in a towel, interrupted them. "Eric, you will help Sig with her theater, won't you? I told her you would ... you're so good at things like that." Without waiting for an answer she disappeared into the bedroom, and Eric looked at Sig.

"I used to think you were just kidding about that theater of yours, Sig."

"Well, I'm not kidding, I'm serious. Somehow I'm going to have it."

"Still the same dream?"

"What's wrong with that kind of a dream? Theater can develop kids as much as sports. Eric, have you ever stopped to think how many people can develop their talents and their creative ability in drama? We need light technicians, stage people, publicity, scenery, costumes ... organizers ... we all need an opportunity to see what we've got inside us."

"A world of make believe...."

"A world of make believe that lends ideas to real living and gives people an opportunity to get the inside out."

"Maybe it's better to keep the inside ... inside ... ever think of that? I mean this do-your-thing stuff isn't so good."

"That's different than a chance to develop talents you have a desire to develop. You know I've always believed if you have a desire, you also have the talent, if you just develop it."

"But you already have the school and the church."

"The school can do one play a year, perhaps; and the church does a little but its buildings are always being used for other things. We need a place for drama, with the atmosphere of the theater...a place where the performers can feel responsible to put up scenery and leave it ... real theater that we can use winter and summer. How wonderful to be able to put up the scenery from the beginning and leave it until the play is over."

"All right ... I can see you are determined. I never could talk you out of anything."

"If only I had a way of getting people interested, of raising money...."

"Money isn't hard. We can get people to invest ... there's a lot of money floating around, people who need tax write-offs and want to have their name on a seat or a panel...."

"Oh, Eric, do you suppose?"

"Sure, I suppose ... do you think you could find an old barn or an old building?"

"I don't know ... not one that wouldn't need a lot of work, that's for sure."

"A lot of work is easy ... you know, there's a kid I met on my mission that has a talent for drama, and he's really good with lights. Maybe ..." Eric stopped talking and looked at Signee closely. "In fact, this guy is almost as rolled in grease paint as you are ... he has morals about like yours, and ... you might like to meet him."

"If he's good at building a theater, I'm sure I'd like to meet him ... but Eric, don't do me any favors and try being a matchmaker, huh?"

"Well, you could use a husband, couldn't you?"

"Not one you would pick out."

"Why not? I know you pretty well."

"Not well enough to choose my husband. Let's stick to the theater for our togetherness, huh?"

"All right, but I think this guy can ... never mind, I'll think about your theater and see what I can come up with."

"Oh, Eric, will you really? Will you help me? When I think of the possibilities, how many kids I can help, the effect it can have on this community ... Eric, if you would...."

"All right, all right ... I said I'd think about it ...." Eric held up his hands in defense. Seeing his action, Signee realized she'd been carried away and was talking loud and fast. She suddenly burst into laughter. Eric joined her.

"So I get heated when I think of the possibilities. Eric, I admit I'm a nut about the whole thing, but every day I see how many more kids need self-expression, and there isn't any better way than drama, I promise you that ... you do see it, don't you Eric ... you get the vision, don't you?"

"Anything you can visualize, you can accomplish ... you taught me that."

"I did?"

"Sure. Remember before we took State and I was so scared my tongue was thick?"

"I only remember the squeaky swing and being afraid you might get caught talking to a girl when you were supposed to be sleeping."

"The swing really squeaked that night, didn't it?"

"And you wouldn't sit still."

"How could I? My stomach was tied in knots. I had to talk to you or explode."

"You took quite a chance, throwing rocks at my window."

"It worked. You came down."

"In my robe and slippers."

"Your slipper had a hole in the toe. I'll never forget that white toe shining in the moonlight."

"What a thing to remember."

"I remember other things, too."

"Like the neighbors throwing the cat out of the second-story window?"

"If that cat had hit me, my face would have given us away."

"The cat was pretty scared. Her claw marks are still on the porch pillar."

"There were other things that stayed. I'll never forget what you said to me that night."

"I couldn't have said anything very important." Signee suddenly felt nervous, almost afraid of what he might say or recall.

"That night you reprimanded me good. I told you how scared I was and all tied up inside, how I doubted myself and the cooperation of the team. And then you got mad at me...."

"I did?"

"Don't you remember?"

"Well, I..."

"You told me you were ashamed of me. You shouted at me and asked me how I dared doubt Heavenly Father's ability to help me."

"I said that?"

"You did. I'll never forget. It worked for me then and a lot of other times when I was on my mission, too. You don't know how often I've repeated those few words to myself."

"I'm glad. I use that idea myself. I didn't know I was brave enough to push it on you." Signee dropped her eyes and smiled, then she looked up again and there was merriment in her eyes. "You know that old swing still squeaks, Eric?"

"Tell me, Sig, how many football players with sick stomachs use my old method of getting your attention?"

"Not too many ... the idea died out with you, I guess."

"You didn't know it, Sig, but you were the big reason I

worked my insides out playing football."

"I thought you lived for the game."

"I did, but football and being in love with the cheerleaders fit together in a nice package."

"You're right, Eric. All the cheerleaders loved all the teams."

"One in particular for me."

Signee felt uncomfortable; getting up, she began to move around the room. "You were never really in love with me, Eric. I'm just your sister ... your cousin ... just a pal ... that's all."

"Don't kid yourself, Sig. I was in love with you then, now, and will always be. You are still so much a part of my life that I ... well, I'd never have made it without you."

"Eric...."

"Oh, don't worry. Alta knows ... we talk about you once in a while. Don't get the wrong idea, Sig. I love Alta; she's perfect for me. I have to thank you for her too, in a way."

"No regrets, then?" Sig began to relax.

"How about you, Sig? Any regrets?"

Sig was thoughtful, looking into Eric's eyes. She shook her head. "No regrets. If I had to do the whole thing all over again, I would do the same thing ... a bit more wisely this time perhaps, with the same results. Loving isn't the same as being in love, is it Eric?"

He shook his head while he bit his lip, a characteristic Signee remembered well. "We did our choosing, Sig, and I know there was a more powerful source that helped us make our choices."

"Thanks, Eric. I'm glad to hear you say all this."

"You doubted? My Sig, with faith to move mountains?"

"Sometimes the mountains get a little big. Sometimes I've wondered."

"Don't you dare let me down, Sig. I learned about faith from you."

"I learned from my parents. You know, I think I lived on the faith of my parents for so long I can't remember when I changed and their faith became mine."

"And I leaned on yours for a long time."

"Who's leaning on what?" asked Alta joining them, her hair shining and still damp from her shower.

"We all lean on each other," said Eric, looking at his wife. Rising to meet her, he reached out and twisted her nose slightly as he laughed.

"Something funny?"

"You're funny, my love," said Eric, putting his arms around his wife. "And your hair is still wet."

"I know, but I didn't want it completely dry. I'm still so warm."

"Warm? Honey, hot is a better word for you...." There was a twinkle in Eric's eye as he held Alta close and smiled at Sig.

"Eric, please...."

"Don't worry, Alta ... Sig knows me."

"I know ... but some things are intimate." She tried to sound angry, but ended up snuggling under his chin.

"She tries to fight me, Sig, but she's too skinny...."

"She's darling, Eric....You're even prettier than you were before you married Eric, Alta."

"See, wife, I told you I'd improve you. Well, we can't stand here necking ... we've got to get moving."

"Eric, you did help Sig with her theater, didn't you?"

"Not yet, wife, I'm thinking about it." Pulling Alta toward the door, he looked back at Signee. "You'll be hearing from me, Sig ... in the meantime, look for that barn or old building or something that can be fixed up."

"I will, Eric ... what a good idea. Thanks...."

"Sig?"

"Yes, Eric?"

"You are happy, aren't you?"

"Oh, for system's sake ... why is it that you married people always think everybody who isn't married is miserable?"

"Well, marriage is heaven or hell, and you never can tell which one you're going to have today...." He smiled and ducked as Alta pretended to swing at him.

Watching as Eric opened the door and let his wife go out ahead of him, Sig couldn't help thinking how much Alta had changed. She had more confidence than she'd known her to have before. And yet there was that hurt in her eyes, that insecurity that came whenever she talked about having a baby.

Chapter Four

Minta waited outside the fieldhouse even later than the regular time the cheerleaders practiced. Her wait was rewarded when Deek came out of the locker room alone and found her there. He crossed the parking lot and Minta started her car as he approached, leaning out of the window to call to him.

"Deek, you said if we won the game you would take me to the dance. Why didn't you?"

"I didn't say which dance, did I?" He stepped back as she screeched to a stop in front of him.

"I meant the victory dance following the game, and you know it."

"You didn't say that after the game."

"How could I? You disappeared. I couldn't find you."

"I didn't want to be found."

"Why not, Deek? Why not? Is there anything the matter?"

"Minta, don't get emotional."

"But I *am* emotional, can't you see that? I always get emotional when I'm upset. Don't you?"

"Not the way you do."

"Don't you want me to care about you, Deek? Who did you go

with after the game?"

"One question at a time, Minta."

"All right ... do you want a ride home?"

Deek looked around the parking lot; it was almost vacant. "Well, it isn't far to walk, but yes, if you want to give me a ride ... sure."

"Well, don't be enthusiastic or anything."

He opened the door and got in beside her. She hit the gas and the gears, and they were off. She swung onto the street in front of the school and down three blocks to where Deek lived. But she didn't stop; instead, she pushed the gas harder when his house was in sight and went right on by.

"Minta, I said home, not dragging cars with the gang."

"What's wrong with that? Oh, Deek, you are such a bore I don't know why I bother with you."

"Neither do I. Why don't you just forget about me?"

"Do you really want me to?"

"I don't know. I like you, Minta, I have to admit that. But you are so blasted available and changeable that it isn't worth the effort."

"Well, I like that. If that's the way you feel, why don't you get out right now?"

"Why don't you stop so I can? Why didn't you stop at my house?"

"I don't know why I like you," she said, and made a quick turn to the right, just missing the curb as she rounded the corner.

"Minta, you are the worst driver...."

"You made me mad. Why can't you be nice like you used to be?"

"Why can't you let me be nice like you used to?"

"What do you mean by that?"

"Think back, Minta. We didn't ever go out very much, but we had fun. I enjoyed talking to you and you were a happy person to be around, and I liked that ... then suddenly you began to move in on me."

"I haven't moved in on you. I only want to see you sometimes and talk. Other boys like me; why don't you? What do I do different with you?"

"Other boys may want different things out of life than I do.

40

I'm not ready to have a steady girl, Minta, and you won't be casual."

"I don't feel casual."

"Then pretend."

"Pretend? I thought you said boys didn't like girls who pretended. Realism, that was what you said . . . simple and real."

"I still say that. You just don't understand."

Minta jerked the wheel to one side and made a fast left. Deek reached over and grabbed it to correct the turn from going too far.

"Minta, who taught you how to drive? Who gave you your driving test?"

"Who do you think?" she said, shoving his hands off the steering wheel.

"It would have to be Jones; he's probably the only one you can dazzle."

"Then you do think I'm capable of dazzling someone? And where did you get an old-fashioned term like dazzling? That's from my father's day."

"I get my old-fashioned words from my mother; she tells me about her generation. And yes, you are capable of dazzling quite a few, so why not work on them and not me?"

"Well, somebody's got to look after you. Honestly, Deek, you do the dumbest things."

"Right. Now turn the next corner carefully and take me home, or so help me I'll move you over and drive myself."

"Would you really?" She smiled, taking her eyes off the road to look at him. He grabbed the wheel again.

"Minta, look at the road. Stop making eyes at me and sounding like you'd like to mother me."

Minta didn't answer, but she turned the corner and drove to Deek's house without saying any more. She stopped the car in front, and Deek opened the door to get out. Minta stopped him with a question.

"You really don't like anything about me, right?"

"I didn't say that."

"It's obvious. I won't bother you anymore, Deek." She dropped her eyes, turned her face toward the front, and waited. Deek thought she might be crying, the change in her voice was so sobered and serious. He shut the door but he didn't leave. He leaned on the window and looked at her. There was a softness in his voice when he spoke.

"Look, Minta. You're a very pretty girl ... a nice girl, too, if you'd let yourself be natural."

"Don't give me a father lecture, I've had enough of those. You've made yourself clear; you don't like me."

He was silent a moment as his eyes studied her. "No, I can't say I don't like you."

"You mean you care?" She suddenly brightened and he could see she hadn't been crying at all. His voice was sharp.

"Yeah, I care...."

"Well ... tell me...."

"I don't think you want the details ... they're all physical."

"Oh." She almost spit the word at him. "You are rude."

"Do you want the truth, or do you want me to lie to you?"

"Don't give me the details; just tell me why. Why, Deek? Can't we ever have fun again?"

"Maybe, if you weren't so intense."

"What do you mean by that?"

"I mean everything is such a big deal with you, and you want to do the bossing."

"That's what Siggie said."

"You've been talking to Siggie? Pretty neat, isn't she?"

"Is that what you think?" Minta looked at him accusingly. "So, you are in love with Siggie." She hit the steering wheel with her hand. "How can you, Deek? ... an older woman."

"You see what I mean, you're always making a big deal out of everything. No, I'm not in love with her ..." His obvious disgust suddenly changed and he smiled, "But that's not saying I couldn't be. I like Siggie."

"If that's the way you feel, you don't need to ride around with me anymore."

"Excuse me, but you asked me, remember?"

"Well, I won't anymore. Enough is enough, like my father says. You don't like me and I won't like you, so..." She started the car. Deek reached in quickly and turned off the key.

"Wait a minute, Minta, maybe we'd better talk, huh?"

"Don't put yourself out."

He ignored her sarcasm. He got into the car and sat beside her again.

"You mean you are really going to talk to me?"

"If it's talk you want and not just chatter."

"Maybe I don't know the difference."

"We'll see. You listen and I'll talk first, then you can have a turn. Minta, I don't mean to be rude to you. I like girls, and I have a deep respect for most of them."

"But not me?"

"My turn to talk ... you listen. You see, Minta, you want to get serious and I'm not ready. It's as simple as that. Sure, I could like you—maybe, if the time was right."

"For me the time is right."

"No it isn't. You're a spoiled girl who has had everything she wants. Right now you might think you want me, but you don't."

"Let me be the judge of that."

"No. I'm the one who decides who I like and when. Minta, you're too easy. If I went with you we'd be ready for marriage too soon, and if I married you I'd be sorry."

"No you wouldn't, Deek. I'd be anything you'd want me to be. Truly, you're the only one I've ever really been interested in."

"Minta, I'm the toy you haven't got yet ... I want a wife that isn't easy to get, a strong...."

"You mean you want me to play hard-to-get?"

"No, I don't believe in playing games. I mean I don't want to be possessed the way you want to do with everybody and everything. It isn't a matter of playing games, it's being interested in things and people and filling your life with other things. Boy, I'll bet you won't let your husband breathe without you."

"Why should he?"

"You see what I mean? No, you don't." He opened the car door and got out again. "We had fun once, Minta, but it's all over now. I'm glad we didn't ever get physical so we haven't any regrets. We won't be going together at all, Minta. Too bad; you have a lot of qualities I admire. When I get back from my mission in about three years, if you're still around and have your emotions intact, I'll look you up."

"No you won't." Angrily she turned on the key, put the gears in contact and took off, squealing the tires as she went. Deek stepped back just in time and watched her go.

As she left Deek, the tears stinging her eyes, she turned onto the highway diagonal to the school. She didn't know where she was going and didn't realize how fast she was moving. She was only aware of saying to herself over and over.... "I've lost him before he was mine ... I'll never love anybody else ... oh Deek ... " Rounding a curve, she was vaguely aware of something shadowy in the road ahead, an animal ... a cat or a small dog ... she swerved; the car went out of balance. The next thing she knew the car was whirling around in the middle of the street as if she'd hit black ice; but the streets were dry and warm. She came to a jolting stop, her front wheels over the bank of the creek that ran along the side of the highway. Her head hit something hard and she blacked out.

Later, Minta didn't even know how much later, vaguely she heard a man's voice.

"Hey, honey, are you all right?"

"Uh...." Minta lifted her head and looked at a face she had never seen before.

"You took quite a spin, honey; your tracks are clear across the road. Is there someone I can call?"

"No, I'm all right...." Minta tried to lean back; a pain in her chest caught her. "Oh...."

"Let me call an ambulance ... or the police?"

"No...." Minta tried again and this time she could lift her shoulders, but when her head went back she groaned again. Then she felt the stranger's hand on her head.

"You've got a pretty bad bump there, must have hit the windshield with your head."

"I'm all right. Is my car all right?"

The stranger, who Minta noticed was young and good-looking, backed away to look at the car. He walked around it while Minta pulled herself out from under the wheel and stood up beside the car.

"Everything looks all right. Good thing there was a bank on the creek or you'd have gone in ... or if you'd been driving faster...."

"Can I back out of here?"

"I think so. Want me to try it for you?"

"Thanks." Minta stepped back while the man stepped into the car; and with a few roars and a few tries, her car was back on the road.

"I think everything is all right. But what about you? That bump on your head should be checked. I'll be glad to take you to the hospital or call your parents."

"No, don't call my parents. Mother, sweet and lovely, knows all the social things except how to teach me to impress the right guy...."

"What?"

"Don't mind me, I'm reacting to the bump on my head, but I'm all right." She got into her car and started the engine. "Thanks, stranger ... I'll be just fine now ... at least physically...."

"I'll follow you home. You live here in town, don't you?"

"How did you know?"

"Your license ... I know a little about this area."

"Well ... we're all smart but Minta."

"Minta?"

"That's me."

"Minta, are you drunk?" The question was direct and blunt.

"No, I am not under the influence of alcohol."

"Then that bump on your head...."

"No, we can't even blame me on the bump on my head. I am simply a rejected woman, and the emotional strain is too much for me. I'll be all right when I get used to the idea and the shock. 'Bye."

With a sudden jerk, she was off again. The stranger got into his car and followed her. Minta was aware that she was a little dazed but capable, and when she rounded a corner shakily she was almost glad the stranger had insisted on following her. As she drove into her own driveway he parked in front of the house, got out, and reached her car door before she could open it. Minta looked up at him.

"I told you I'm all right. You see, I drove home very well."

"A bit wobbly ... come on, I'll help you get into the house. Will I frighten your parents?"

"Nothing frightens my parents unless you use improper grammar or pick up the wrong fork at dinner ... or, perhaps, if you voice an opinion on the political situation in our beloved Green Village."

"I'll be careful not to say a word. I'm new here, anyway."

"Good thing." Minta took hold of his arm as she stood on her feet, felt her head swim, and leaned on him a lot. "Maybe it's a good thing you followed me home."

"My pleasure," he said, taking her elbows in both his hands and guiding her to the front door. Leaning forward, he was ready to turn the doorknob when the door opened before he touched it.

"Minta...." said a stylish, middle-aged lady.

"Mother, I'm sorry I'm a mess, but ... well, I didn't get my hair combed but I came home anyway." Her tone was sarcastic.

"What happened? Minta, are you all right?"

Her escort answered, "She's a little shook and has a bit of a bump on her head; other than that, I think she's all right."

"Who are you?" asked Minta's mother, looking at the young man.

"I'm Barney Tremon...." he looked at Minta significantly, "if anyone is interested."

"Were you out on a date with my daughter?"

"No, sorry, but I wish I could have been."

"Mother, please," said Minta, irritated. "He is not my date. I had an accident, and he followed me home."

"Did he run into you?"

"No, Mother. He was nice enough to stop and help me."

"Did you need help? Minta, are you all right?"

"I thought you'd never ask, Mother. Yes, I'm all right. Thanks, Barney ... Barney...."

"Barney Tremon, and I go to the University."

"All right, so you aren't Minta's date."

"Minta," said Barney quietly, as he looked from her mother to Minta again. "Minta is a very pretty name." Then looking back at her mother, he added, "Did you create that name, Mrs. ... Mrs. ... "

"Morgan. Yes, I did...."

"Minta Morgan," said Barney, almost in a whisper this time, as he looked back at Minta. "A pretty name for a pretty girl ... may I call you later?"

"Well, I ..."

"Just to find out if you're all right ... of course."

"Fine with me."

"Well, it isn't ... " her mother started to say. But Barney took over again.

"And it was very nice meeting you, Mrs. Morgan." He

46

emphasized the name as he glanced quickly at Minta. "I was glad I happened along just in time, and glad she wasn't hurt. You'll be hearing from me." Barney turned and left quickly.

"But I...."

"It's no use, Mother, he's gone. Now if you don't mind, Mother, I'd like to have a hot bath and dinner in my room."

"Of course, dear. Your father and I were going out anyway. He has some political meeting."

"Of course, when did he ever stay home? We're never bothered with family night. Not us... Sometimes I wonder why you and Father ever joined the church."

"We were born in it, my dear, and we go... you know we do."

"When it doesn't interfere with anything else."

"Now, that isn't true...."

"I don't want to argue, Mother. I'm tired, I'm shook up, and I want to go somewhere and cry all by myself. So go on. Please go away."

"Minta, I have never been able to teach you respect for your parents or your home. I guess I'm a failure, but goodness only knows I've tried...."

"When did you try, Mother? When you call this empty group of rooms a home? You defile the word." Minta headed for the stairway, found herself a little dizzy, grabbed the railing and pulled herself to the top of the stairs, across the hall and into her room. She kicked the door shut and locked it.

Later, after a tub soak, Minta lay on her bed looking out of the big second-story window. The sun had gone down, leaving traces of red and gold in the sky, and here and there a tiny star was just beginning to show through. Minta thought of Deek, the only star in her sky, the only light in her life. She remembered the first time she ever saw him. She was a sophomore; her family had moved to Green Village in the beginning of that year of school. Being a new girl in a small town, whose father was the new principal and had more money than the average citizen of Green Village, she was immediately the center of attraction. There were plenty of boyfriends around from the very beginning, and Minta had been flattered. But that day, the first time she had really noticed Deek was in the sophomore game. He was playing tackle that year; he was big for a sophomore, and he'd rolled a player out of bounds, almost hitting the stand. He looked up, and Minta was just above him. He looked tough and hot, but he returned her smile anyway. That night at the dance he'd danced with her several times. They'd laughed and laughed, laughed at nothing and everything. It was crazy and fun and . . . that was what Deek had meant when he said she didn't laugh anymore. But that was before she really cared. Why had she cared too much? Why had she blown it? It seemed like suddenly he was just saying insulting things instead of being fun. Or was she the one who had changed? Well, he had been right about one thing he'd said before she left him, before the accident. She was too serious, and she would be easy for him to get. That's what Siggie had said, too. Siggie? She'd offered to help. . . .

"It's a chance," Minta said aloud to herself. "What have I got to lose? If I don't do something different, I've lost him for good. I'll go see Siggie, even if I have to take back everything I've said and thought against her. I've got to try and get Deek back."

Chapter Five

True to his word, Signee heard from Eric, and much sooner than she had expected. His short note was typical of the old Eric who was always full of ideas, well organized and positive:

"Dear Sig:

"To find available land or an old building or barn, put all the kids you can get ahold of to work. They'll come up with something. As soon as you've located something you think will do, let me know the price and terms the owner wants, and then I'll send you some more instructions. Remember the guy I told you about? He'll help. He's everything you'll need to get things going. Sig, when the time is right he'll be there. Happy hunting ... Alta sends her love with mine.

Love, Eric"

Signee folded the letter and couldn't help smiling at the familiar signature, wondering if he also signed all of Alta's cards and flowers with the same "Love, Eric." Good old wonderful Eric, she was thinking as she put his note back in the large envelope and slipped it into her desk. She sat there a few minutes, just letting herself get excited. She could depend on Eric, she knew that; and if anyone could teach her how to ...

there wasn't time to think back anymore. The drama class filed in.

Walking to the front of the room as the second bell sounded, she broke into her surprise without introduction.

"In this class we have talked a lot about a theater ... a summer-winter theater of our own. I am happy to announce today that we are going to make that dream a reality ... if you will help." The kids started to comment, but she raised her hands for silence and went on. "What we need is an old building, a barn, or even a place for an amphitheater ... someplace we can put up lights, make a stage, build some dressing rooms, and have room for the people who buy the tickets. We have some men that will help us if we can just find a place to start working on. It may take more than one year, but the time can be shortened if you'll all help. What do you say?"

The reaction of the students was in the affirmative, and even though Signee warned them of the hours of work involved, their excitement only grew. As she talked, the tears came to her eyes and a lump in her throat made her falter. Finally, all she could think of to sum up her feelings was: "You guys, you're great! You know that? You're just great!"

They all laughed. Signee had used her favorite un-grammatical sentence and they responded. By the end of the class period, she had assigned areas to be explored for possible sites. When the class ended, it was Deek who came to her desk for some private chatter.

"Siggie, what are you going to do when you get your theater?"

Signee turned quickly in her chair to face Deek, her eyes clear with excitement, her face radiant with anticipation and challenge.

"Deek, we are going to put on a three-act play. We are going to put up the basic scenery the first week of rehearsal, and long before the show is ready to be made public, we will have our lights, props, scenery and everything we need to work with right on stage. Deek, you are going to love acting if we ever complete our theater."

He tilted his head and bit his lip. "I guess I could go for that."

"What?" Signee looked at him squarely, unbelieving. "You mean it? You would really be part of our theater?"

"Even to acting, if that's what you want."

"But Deek, you said you couldn't be interested in drama. You said you were a football lover and you said the two didn't mix. Didn't you say that?"

"That's only sometimes, Siggie. You sort of make us all come alive. I can be as enthusiastic about acting as I am about football; it just depends who's watching."

"I'll be watching. . . ."

"That's good enough for me."

"And your parents . . . you can count on them, can't you?"

"Always, for whatever I'm doing. My fans . . . sometimes they even embarrass me with their attention. I've got a cousin that used to play football for Green Village . . . he remembers most of the plays and sometimes he tries to outthink the coaches and run the game from the bleachers. Yeah, I guess they'd come and watch me act, if I can act. Do you really think I can, Siggie?"

"Haven't I told you often enough? And, judge for yourself . . . come out and tryout."

"How long will it be before we start this acting?"

"When we get a stage or part of one . . . could be next year."

"That will be a little late. I think we ought to get going on the whole project right now."

"The first step is to find some land or. . . ."

"I know . . . an old barn. Don't worry, Signee, you'll have your old barn . . . I know about one my grandfather owns. No one uses it now, and there is just a chance. . . . We'll get a place; don't you worry, Siggie."

As Signee watched Deek go, she thought what a beautiful specimen of a man he was. The way he walked, the carriage of his head . . . he had confidence and knew what he wanted out of life. "No wonder Minta wants him," thought Signee, as she cleared off her desk. This was her one free hour of not teaching, and she was anxious to organize her plans.

"I see you had your little closed session with your favorite student again." Signee looked up to see Minta coming toward her.

"How long have you been standing there?"

"Long enough. Why? Did you say anything I might find detrimental to your character?"

"Afraid not. We were just having a little conversation about our new theater."

"Anything I should know?"

"Something you might like to be in on. I think we're going to get our theater at last."

"And will I be the star of your show?"

"That depends."

"On how much money I can raise? My father will give a lot to keep me happy and out of his way."

"Minta, don't you think you are unkind and even unfair to your parents?"

"They are both unkind and unfair to me. They are the elders, therefore it's more their fault than mine."

"Well, I see that it is feel-sorry-for-Minta day today, so there's no use our talking about that."

"Oh, well...." said Minta, shrugging her shoulders. "I came about another matter."

"All right. How can I help you?"

"There it is ... that beautiful spirit of serving, giving of oneself."

"It sounds like you don't approve."

"I don't."

"Then why are you here?"

"Because you seem to think you know all about men, and I need a man method right now."

"I didn't say I knew all about men...."

"Well, maybe you didn't use those words ... anyway, I want to know how you ... what method you would use ... what little games you might play to capture the man of your dreams."

"My dreams or yours?"

"I think we are having duplicates these days."

"You are referring to Deek, of course."

"Of course. Who else? You do like him, don't you? When I saw you together just now...."

"What you think you saw and what was there are two different things. I like Deek very much. I love him even, but it's a kind of love you wouldn't understand. Deek and I are attracted to each other because we have the same kind of background. Our parents are very much the same kind of parents. He has been raised with the same kinds of ideals and goals as I have. In other words, we are both products of the Gospel; we see things

52

very much the same. He is a secure person, he knows what he wants. . . ."

"You don't have to sell me on Deek. Just tell me how to bring him around. Give me the games now."

"That's another thing you won't understand. I don't play games. Games are untruthful and deceptive. Whatever you do, you must be honest and just."

"Honest and just when you deliberately set out to capture a guy? Not even I am dishonest enough to say that's honest; but if it works, I don't care."

"I can't help you if you have that attitude. You don't set out to capture a guy; you become the kind of person he will be attracted to."

"You mean I have to change and be something I'm not?"

"Minta, you must be a better person than you want me to think you are, or you wouldn't admire Deek so much. We can only change ourselves, not anyone else. Were you thinking of trying to change Deek?"

"Well, I . . . yes. . . ."

"If you could change him, you might not like the product. Do you love Deek?"

"Yes I do, and I don't mind admitting it."

"Then you must love what he is. He wouldn't be what he is if you changed him. I'm not saying there isn't reason or need for improvement, but if you try to change him he will resist with all his humanity and masculinity."

"Don't use big words with me. I can't understand them."

"I'm sorry, but those aren't big words, just explanatory words."

"Then explain them."

Somewhere a bell rang and reminded them school was out. Signee didn't want to lose the opportunity to get closer to Minta, but her obligations pulled at her. She could tell the bell had made Minta nervous, too. Signee happily realized that Minta was more sincere about this communciation she hoped to attain than she had guessed. A sudden thought began to form in Signee's mind.

"Minta, you have cheerleading practice tonight, haven't you?"

"Yes. But I don't care if I don't go."

"As advisor, even though I don't have to be there tonight, it wouldn't be quite right for me to be the one to keep you away." She put her arm around Minta's shoulders and felt her tighten. She ignored the reaction and pulled her arm around her a little tighter.

"Look, I have an idea. What about you having dinner with me tonight? I have a meeting right now, and...."

"I don't want to take your precious time." Her remark was sarcastic, which gave Signee another clue as to how much she was feeling the need of help. She ignored the sarcasm.

"My time isn't that precious; I just have an obligation to those at the meeting, especially your father."

"What could my father say to any teacher that would be helpful, when he doesn't even know how to talk to me?"

"I don't know what has broken down communication with you and your father, but he's a good principal. He's a wise man about his job."

"Then let him do his job," said Minta quickly. Signee was quiet, trying to think of how to help her understand her father. Minta softened in the silence with Signee's arm around her. "Oh, I don't blame Dad. I love him, but Mother keeps him so busy he hasn't any time for me. Dad really doesn't care a lot about social things; it's Mother...."

"Then why not call your mother and ask if you can stay at my place tonight?"

"All night?"

"Why not? I have plenty of room. We could eat and talk as long as we want. We can talk about you and Deek...."

Minta smiled. "You talked me into it. Mother probably won't be home, but I'll call her if you say so."

"I say so. It's part of our new program ... being an example of what you want others to be...."

"Oh, Siggie, you are too much."

"Hey, I'm late. If you have a few minutes, how about locking up for me?" Signee took the keys out of her pocket and Eric's letter fell on the floor. It fell open and Minta picked it up. Eric's "Love, Eric" was sprawled all over the bottom so that no one could miss it. A look came over Minta's face. Signee caught the worry.

"Oh, that's Eric's letter about my theater. Read it."

Minta glanced through the few words, then looked up. "What does he mean he's found a guy that has everything you need?"

"Oh, that ... he must be a person that knows a lot about the theater."

"Doesn't sound like that to me; sounds like he's trying to match you up. What's your connection with Eric? I heard some of the kids say...."

Signee touched Minta's face with her fingertips. Minta looked up, and with all the sincerity she knew how to use, Signee said: "Don't make a big deal out of nothing. I'll tell you about Eric when we talk tonight, if you want to know. After we talk about you and Deek. All right?"

"All right, and you don't have to. I mean, tell me about the letter, if you don't want to." There was a new trust in Minta's voice that made Signee tingle inside. She took the letter from Minta and placed the keys firmly in her hand.

"I've got another idea. How about taking my car home ... to my place, if you get out of cheerleading practice before my meeting is over, and you probably will. So instead of waiting, why don't you drive to my place and start our dinner? You do like to cook, don't you?"

"Yes, but...."

"Then look in the fridge and put together anything that pleases you. There are lots of things for salad; I've got some tomato soup ... or whatever. I like everything. All right?"

"All right." Minta's eyes widened into disbelief, but there was a new glow in them. She jiggled the keys in her hand. "I'll lock up everything and meet you ... but I hope you like my cooking."

"I'll love it." Signee moved quickly into the hall going in the direction of the faculty room, Eric's open letter still in her hand. She glanced down and re-read the words "Remember the guy ... and he's everything you'll need to get things going." What had Eric meant? Surely he wasn't going to be like other old friends and try matchmaking with her? No, that couldn't be Eric. She wouldn't think about that, only the theater. After all, she knew Eric would be the first one to say ..."don't make a big deal out...." She'd used the expression with Minta, but she had learned it from Eric. "That's good advice," she said out loud, without realizing she had spoken out loud.

"What's good advice?" said a voice behind her. Signee turned to see Minta's father, Principal Morgan.

"I guess I'm learning to talk to myself. I wonder what that's a sign of."

"A mind too full ... if one's mind can be too full," he said with a friendly smile.

"I guess it also means I'd better reorganize mine."

"Good idea, I need that too. Say, ..." he said as he fell into step beside her, "I've been going to tell you that though I was warned against hiring you and had some concern, all my fears are gone. You are about the liveliest small bit of teacher we've had in this school for a long time."

"Well, thank you. I didn't know I worried you."

"Well, you know, a local girl, small and pretty ... who all the boys know ... I thought you might have a discipline problem."

"Sometimes I do; but I still hold the grade book."

"Good. And do they bug you about not being married?"

Signee nodded.

"That doesn't bother you?"

"It bothers me, but I'm not ready to do anything about it."

"That's what I wanted to know. I've seen some of the football players spending a little extra time in drama and English than I've noticed before...."

"Don't worry, Mr. Morgan, football players aren't as tough as they look." Signee made light of the comment, but she instinctively knew that Minta and her father had had some kind of communication, and Minta's worries had come out.

"Well, if you need assistance," Principal Morgan said lightly, "we can always advertise and get you a husband."

"I'll let you know if I have a problem."

They entered the room together but separated at the door, Principal Morgan taking his place at the head of the long faculty table and Signee taking hers at the side. But her thoughts were whirling. This was all getting a little too obvious. Marriage was something she intended to handle herself, and the man she would marry would certainly never be one Morgan and his advertising might bring up, or Eric and the guy who had everything she needed. Then, as quickly as the thought had entered her head, she knew how foolish it was. Morgan had been kidding about the ad, and the Eric of old certainly wouldn't be trying to find her a husband.... "Signee, you are getting too sensitive," she reminded herself as the meeting came to order. Then she remembered what Morgan had insinuated ... the football boys—meaning Deek, of course. Surely he couldn't be worried about her with these high school boys.

Chapter Six

"What a date Siggie would be," said Deek as he joined his friend Corey in front of the lockers as they finished dressing after football workouts.

"She's a cute gal," agreed Corey, who didn't often go with girls but liked to discuss them.

"Yeah, I think I could really go for her," smiled Deek.

"You serious? She's too old for you."

"What's a few years? She really turns me on."

"Oh, for flippin' sakes ... act your age, Deek."

"I'm trying ... I feel older than the rest of the guys."

"You sound like Mr. Big who's dated the world."

"I haven't dated many girls, that's true, but girls are so dumb. Now you take Siggie; she has a head on her cute shoulders."

"Are you serious?"

"About Siggie?"

"Who are we talking about, anyway?"

"No, you dumb head. I'm not romantic about Siggie. But I sure do like her, and the girl I marry someday is going to have to be a lot like Siggie ... in fact, if she's still around after my mission, I just may consider dating her."

"That's better ... after your mission you should have more brains."

"I've got brains now; that's why she appeals to me. But there is something I'm going to do for her right now, before I go on my mission."

"What's that?"

"I'm going to get her that theater she's talking about. You know, she's really crazy about that idea, and she's got lots of ideas of what to do with it."

"How are you going to manage that?"

"You know that old barn at the bottom of the canyon on our land?"

"The round-topped one?"

"Yeah. That thing used to hold tons of hay. I remember riding the derrick that put it up in the loft. My dad used to ride the derrick before me."

"That's way up there...."

"I know, but there's a road that goes through the canyon and cuts off there. When she was talking today, I began to think about that barn; and if my dad will let me...."

"You think he might give it up?"

"He doesn't use it anymore. It's worth a try. When Dad knows how enthusiastic Signee is and the good things she wants to use it for ... I think he'll come around."

"Deek, you are nuts."

"I know, but I want to do something neat for Siggie, and that's all she wants."

"You'll have some competition; half the drama class is out looking for land or barns ... some good-sized competition."

"You see, a lot of the guys dig her. There might even be a few that have acting ability, too."

Together the boys raced to the end of the blacktop parking lot, where they separated, and Deek ran on home. It was late, almost dark; football practice had been driving into the shortening days until it was hard to see the football in the air before they ran for the showers. Deek had been getting home too late for dinner, but he knew he could depend on his mother to leave him something he could put into the microwave and have a hot dinner. It was quiet as he entered the back door, and in a family of six children that was a rarity. Deek was the third in the family. His oldest sister was married, had a baby boy, and lived close. She was usually on hand once or twice a day. His oldest brother was on a mission in England, and the three younger children were two fighting boys and a cute little sister, spoiled with too much attention but sharp for her age. He looked around for a note; his mother usually left one for him if his parents were going to be away. There wasn't a note this time. Deek put the expected plate of food into the microwave and started exploring the house.

"Anybody home? Lights and nobody home?" he called, mimicking his father. Then he heard a voice; his father was talking on the phone in his study. He opened the door and put his head in.

"...and if you want me to take that group to the canyon on Friday, I guess I'll be able to manage that too. Maybe I can get Deek ... oh, there he is now, just a minute...." Putting his hand over the phone, he looked up at Deek.

"Where is everybody?" asked Deek before his father could speak.

"Watching your brother perform in a junior high play. They waited as long as they could, but you were too late. You can go with me if you want to ... in a minute ... say, this is the bishop. Will you be available this weekend to go on an overnight trip with the scouts?"

"Count me out, Dad ... football every night and all day Saturday."

"Oh, ..." was all his father said, and then went back to talking on the phone. Deek went back to the kitchen to eat his warmed plate of food. It was bad, turning his father down when he was just getting ready to ask a favor. They had a policy of cooperation in the family, and even though understanding was stressed, it was sure a lot easier to get a favor when a favor was given. Deek took his plate out of the oven, put it on the placemat his mother had left out, and washed his hands in the sink before he sat down. His mind was trying to contemplate how to explain to his father what he wanted to do for Signee.

"Found your food, huh?" Deek's father was tightening his tie as he walked into the kitchen where Deek was eating.

"I'm glad Mother doesn't forget. You know, Dad, she's a darn good cook. I've eaten at other guys' houses, and I know."

"I've eaten out and I know, too. Want to drive over to the junior high with me?"

Deek was about to tell him he couldn't go. Then he remembered he wanted to talk; and a favor, even a little one, he decided, might help communications.

"Sure. I'm not much on plays, but I'll go with you. Will it be late? I've got some homework."

"No, and we won't see it all. But your brother will know we are there, and that's what counts."

The junior high was on the other side of town, so there was time to talk a little before they got there.

"Father, you know that old barn in the upper pasture at the foot of the hills?"

"My father built that barn, helped his father when he was little."

"Yeah, I know the history. But it isn't good for much anymore, is it?"

"Good and solid. There's some good wood in that barn yet."

"That's what I was thinking, and that old house next to it up there where Grandma lived. I was thinking if we took the lumber from the old house and reinforced the old barn, it might be good and strong again."

"Maybe. What do you want it for?"

"I want to give it to Siggie."

"Why would you want to do that?"

"She wants to make a theater out of it."

"It would take more money than it's worth."

"I'm not asking you about that. I just want to know if I can give it to her."

"How would you give it to her? The land where it sits is very valuable. If you moved the buildings, they would crumble."

"I want to keep them there ... can't we fix it legal some-way, and let her use the old barn and fix it up, and let her have it for as long as she wants to use it for a theater, but make it so she can't sell the land to anyone else, or something like that?"

"I suppose we could do that."

"She wants it for a good cause, Father. She's a good person and wants to help kids. She says drama can build people's lives, and...."

"I know Siggie. I've known her since she was a little girl. I

62

knew her parents even before they moved into that house they are living in now. She's a good girl, at least I haven't heard anything against her ... there has been some talk, and I wouldn't want you to get mixed up in any of that."

"Oh, for heck sake. You think I don't know what I'm doing? She's a good girl, Father. I don't know anything about the talk, but I know she's as good a person as I've ever known in my life. She's like Mother, and...."

"Wait a minute. Maybe I'd better find out just why you want to give her so much."

"So much ... you call an old run-down barn much? It may turn out to be more valuable than the land it sits on when she gets through with it, but she deserves some help if this is what she wants to do. And I want to help her."

"I think that's very admirable," said Deek's father thoughtfully.

"Then I can have the old barn?"

"Have it?"

"Have it ... lease it ... whatever I have to do to make it available to Siggie."

"But do you think that's wise?"

"What do you mean?" Deek's hope suddenly turned to surprise.

"You seem to be so intense about Signee, and if you give her the barn, won't people think...?"

"What are you suggesting, Father?"

"I'm not suggesting anything, but I do want to protect you from even the appearance of anything that might be suggestive to others."

"Are you trying to say you think there's something between Siggie and me?"

"I'm trying to say there are people who will think that, and I'm asking you if you've considered that possibility and if you are prepared to handle that kind of talk."

"Well, I ... " Deek was getting angry, and his breath came in short gasps as he struggled for words.

"Just a minute ... " Deek's father put his hands firmly on the shoulder of his son. Deek tightened!

"My own father ... I didn't expect this from you."

"I'm not saying it ... just take it easy, and let's discuss this."

"I don't want to discuss it."

"Just what I thought. You aren't ready to give a gift to anyone because you aren't ready to face what might happen in the minds of others."

"I'm thinking about the mind of my father. I've changed my mind about going to the play. If you'll pull over, I think I'll walk from here."

"I'll pull over in a minute ... but before you run off in your anger, don't you want to hear me out?"

"I don't want to hear you out. I thought I could talk to you about anything, and I find out you don't trust me."

"I didn't say that."

"You didn't have to say it ... I'll find some other way of getting one...."

"Easier than talking to me?"

"Yes."

Deek tightened his arms around himself and sat like a rock. His father pulled into the parking lot of the junior high school and brought the car to a stop, but he didn't make a move to get out of the car. His voice was calm as he spoke to his son, and as the words poured out, even a stranger listening in would have been moved by the firm concern in his voice.

"Deek, you haven't asked me for counsel. You've only asked me for the old barn to help a young lady with a dream, and I think that's admirable...."

"I can see you do," said Deek, his voice sarcastic. His father went on as if he hadn't noticed his son's tone of disapproval.

"Deek, that old barn is on the very piece of property I have divided in my will to be yours someday. I really don't care if you want to turn it into a theater. Land is valuable; the barn is probably worth quite a bit, and if others put money into the barn we can have some legal problems if it isn't handled correctly. But the land and the barn aren't my first concern. I care about you more than all the land."

"And you don't trust me, right?"

"Wrong. I trust you not only with the land and that old barn and my life ... but I trust you with yours, which is more important to me than my own."

"But not enough to let me do with my life what I want to do, huh?" Deek was relaxing a little but still very defensive.

64

"Yes, I even trust you that way ... or would, if I had the right to give you your own free agency ... but I haven't that right. You were born with your free agency, to live your life as you choose. But I'm trying to be true to myself by being a good father and giving you the counsel you need."

"Take my word for it, you've been counseling me since the day I was born; and since I'm getting ready to leave home next year for some place in the mission field, perhaps you'll stop pushing me and let me think for myself."

"Exactly. That's the very reason for my questions that made you so angry."

Deek turned and looked at his father. "You're playing games with me, just to see if I still have a temper?"

"Just to see if you can prepare yourself for talk that might occur in a small town, talk that can cause a lot of hurt. The questions I've asked you, Deek, are the questions that could go through the minds of other people. You should know what you're facing."

"Then you don't think ... ?"

"I think I know a little about my own son. But you need to be prepared to arm yourself." He put his hand on Deek's shoulder again; this time Deek felt the understanding that went with that touch, and turned to look at his father as he continued. "Son, I've been aware for some time now that you admire Signee. I haven't found anything wrong in that admiration, and I haven't had any reason to question your motives. Others might. My first reaction to your enthusiasm was a concern for you, and I wondered if you thought you were falling in love."

"But Father, you know I'm not going to go for any girl until I get home from my mission."

"I know that's what you want. But emotions get out of hand without our wanting them to if we don't set up a guard, and I wondered if ... "

"If I was going overboard for a girl older than myself?" His father nodded and Deek smiled, relaxing, glad the communication was coming back. "Well, maybe you're right. Maybe I do think of Signee, but I'm not stupid enough to push that. She'd be a wonderful person, Father, and if she were my age I might try to tie her down even before I go on my mission. But I know that wouldn't be right. I should know; you and Mom have told me often enough. Besides, I'm a coward, I don't want the responsibility of a commitment. But she's wonderful, and I do want to do something to help her ... besides, she has a way of bringing out the best in me. You know, she's talked me into thinking I can act."

"And why not? You've always been a mimic."

"Yeah, but not on stage."

"The whole world's a stage ... haven't you read Shakespeare?"

"Can't say I have ... never met the man."

They both laughed and the strained emotion between them was all gone. Deek ventured the question again.

"What about the barn, Father?"

"I give it to you to do as you will. I caution you that legal problems are difficult to work out later, so they should be handled now. If you mess up the job, you'll be the one who has to work out the mess. I'll give you that section of land in your inheritance when I get through with it ... that means when I'm dead. And probably by then you'll have more land and money than I have. But anyway...."

"I'll make my own, Father. That's one thing I've learned from you ... when you make your own, you do with it what you want to do with it...." He mimicked his father's voice.

"That's right, and don't you forget it." They laughed again. "And now," he said, "if we don't get inside to see that play, we'll never live it down with your brother."

"Thanks, Father; I'm sorry I lost my cool."

"Well, son, I hope you don't react that emotionally to everybody who says what they might think when you go overboard at doing good for a pretty teacher."

"But I told you...."

"Wait a minute ... I'm convinced, but others will never understand, or even want to. Some people like to find a juicy story ... if you get upset, it just emphasizes what they'll say. Your reactions and actions will kill the story. You'll have to toughen up a little; Signee's had to live through some of that already."

"What do you mean?"

"There've been a few stories...."

"What stories?"

"You don't want to hear stories, Deek."

"I'd like to know what people are saying."

"It's more important how *you* feel. There are always good reasons why people do what they do, and stories only say what people think they do. Besides, the old saying that the 'proof of the pudding' ... you know, and I believe Signee is a very fine person ... as you have told me a about couple of ... well, a few 'wonderful' times."

Deek opened the car door on his side, and the two of them got out and walked toward the junior high auditorium together.

"Thanks, Father. You don't know how much I appreciate the barn."

"I hope it does the good Signee wants it to. It should be fun to see if you can raise enough money to make it any good."

"Father ... it's neat that you trust me."

"I sometimes need reassuring ... thus the quiz ... you did what I expected. I guess that's why we have to trust you, Deek ... because you have always lived up to the best in you. I don't mean you haven't made mistakes ... and you're allowed a few...."

"I've made plenty, and...."

"But the little ones ... well, that keeps us repenting, doesn't it?"

"I guess ... but I don't want to have to repent. It wastes so much time."

"That's one point of view ... hey, there's the applause. Do you suppose we've missed the whole thing?"

They started taking the steps two at a time.

"You know, Father ... if this play doesn't last too long, I think I'll drop by Signee's and tell her about the barn."

"She's living alone ... what will the neighbors think?" His father smiled.

"I'll watch her reputation ... and mine. Maybe I'll use a walkie talkie for communication."

They both laughed and hurried toward the doors, where the applause told them the play was a success.

Chapter Seven

"I love cream of tomato soup," said Signee, leaning back against the pillow, "and what a good idea to light the gas log in the fireplace. I love getting snuggly in front of the fire."

"I'm glad you don't mind me taking over. I've really enjoyed myself fixing things. I didn't know I liked to cook, but when it's for something special ... like this ... it's fun."

"You're special for me. I don't like living here alone."

"I wish I could live with you, Siggie."

"Are you serious?"

Minta hesitated, looking up at Signee from her squatting position on the floor in front of the fire. "Yes, I am. I didn't know I was feeling that; it just slipped out. But yes, I wish I could live here with you...." She dropped her head. "But you probably wouldn't like that; I'm not easy to get along with."

"Nothing worthwhile is easy. But maybe your parents wouldn't like the idea, since you're the last one at home."

"Last—that's me, spoiled, doted on, bossed, not able to draw a breath of my own that I don't feel guilty about."

"Why do you feel guilty?"

"Because I have never been able to do anything good enough to live up to my good name. So my father and my mother remind me constantly."

"A heritage problem, huh?"

"Nothing I'm so proud of, but maybe I could be if I didn't feel so guilty. Great-grandfather Morgan was one of the original Saints back in Nauvoo and came across the plains. He married Great-grandmother, no less a valiant soul, and the generations have been climbing ever since. Of course we don't talk about Aunt Betty, who ran away and married a gambler and was excommunicated from the church; and Cousin Corey, who died of alcoholism ... and a few other wayward relatives ... the exception of which our family genealogy sports some of the most noble of the genteel gentlemen of our time. Maybe if I was a convert they'd think I was neater. I'd like to be a convert to something or other, to make my parents take notice."

"I think when you approve of yourself you won't have to worry about their approval."

"Sounds like the beginning of a sermon."

"You're just touchy. It's the beginning of a discussion, that's all, and only if you want to discuss."

"I don't mind discussing if I get to give my side of the discussion."

"Isn't that what discussion means?"

"Tell my mother that, huh?"

"By the way, did you call your mother?"

"I left word. I drove by and left her a note. Somehow when I tell her anything we end up in an argument or with me feeling like I should apologize for something. I try to avoid that feeling."

"If you are having problems with your parents, maybe it would be good for all of us if you move in here with me. You can have your own bedroom and bath, but it isn't fancy like that big house of yours."

Minta's face brightened. "If you really mean it, I'll bring my closet over tomorrow."

"If you have your parents' permission."

"I can cause a little trouble, and they'll be glad to ..." Looking up, Minta saw Signee's face cloud up and hurried to make amends. "No, I won't do that. But I'm confusing to my parents; I'm sure they'll be glad to have me out of the way for a while. As long as I call them, they won't object." Minta laughed a tight little laugh. "I don't know why my parents had me; they really don't like children. Father tries. He's a principal, but his family looks down on him for that ... he's the only one of his brothers who doesn't make big money."

"You seem to have plenty."

"Money isn't our problem; mother has an inheritance. But I don't think they like each other very much."

"What makes you say that?"

"I never see any signs of love ... no kisses...."

"Maybe they have a different way of expressing their feelings."

"How many ways are there? Can I live with you?"

"If your parents approve. You'll have to do your share of the work." Signee smiled at Minta, and there was a warm feeling that seemed to flow from her smile. Minta responded.

"I'll pay you rent, too."

"That won't be necessary. I don't pay rent to my parents, I just keep the house up."

"Siggie, I'm so excited. I think I'll like my parents better if I don't have to live with them. And Mother should be happier too; she likes bridge better than she likes me. This way, her responsibility is removed."

"Minta, maybe I'd better call her tomorrow. You do have permission for tonight?"

"Sure."

"Well, then, let's get these dishes taken care of. I feel like a hot bubble bath."

Together they started picking up the dishes from the low glass table Minta had placed in front of the fire.

"Why don't you let me do these dishes while you take your bath, Siggie, and then ..." she hesitated, "maybe we'll have time to talk about ... "

"Deek?" Signee supplied the name and Minta nodded. Signee picked up the placemats. "Sure, I love to talk while I do my nails. Minta, I can see that you and I are going to get along beautifully."

"What if we fight?"

"Our fights will all be healthy, and we'll work them out. Just one thing ..." She stopped and looked at Minta. "Always tell me how you feel, not what you are supposed to feel or what you think I want you to feel, but exactly how you feel. All right?"

"Just what I feel? Are you sure? What if my feelings make you mad at me?"

"If I should be upset about anything, or if you should be upset about anything—we'll talk about it until we each allow the other her own point of view."

"And you won't hate me if I don't think like you think?"

"I won't hate you. I promise I won't hate you."

"How can you promise you won't hate me?"

"Because I'm always going to love you. I've made up my mind."

"I can't believe you, but I hope it works. It doesn't work for my parents." Minta stood quietly looking at Signee.

They were in the bedroom now; Minta had followed Signee around as they talked. She watched now as Signee slipped off her shoes and went on talking.

"It isn't always easy to say what you feel, Minta, or even to know what you really feel. It takes practice."

"All right, I'll practice. If it works with you, maybe it will work with my parents. I hate to be a mess for them all the time."

"You're not a mess, Minta...."

They smiled at each other again, and the magic was there. Signee got out her robe and started the water running in the tub.

"Sure you don't want me to help with the dishes?"

"Siggie, I'm not a baby. There's only about four dishes; you can trust me with those."

"I wasn't thinking of trust, but feeling a little lazy letting you do them alone."

"Don't worry. I'll get them washed and put away while you're in the bubbles." The doorbell rang.

"Who can that be this late?"

"It wouldn't be my parents; they don't care that much. Even if Mother didn't find the note yet she won't get upset, because she only relaxes when I'm not home."

"Don't you think you're a little hard on your parents? I'm sure they love you."

"I suppose," said Minta as she went to answer the door. "What if this is my mother, with a change of heart?"

"What if it is?" came Signee's answer.

"What if it is?" said Minta under her breath, as she opened the door to see Deek standing outside. Surprised, she stepped back. "Deek, what are you doing here?"

"I came to see Siggie, what else? What are *you* doing here?"

"I'm ... I'm. ... " she stopped, her mind racing, and suddenly she felt foolish. "Do you come here often?"

"When I feel like it," said Deek casually. "But this is the first time I've met you here. What's the deal?"

"None of your business."

"You're right. Can I come in? Siggie is here, isn't she? Her car is outside."

"I drove her car ... but yes, she's here."

"In that case, I'll wait. Can I sit down?"

"Certainly ... where are you used to sitting? The couch all right?"

"That will be fine." He walked past Minta casually and sat down on the couch as if it were a natural habit. "You'll call Siggie?"

"I certainly will," said Minta, her lips biting the words as she said them, and turning, left Deek to knock on Signee's bathroom door.

"Yes?" came Signee's reply over the sound of the shower.

"You have a caller."

"I'll be out in a minute; please ask them to wait."

"It is not a 'them', it is a he...."

"All right," said Signee, puzzled at the sound of Minta's voice, "ask him to wait, please."

Minta went back in the front room to deliver the message to Deek. She did so stiffly.

"Miss Short will be with you as soon as she can. She has asked that you wait." She turned to leave.

"Aren't you going to talk to me until she comes?"

"And then disappear quickly so that you two can be alone?"

"Y-yes, I think that will be all right." Deek knew what Minta was thinking, and couldn't help remembering his father's warning. He wanted to laugh out loud, but he was having too much fun watching Minta squirm. "Why don't you sit down,

Minta, and tell me what you've been doing?"

"Because I'd rather tell someone who might care."

"It will make good conversation."

"I don't need your bits of conversation. You made it very clear that you aren't interested in me, and...."

"I didn't say that, Minta. I said you are too obvious and you should back off."

"So I've backed off. Anything else?"

"Yes. Sit down and forget to be sarcastic."

"When did you start having anything to say to me?"

"Oh, come on, Minta. We're friends. I've been wanting to tell you, that you did a good job of cheering at the last game. You guys really work hard for us ... we're grateful."

"Thanks," she said quickly. "I'll tell the cheerleaders we have your approval."

"Still upset, aren't you? Just relax ... reach behind you, Minta; there's a checkers game on that shelf. How about having me a game while Siggie is in the shower?" Minta looked surprised. "Oh, I heard the water when I came in. She is showering, isn't she?"

"Yes, she is," she said, handing the checkers she found on the shelf behind her to Deek. They played checkers, and Minta began to relax when Signee appeared in her robe and slippers, her hair done up in a towel.

"Deek. What a surprise. Minta didn't tell me it was you."

"You didn't ask," said Minta under her breath, and thought: "I'll bet it was a surprise."

"Little teacher ... have I ever got something for you." Deek pushed the checkers aside, and his eyes lit up.

"Tell me about it, Deek. What's up?"

"You said you wanted a barn for a theater?"

"I did. Have you found one?"

"I have ... and you can do whatever you want with it. It might need a lot, but it's yours."

"Deek, ... where ... don't worry about how much we have to do; we'll get it done. Tell me, where?"

"The one above our house in the upper field. I know you've seen it...."

"The old red one near the hill?"

"Sure. What do you think?"

"It's a ways off, but ... Deek ... how did you manage it?"

"It's part of the family, and now it's yours. If you want it."

"Is that what you came here for tonight?" asked Minta.

Deek smiled and turned to Minta, chucking her under the chin.

"Sure. What did you think?"

"Well, I. ... "

"You what?" But Deek didn't wait for her to answer; he moved past her to the door. "Siggie ... I just thought you'd like to know that your worries about a place are over. If you want the old barn, it's yours."

"Can we go look at it after school tomorrow?"

"We can ... you and me and your whole team of drama kids, if you want. I'll go ahead in my truck and open the gates while I sort of see if the old road is passable."

"Deek, I can't tell you how excited I am ... thanks ... I really mean that. After we look at it we can get in touch with Eric and see ... oh, Deek, I thought it would be weeks before we could report a place. I hope it will work."

"We'll make it work, Siggie...."

Deek left them, with a mischievous smile at Minta, and Signee whirled around in her excitement. "Just think, Minta, we're on our way. I've seen that old barn a hundred times; I don't know why I didn't think of it before. But then it's so far up there ... but that won't be bad ... we can cut the road a little deeper ... we can get ... oh, Minta. Isn't that Deek of yours a darling?"

"Deek of mine? I thought for a minute he might be yours."

Signee stopped and looked at Minta. "What are you talking about? You haven't been...."

"Well, what was I to think? He came here and walked in like he knew the place...."

"Minta, sit down." Signee's voice was sterner than she wanted it to be. "Sit down; you and I are going to have that talk, and right now. We can't start off distrusting each other."

"I don't think it will work out ... me living here."

"Yes it will. Sit down, Minta."

Minta sat down, and Signee pulled a chair up close to her. "Minta, we'll talk it all out ... you can ask the questions, and I'll answer whatever you want to know."

"I don't know what questions to ask. You say I don't know how to handle boys, and then I find Deek at your front door. And people say Eric and you ... Maybe I don't want to handle boys, I just want to be honest and not play games. I ... I just want Deek to care about me the way he used to." Minta started to cry. Signee put her arms around her and let her cry on her shoulder.

"I can see why you are confused. You cry, Minta, and when you are through...." Minta suddenly raised her head.

"I'm through now. Crying won't help; I know that much."

"All right ... make yourself comfortable. I'll tell you about Eric and me, and then maybe you'll understand some of the stories people tell, and maybe understand Deek a little better. My story isn't unlike yours, except I was the strong one, and with you Deek is the strong one. You can't get him to go against what he is or believes, can you, Minta? I know you've tried "

"I did...."

"I'm not trying to blame you; just look at the results. You see, Eric and I were just like you and Deek. He was the football player and I was the cheerleader, and we went together ... we'd grown up together. He was big and neat and ... well, I thought he was the one for me. I thought we'd be married when he came home from his mission. Eric came from a family that wasn't very active in the church; and even though he went to church with me and the rest of the kids, he wasn't raised to go on a mission the way really active families teach their boys. And I knew if I said one word, he'd stay home with me. I really didn't want him to go away; but all of my brothers had been on missions, and I knew what a mission meant to a boy and his family. I wanted Eric to have what my brothers had had, and I didn't want to marry a man who hadn't been on a mission."

"Why? What's so great about a mission? Two years away from everybody you love ... there's church work to be done here, too."

"You don't understand, Minta. The prophet has said that every young man should prepare himself and go on a mission ... it's a special time given to studying the Gospel and taking the message to the world. There are so many things a boy learns on a mission. I've heard my mother say, they go out boys and come home men ... and I've seen it happen with my brothers.

Anyway, I wanted Eric to have that experience; I didn't want to be the one to keep him from that. So I told him the way I felt, and when he knew I meant it ... he went."

"You were crazy, Siggie ... you sent him away when he wanted to marry you?"

"Yes, I did."

"Did you promise to wait?"

"No. We didn't make any promises, only to see how we felt when he came home."

"And how did you feel?"

"Well, I was away at school when he came home. Alta was here, and he started going with her ... "

"And you lost him. Is that what you want me to learn about handling men?"

"I haven't finished. Yes, he married Alta. But by that time I was going with Jimmy, and I thought I loved Jimmy. I came home to see Eric, to go with him and see how we felt. But I didn't have to go out with him. I saw him with Alta. She had always loved him. She wrote to him all the time he was on his mission."

"Some friend ... taking advantage while you were away."

"No, Minta, she didn't do that, either. You see, every woman wants a man she can follow, a man she can look up to, one strong enough to be the head of her home. Eric came home from his mission with a strong testimony of the Gospel, and I loved him ... loved him more than ever because of his humility, and ... it's hard to explain, but I knew that I loved him only as a sweet person, a dear brother, not full of dreams and sparkle like I want to love my husband. Oh, I think we could have made it, and maybe we would have if it hadn't been for Alta. But when I saw them together I knew what they had was real and Alta needed him. What I wanted, and would never have had with Eric, was someone stronger than I was to look up to and follow."

"Why couldn't you have had that with Eric? You said if it hadn't been for Alta...."

"No, it's not that way. You see, with Alta, Eric was the leader, the wise man of the Gospel. She always thought he was so great. But with Eric and me ... well, I'd have always bossed him and he'd have let me. We just weren't right ... I knew that then and I know it now. You want a man that's strong, that has a dream, some principles he fights for and cares about even more than he cares about you. You know what I'm talking about. That's why you love Deek. Deek is strong and won't let you push him around."

"I know he won't. He's determined to go on his mission."

"You see, any other boy you've been with wants just to please you. Deek is different...."

"I'll say he's different." Minta was thoughtful, a faraway look in her eyes; then she came back to the present. "What about Jimmy ... what happened to him?"

"Well, Jimmy is another story."

"Why didn't you marry him?"

"Because the love I felt for him was more sympathy than love. I know that now, but at the time I almost married him. It's so hard to know the different kinds of love."

"You say 'Jimmy' kinda special. Are you sorry you didn't marry him? Isn't it better to be married, even if the love isn't perfect?"

"I've thought that more than once. Sometimes I still think that when I get to feeling lonely. But no, I don't want to settle for less than my parents have." Signee unwound her feet from where she'd tucked them in the bottom of her robe underneath her on the chair, and stood up. "No, Minta, I'm not sorry I've waited, and I know that somewhere there is a special person just for me, and if I do the things I'm supposed to and have faith, that someday Heavenly Father will let me know who and where he is."

"Well, I'm not ready to let Heavenly Father decide who I marry."

Signee laughed. "Don't you think Heavenly Father knows whom ... " and she emphasized the grammatical correction, "is best for you?"

"Oh, I don't doubt that He does. But He and I aren't on very good talking terms, and I'm not sure I can understand His language. And in the meantime, I might lose Deek ... Deek ... as if I had him to lose."

"You might have."

"How?"

"By keeping busy developing your talents and not being there every time Deek turns around. You have to be a person with principles and goals, too."

"You mean we're playing games?"

"Not really games ... but sincerely find a way to be so interested in developing yourself to be a good wife and mother that he has to look for you."

"That will be the day, when Deek looks for me."

"When you have completed your goals, after you set them, you will be the kind of a person any Deek will be proud to go looking for. It's called being the kind of person yourself that the man you want to marry is. Does that make sense?"

"No. But maybe you can show me how this works; then I'll understand you. Anyway, what have I got to lose? I can't even get a conversation out of him for anything but checkers right now."

"It will come. Now, let's get some sleep. Since you're going to come and live with me ... I hope ... we'll have time to work out the details. In the meantime, we've got a theater to plan. That will keep you busy. You know, Minta ... I just think I'll make a leading lady out of you."

"You're kidding."

"No, I'm not. You have all the qualities and standard equipment ... we just have to teach you how to use them."

"If you can make an actress out of me, Siggie, I'll believe all the rest of this stuff you've been saying."

"I accept the challenge." Signee pulled her robe tighter around her and started for her bedroom. "Your bedroom is there, at the top of the steps. I turned the nightlight on for you."

"All right, Siggie." Minta started for the steps but stopped halfway up. "Siggie?"

"Yes?" said Signee from her room, where she'd started to open the bed.

"You don't mind me calling you Siggie, do you?"

"Call me whatever you like, as long as you don't feel disrespectful. Siggie will be fine."

Minta went up a few more steps, then turned to call back down. "Siggie?"

"Yes, Minta."

"You don't really love Deek, do you?"

"Why do you ask?"

"Because I saw the way he looked at you tonight, all excited and...."

"That was because he found my barn."

"Do you love him?"

"Of course ... very much." Signee stopped and waited for Minta to say something. Only silence. Then Signee stepped back into the hall and looked up the steps where Minta stood. "Minta, I love Deek very much, the way I love Eric, Alta, and my brothers."

"But does Deek know he should love you like a sister?"

"If he doesn't, my Minta, he will know when he finds the girl who is going to be his wife." She paused for a long minute while her eyes looked into Minta's, then tossed her head and let a smile cover her face. "Goodnight, my Minta. Sleep well."

"I will. Besides," added Minta, as an afterthought that caught Signee off guard, "if I can't have Deek, I'm sure I can have Barney."

"Who's Barney?"

"He's a college boy. He's mighty handsome, and he wants me to be his girl."

"How do you know that?"

"He calls me all the time."

"What's he like?"

"I don't know, I haven't been with him yet. I'm sure he's experienced."

"What do you mean by experienced?"

"He gets what he wants."

"How do you know that?"

"I can tell. He frightens me a little."

"Then you're wise not to go with him."

"I haven't had to yet."

"Is dating a 'have to'?"

"Well, you know, I'm still after Deek; but if I can't have him, it's nice to know someone wants me."

"Nice, but frightening. You're a pretty girl, my Minta. Build your character to be as attractive as your beauty, and you can have anyone you want."

"You know who I want ... 'Night...." Minta turned and left, Signee still looking up to the spot where she had stood only a second ago.

"Yes, my Minta, I know who you want. I do hope you've got what it takes to get him, and you won't get impatient and waste yourself on someone less worthy." Signee waited as if she'd expected Minta to answer, thinking perhaps she'd heard the softly spoken words. But all she heard was the water turned on in the bathroom upstairs.

Chapter Eight

"Minta, it's all fixed with your parents," said Signee when they met at Signee's house the next day. "I hope you don't mind, but I had a chance to talk to your father this morning after our board meeting, and he suggested I call your mother. So I did . . . and it's all right."

"Glad to get rid of me, huh?" Minta kicked off her shoes and turned on the stove to start dinner. "Let's see . . . we can have . . . I hope you don't mind me planning our dinners all the time."

"Oh, no. . . ." said Signee, washing her hands after depositing her books on the desk. "I love it, I told you that . . . and Minta, you're wrong about your parents not wanting you. They love you very much. Your mother said she hoped this arrangement wouldn't be permanent, but as long as you were happy she didn't mind."

"Mother's social position expects her to love her only child and say she wants me home."

"Minta, I'm getting used to you. All these things you say just aren't you."

"Don't count on that, Siggie . . . I'm really not the good girl you think I am . . . underneath I'm just as ugly as I sound. . . ."

Minta stopped setting the table and was thoughtful. "But you know, Siggie, I think I'd like to be the kind of a person you think I am."

Signee, coming back into the kitchen after getting an apron, smiled and threw Minta a kiss happily. "Then you will be, my Minta. Whatever you have the desire for, you also have the talent to become ... my mother taught me that, and my mother was always right. How about chicken to go with what else you've planned tonight? I have some frozen pieces."

"I like chicken, but I can't cook it."

"Then I'll cook the chicken while you do your thing." Signee took out the chicken pieces and put them in the microwave oven to thaw. "Minta, I'm so glad your parents let you come and live with me. We're going to be good for each other; you'll see. Love your parents for letting you stay, please."

"That's one thing I can love them for."

"That's a big blessing."

"Now what are you talking about, Siggie?"

"The blessings that come from keeping the commandment about honoring your parents. For every rule of the Gospel we keep there is a special blessing, and the ones that go with honoring parents are big ones. You'll be entitled to them if you remember to honor your parents."

"Siggie, you spout ideas about the church like they were golden rules at school for which we all get a good grade. You make them sound so common."

"But Minta, they are. Heavenly Father is just like an earthly father, only much more intelligent and wise, and capable of loving us more than an earthly father. Just think how wonderful it was of Him to make sure we have the books so we know the rules."

"Honestly, Siggie, do you think I'll ever understand the Gospel the way you do?"

"Of course you will ... just work at it day by day and do a lot of praying." Signee dipped the thawed chicken pieces in seasoning and melted some butter in a pan. "I'm glad we have a microwave oven; it would certainly take too much time for chicken tonight if we had to cook the conventional way. Do you like your chicken browned?"

"Of course. Browned and crisp."

"Will you settle for browned and tender?"

"If I have to."

"Good girl, Minta." Signee turned to put butter on the table and she and Minta bumped into each other, the butter flying out of Signee's hand and landing in the middle of the floor. Minta, holding a pitcher of water, spilled the contents. There was a gasp from each, and then they looked at each other and laughed. Then suddenly Signee opened her mouth wide. "Minta ... I almost forgot ... have you any boots in the stuff you brought from your closet?"

"I haven't. Why?"

"Minta ... tomorrow, right after school, we are joining the drama students and all the other kids who are working on the barn for a tour. We're going to find out what the place looks like, and you'll need boots. The mud in the field hasn't dried up ... so Deek informs me."

"You mean I'm going, too?"

"Of course. You're a barn worker, aren't you?"

Minta shrugged. "I guess so, if you say so."

"Besides, you'll want to go, Minta. Deek is going to be there."

"Now who's telling me I can chase boys?"

"It isn't chasing to be where you should be, and it's a good opportunity to let Deek see that you can have fun with everyone."

"But I don't have fun with anyone but Deek."

"Then Minta, pretend to have fun with everyone until you learn how."

"Why should I, Siggie?"

"Because that's part of keeping yourself busy. You need to concentrate on friendship and not romance; you need to care about education and acting, and, and, and ... so many things, Minta. It's a wonderful world, and you'll be happy with or without Deek if you can learn to develop your talents."

"I'll never be happy without Deek."

"Of course you will. While Deek goes on his mission, you'll be helping me with the theater ... we'll have play after play, and you can take bit parts and leading parts, help with costumes and make-up. You'd be very good at make-up, Minta."

"Are you trying to say I wear too much make-up?"

"Not at all. You have a very nice way of putting on your

make-up. It looks very natural, and that's good. For stage, we just put on a little more."

"Siggie, you really are excited about the barn, aren't you?"

Signee stopped cleaning up the water they were both mopping at and looked at Minta seriously, her eyes shining. "I really am, Minta. I always dream, but I thought the dream was years away. And now, suddenly it's right here, right now... my own theater... and it belongs to all of the kids who will work on it, too ... I don't want to be selfish."

"You couldn't be selfish if you tried. That's my department."

"There you go again, running yourself down. Don't do it, Minta."

"All right; I'll try and learn to be positive, even about me. But truly, Siggie, wouldn't you rather be married than directing plays and building theaters?" Signee's face clouded, and Minta rushed to explain. "I'm not trying to hurt you, Siggie, really I'm not. I just want to know."

Signee reached out and patted Minta's hand. "I know you just want to know." She sat back on her feet, still holding the wet cloth in her hand. "I'll tell you truly ... of course I want to be married. I've always wanted to be married. Being a wife and mother is my first dream; but that hasn't happened for me yet. He'll come along someday. In the meantime, I'm going to enjoy every minute of my second dream ... the barn ... my theater, and helping kids have a chance to express themselves, to find out what they have inside of them. Do you understand what I mean?"

"I think so. But I want to be married more than anything else. I want to marry Deek."

"I know, Minta. But first you have to deserve him, and that's what we're working on now. In the meantime I'm going to make an actress of you."

"Are you really, Siggie?"

"Of course. You will be good on the stage, you'll see ... you have the talent, I'm sure of it."

Signee was singing a lively tune to herself the next day as she pulled on her boots outside the drama room while she waited for the drama class to gather. She felt good about the barn idea; she felt good about Minta; and she was excited beyond the point of being a quiet, dignified school teacher. She was feeling like the students acted as she climbed into the truck beside Deek and Minta and they started on the trip to the barn. They sang, talked, and laughed all the way until Deek turned off the road and cut through the fields.

"We'll have to cut a road through here," said Deek, as the truck bounced the girls around and the kids in the back complained. "I know Charlie's father has some road equipment we can get him to donate ... if you can give Charlie a part in the first play."

"Then Charlie shall have a part," declared Signee.

"Maybe he can't act," suggested Deek.

"Then we'll teach him."

"That's true faith. I know Charlie can't sing," said Minta.

"Then we'll give Charlie a part he doesn't have to sing." They all laughed, and their laughter echoed above the singing voices in the back of the big truck.

Deek led the way, cutting in and out through the field. The cars behind followed him, until suddenly the truck made an exit into a grove of trees. On the other side of the trees was a clearing where stood the old barn and the small log cabin next to it.

"Who lived in the log house?" asked Minta.

"My great-grandmother," answered Deek proudly. "That log cabin was a favorite spot for my father when he was a boy."

"She should have lived in the barn and put the cows in the house; or was the barn for horses?" Minta was having fun.

"I don't know. I guess all the animals had their turn."

"Deek," said Signee, "I can tell you haven't done a lot of farming. But I am thrilled with this setting. Look, Deek ... look at the clearing beside the barn, it's perfect for parking. I love this whole place; we'll have a unique setting for our entertainment. There must be some way we can put a stage on the outside for summer scenes."

"We'll build whatever you say, Siggie."

"I'll have to have some help planning this ... I want all your ideas, and then we'll get somebody to help us make it work."

That was the beginning, just seeing what they had to work with. Then all the kids piled out, and with their brooms began to clear away the dirt and what was left of rotting hay. It was exciting to discover the possibilities, and the kids had fun jumping out of the hay loft. Signee worried about that and tried to get them to stop before anybody got hurt. They laughed at her and said they would jump at their own risk. Then, when the workers began to drag a bit and the sunlight was almost gone, Deek brought in a lantern, and the girls served donuts and hot cider from thermos jugs. Soon after the food was served, the cars began to leave for town. Deek, Minta and Signee stayed after all the others had found rides home.

"You have to be at school early, don't you, Deek?" Signee was concerned.

"Football after school, not before. I thought we'd better clean up the mess and get it ready to set fire to when I get home from school tomorrow. I hope the wind doesn't blow tonight and undo all all our work." Deek was gathering up garbage to haul back in his truck.

"You've had some good training at home, Deek," said Signee, holding a plastic bag while he piled in the paper plates and cups they'd used to serve the refreshments.

"My sisters usually do this kind of work. I stayed to do this tonight because I'm not ready to go home yet."

"At least you're honest," said Minta. "You can drop the act now that we know your motives." Her words were products of habit, but her tone was teasing and not sarcastic as it had been before when she had talked to Deek.

"Well, I don't mind the clean-up, but I really wanted to talk about the stage."

"Oh, sorry," said Minta. "It sounds like the conversation is for you two, and not me."

"You're part of the theater too, Minta," said Signee. "In fact, my deah ... you are going to loooove ... the theatah...."

"Sure, stick around," said Deek.

"I think I will," said Minta, and picked up a broom.

After the clean-up and darkness settled in, the three of them drove home together. When they reached Signee's house, they were still talking about the possibilities of what they could do with the barn. Without thinking, he followed Signee and Minta in, and they all sat down to discuss again in the middle of Signee's front room.

"Look, women ... the way I see it, the barn is basically good. If we can organize the girls to scrub and clean after the guys get all the rest of that junk out and burned, then we are ready to start building. You do like the place, don't you, Siggie, even if it is old?"

"How can you ask? I love it, Deek."

"All right, I've got this idea. I think I can organize the guys, and meet with some businessmen in town and get them to donate for free advertising on the barn, and for a tax break for those who don't want to advertise ... and we can raise some good money. I would like to be the one to organize and get the bids, Siggie ... if that's all right with you."

"Great, Deek ... as soon as we get the whole thing drawn to scale. I don't know who I'll get for that, but Eric said he'd help. I'll write him the details tonight."

"Good. I will do the footwork. Just one thing bothers me."

"What's that, Deek?" Minta and Signee asked, both at once.

"How are we going to work school and basketball into our schedule?"

They all laughed, and Deek got up to leave. "I guess I'd better get home and think that one out. Siggie ... this is a great idea of yours. I haven't seen the guys so excited about anything since we took State last year."

"You'd better take State this year, too, or I'll probably get fired."

"We'll take State. If Minta can keep the girls cheering, we'll take State...."

"I'll do my job, Deek. I promise."

"Great. Well, I'm glad the barn is going to work out. And don't worry about the legal things, Siggie; I'll take care of that too."

After Deek left, Signee and Minta plopped on the couch again.

"I'm too tired to move, Minta."

"Me, too. I'm not used to this kind of labor. But what gets me is Deek."

"What about Deek?"

"I've never seen him so enthusiastic about anything but playing ball before."

"He is excited, isn't he? It's a good thing. We wouldn't even be started yet without his barn."

"I think he's enthusiastic because of you, Siggie."

"Now, Minta, we aren't going to start on that again, are we?"

"Well, you explain why a boy who has never liked drama is suddenly Mr. Big in the business of theater."

"Maybe it's the building or the business he likes. Anyway, hang around and see how it all works out, Minta. It might be fun."

"Don't worry, Siggie, I couldn't leave if I wanted to. I'm curious."

"Good. I planned on your being curious."

Chapter Nine

Signee wrote details of her theater progress to Eric, and before she had time to realize her letter had arrived at its destination, she received an answer in a most unexpected way. Her doorbell rang very early in the morning, and when she blindly struggled to find her robe and answer the third ring, she opened the door to face a complete stranger. He stood there as casually as if it was afternoon and he'd dropped by for a chat.

"Yes?" Signee managed to say.

"You'll be Signee Short. Right?" She nodded. "I am Kolby Burke. I'm here to solve your problems with the barn. Can we take a look at it right away?"

"Right now?"

"Yes, of course. Eric said this was a rush job, that I had to get on it right away."

"Eric sent you? I just wrote him a letter asking...."

"I'm your answer. Eric hates to write letters."

"I know. But I don't know you...." Then she remembered what Eric had said. "Oh, yes, you must be the one who can solve all my problems."

"I'm the one. I'm the conversion expert. I'm anxious to see

your barn and evaluate, make some drawings, and get back to Eric and report as fast as I can. Can we go now?"

"But I...." Signee looked down at her robe, and Kolby's eyes followed her look.

"Oh yes, your robe. Well, of course I'll wait until you get dressed."

"I am not undressed...." Signee started to say, and then thought better of the poor joke. "Excuse me, Mr., Mr.... what did you say your name was?"

"Burke, Kolby Burke. I'm a friend of your friend Eric. I told him I would help you, but I can't do much good unless I get to see the barn."

"I haven't any objections to you seeing the barn. I wasn't expecting you, that's all."

"Well, I'm here. Eric thought I should take a look at what is and isn't. Don't worry, Signee Short, we'll have things going before you can...." He looked at her robe again.

"Before I get out of my robe and into some clothes. Right?"

"Right. May I just wait?"

"Oh ... yes, by all means ... I mean, do I have a choice?"

"I would like to get to the job as soon as possible."

"I'll hurry."

Signee pushed opened the door to her bedroom and went inside to find Minta stretched out on her bed ready to ask questions.

"Who is he?"

"He's here to solve all my problems. Remember the letter Eric wrote?"

"I do."

"This is the man. I must say I'm not very impressed. In fact, he scares me a little. He is so bossy."

"What is he going to do?"

"I don't know, Minta. He sounds like he's going to take over the whole project. But don't worry; I won't let him take over everything. The kids have worked too hard and want to use their own ideas. I also have a few of my own."

"Don't get upset, Signee. You said we needed help."

"You're right, Minta. I shouldn't get upset."

"You are going to talk to him, aren't you?"

"Yes, I'm going to talk to him, if he'll let me. He does most of the talking. He's the only man I've ever known that could out-talk me." Signee dropped her comb on the dresser. "I won't be home for breakfast. See you at school later, Minta."

Signee didn't talk to Kolby Burke very much as they drove to the barn. She gave him a few instructions about directions, and then sat quiet. Kolby did most of the talking, just as she thought he would, and he didn't even seem to notice that Signee wasn't talking. He was eager and enthusiastic; Signee didn't know why, but his enthusiasm annoyed her.

"There's a lot that can be done with old buildings," Kolby was saying. "I've made some pretty good things out of a few of them. I've never had the opportunity to start from the ground floor like this yet, but I imagine it is similar. Nothing has been done yet, right?"

"Just cleaning, mostly."

"Is everything legal?"

"Mr. Burke, we've just acquired the rights. This old barn belonged to the father of one of my students."

"That's good. Old barns are a good way to go."

"I'm so glad you approve." Signee's voice was a little sarcastic and she reminded herself of Minta in a bad mood.

"The basic structure is the important thing...."

Signee didn't answer, but inside she was thinking: "We know all that. Does he think he is the only one who knows anything?"

"My field has recently become lighting specialties ... this is my big thing. I've been a builder for some time, but I've always been fascinated with lighting effects, and Eric knew I'd like this opportunity to try some of my ideas. It can be very expensive, but...."

"We haven't much money, you know."

"Money isn't the issue. For a project like this, I have connections with a lot of businessmen who need income tax deductions ... money won't be hard to get. The important thing is the basic construction ... and even then, I guess we could really handle that, if ... but I'll wait until I see it."

"We're almost there; take the next dirt road to your left, and...."

"Dirt road? That's something we'll have to do without."

"Do you also have friends that will oil the road?" Signee's tone was sarcastic, but Kolby didn't seem to hear it.

"Oh, yes, we can do this whole project up . . . well, you'll be surprised how fast."

"I'll bet I will. . . ." Signee didn't want to sound ungrateful; she didn't want to be annoyed at the obvious help. But she was; something about this man's attitude just turned her off and made her want to reject anything he said.

"Hey, that must be it. . . ." he said, pointing at the barn that showed over the top of the trees. "I don't think you'll like too many trees, will you? It makes construction very limited . . . a few for color, but that's all."

"That's all?" Signee was suddenly very disgusted with this intruder, and this time it was plainly in her voice. "I like the tree setting. I don't want anything to happen to the trees."

"We'll see . . . if you feel strongly. . . ."

"I feel strongly about this whole thing. Do you have any idea how long I've waited for a chance to design my own stage?"

"Of course, that must be important. . . ."

"It is very important . . . there, turn to the right." She almost shouted, as if he were forcing her to reveal a secret hiding place she didn't want anyone to know about.

"Say, this is very picturesque. This is more than I expected."

"Just what did you expect, Mr. Burke? What did Eric tell you about all this?" She waved her hand to take in the whole countryside.

"He said I was to give you a hand."

"I see."

They didn't talk any more just then, but Kolby pulled the car in front of the barn. Signee hadn't remembered it looking so shabby in the dusk the night the students had come with her.

"Hm . . . it is old, isn't it?" was all Kolby Burke said, and Signee didn't answer him. The way she was feeling, she didn't dare say anything for fear she would explode; and though it might have been fun to tell this talkative show-off that he couldn't run her, she didn't want to hurt Eric's feelings. She opened the car door for herself and walked toward the big double barn doors. Kolby Burke followed her. Once inside, he began kicking the base and center poles.

"It's really old. . . ."

"What did you expect?"

"Something I could work with."

"And you can't work with this building?"

"Well, I don't know...." Kolby began walking around, and for once he didn't say much. Signee followed him.

"I don't see how you can say that; this is perfect for a theater. It's the kind I've always dreamed of. Look: the stage right there ... the first row of seats here..." Signee began walking around on her own, her ideas forming, thoughts coming out of her as if she had already completed the project and opening night was upon them. "I can see the first shows done with a few pieces of scenery, just enough to cover the entrances, the dressing rooms under the stage with short steps up each side, and a stage of levels with a couple of steps leading into the audience. I have never seen such a perfect building..." she stopped in front of Kolby, who was examining the wooden poles that held up the loft. He seemed intent. "But of course you have to have some vision...." He still didn't talk or even act as if he had heard her. "Can't you see what I mean?" She stood directly in front of him. He went right on with what he was doing. "Mr. Burke, aren't you listening to me?" She planted herself in front of him. Looking directly at her, he seemed not to see her. Then he wiped his chin with one big hand and looked above her head into the loft.

"I wonder what we'll find up there?"

"A loft, Mr. Burke, that is a loft. You must be a city man not to know what a loft is."

"Hm..." he said and began searching the walls for some way of climbing up. "There must be a ladder, there is usually one built on the wall close...."

"There isn't a ladder, Mr. Burke, and I didn't let the students go up there because I'm sure there are some loose boards and decaying ... Mr. Burke, you aren't even listening to me." Signee stood in front of him again.

"Miss Short," he said, putting his hands on each side of her shoulders. "You may call me Kolby, that is my name." Then he lifted her out of his way and went on examining the walls. In one corner, there were some boards lying against the wall; he moved a few, and what had been a ladder nailed to the wall clearly showed. He mounted the side, climbed up, and with his hand pushed on the boards overhead. With a lot of dust falling on top of him, a trap door opened into the loft. A few more steps, and he disappeared into the loft above. Signee was feeling put down and bossed, but she followed to where he had disappeared and looked up into the opening. Then, without warning, there was a loud crack; and through the hole, right into her face, dropped another pile of dust and old leaves. She let out an exclamation, more like a yell, and moved back. Silence followed. She waited.

"Mr. Burke ... Mr. Burke ... are you all right?" She started toward the half-broken ladder.

"D-don't come up...." she heard him say as he rolled over and his face came through the hole above her. "I told you my name was Kolby," he smiled.

"I know, but are you all right?"

"Sure ... but you were right about some of these boards ... they are rotten. In fact," he said, scrambling to his feet and coming down the ladder, "this whole place is rotten."

"I don't believe that, Mr...."

"Kolby..." he corrected her.

"All right, Kolby, but just because there are a few rotten boards is no sign I'm going to give up this barn idea. What do you know about my barn, anyway? You and your city ways...."

"Now, just a minute; don't jump to conclusions. I'm almost through checking this place out, and then I'll give you my report. If you can be quiet long enough to let me finish."

"If I can be quiet ... you are the one who has been doing all the talking up to now. You haven't even asked what I want, and you are ready to condemn my barn without...."

"Siggie...." She stopped talking, startled that he would call her by the nickname only her friends used. Kolby put up his hands as if in defense. "Please ... just be quiet and let me finish. You women are all alike." He shook his head and went back to his work.

"What do you mean, we are all alike?"

He put his hands up again. "Please ... quiet ... I'll answer all your questions later." Signee turned abruptly, walked over to an old wooden box, and sat down. There was something so irritating about this Kolby Burke that she wanted to scream at him. It had been a long time since Signee had wanted to scream at anybody, and she knew it wouldn't help her barn theater dream. So she just sat there, fumed inside, and waited.

Kolby did some more kicking poles and some measuring, and then he walked over to and past Signee.

"Come on, I'm all through here. Let's get you back to school and me back to my work." Opening the big, half-broken door, Kolby waited for Signee to walk through it, closed it behind them, and went toward the car. When they were on the way back, Signee stood it as long as she could and then asked the question again.

"Well, what about my barn?" She waited, and he didn't answer for a minute. Clapping her hands together, she went on. "Oh, why am I asking you about my barn? It was my idea, and the kids are willing to help. We can do the whole thing. I should never have told Eric my dream...."

"That's not the idea I got."

"Well, at least he talks ... what idea did you get?"

"Eric says you have lived with this obsession since high school days. I didn't get the idea you had just told him your dream."

"No, but I just told him I was going to make it come true."

"Now we are on the same wave length."

"And now you'll tell me just how you fit into this whole thing."

"I could, yes. I work with Eric, owe him some money and he thinks this is a good way to pay off what I owe him. Besides, he knows I have a few dreams of my own, and gave me this opportunity."

"Your dreams don't include my theater, do they?"

"They could...." He was thoughtful again, then smiled. "But at this point I'm not sure they do include your barn, and I'm not ready to divulge them ... however, this much I am ready to state. Eric asked me to check out this barn of yours and see if it is sound enough to put money into."

"Without telling me?"

"Yes, you see he understands you—and, as a matter of fact, all women—pretty well."

"And I suppose you understand them too?"

"Well, yes, I have had some experience ... but that isn't the issue here. I'm more concerned about the barn. I find it reasonably sound in some areas; however, the upper loft might have to come out...."

"Come out? But that's the most picturesque part of...."

"It might have to come out before we start to build, if we are going to build, or it might come out on top of the heads of those who watch your shows, if you do shows . . . unless we take it out now."

Signee was suddenly furious. "*If* we have a show, *if* we build. You know, I'm beginning to have just about enough of you. When you first knocked at my door I thought you were just a curiosity, but now you are more than that. You are a threat to my theater. Well, you aren't going to spoil it for me. I'm sorry I ever told Eric, because he wants to interfere. You see, I know I'm going to have a theater because I've got to have one. There are a lot of young people in this town, young people with dreams and ambitions that get discouraged all too often, who won't read Shakespeare or get any culture or diversion. In a small town, the youth too often try to get away from it all instead of enjoying the freedom and beauty of more space. They need something to keep them active, busy, and seeing culture in action. I have one girl right now, especially; if I can get her into a play she might get over this romance of the moment and go on to bigger and better things. She has talent, money, and drive, and she needs to put those energies to work while she learns how to develop her talents and feel what it's like to approve of herself. I'm going to have this theater, Mr. Burke."

"Kolby."

"Kolby, or whatever your name is . . . I don't need you and your discouragement. I don't even need Eric. I have a whole town full of energetic kids who are willing to work and raise money and put in hours and help design, and they need that as much as they need the dramas that will be put on the stage. And I don't want you or Eric, no matter how righteous your desire to help, taking anything from those kids. So say whatever you want about my theater; I'm going to have it."

"Even if it comes down on their heads. . . ." added Kolby quietly.

"It won't come down on anybody's head . . . I'm not dumb. I know we have to brace it and build it to be solid . . . somehow we'll get it done."

"Now we are back where we started from . . . the reason I came here. I will make my report and let you know."

Signee took a deep breath. "You are the calmest, most

stubborn man I have ever been around. Are you married, Mr. ...Kolby?"

"Not at the present, no ... though I fail to see what the status of my marital life has to do with the issue of your country barn."

"I was just thinking that you must not be married, or you wouldn't be so set in your ways and hard to get along with ... excuse me, I mean that only in an observant way. I'm not trying to offend you."

"You didn't offend me, Siggie, but I could turn that question to you. But I know you aren't married, so I guess that's what makes you so dogmatic and hard to get along with...." He smiled. Signee bit her lip and remained quiet.

Chapter Ten

"We're going ahead with the theater," announced Signee to the drama class, while she added under her breath, "no matter what Kolby's report is." Then aloud she continued, "We'll need your help and the help of some good carpenters. Deek has offered to organize and get everybody going so if you want to be involved, sign up with Deek for working on the building or business, and with me for plays, directing, and anything else we haven't found a department for yet. We're going to have a lot of fun along with a lot of learning experiences with our theater. We'll probably make a lot of mistakes, but mistakes are only methods of learning. So everybody gets a chance to learn."

Laughter followed Signee's remarks to the class, but the response was overwhelming and brought tears of gratitude and excitement to her eyes. Already she was getting to know individual personalities of the students she had been teaching; already she was finding new talents in students she hadn't ever seen before. And as the work picked up momentum, Signee found her eyes often full of tears that choked her up, but the rest of the time she was riding high with excitement. Every day was anything but dull, and each evening she had new problems to pray about.

Eric wrote that Kolby was working on the plans and they would be ready soon. That was one problem that began to worry Signee. She didn't want to seem ungrateful, and she really needed their help, but neither did she want Eric and Kolby taking over. It was her dream, and the dream of all those students and young people who had joined her. Even the parents were beginning to be part of the planning. Signee knew she had to move carefully if she was to keep the loyalty and enthusiasm of everyone. In the meantime, she felt it was time to get a play started. She couldn't get away to read and select plays herself, so she approached Minta.

"Minta, how would you like a special assignment for our theater?" They were eating crackers and soup after an exhausting day. Minta had been cheering, the team had been out of town playing, and Signee had worked all day at school and put in more hours after school at the barn.

"What have you got in mind, Signee?"

"We need to have some plays selected. Would you like to be the one to pick out a few?"

"What do I know about plays?"

"You know what you like, don't you?"

"Yes, after I see it on stage."

"Minta, you could choose a bunch of them and we could look them over in the evenings after our many jobs are finished."

"Anything for Siggie ... but I warn you I don't know what I'm doing."

"Minta, the way you say that makes me feel foolish."

"Just mimicking Deek. No offense."

"Then would you like to drive into the city on Saturday, and take some time to look and select?"

"What car do I take? Ever since I ran off the road, my parents haven't been too generous."

"Deek and one of the guys are driving in on Saturday to pick up some lumber and a few parts. I thought you might like to go with them."

"Oh, oh ... there you go again, setting it up for me with Deek. How come you can chase boys and I can't?"

"My age ... they know I'm not after them. There are some very nice advantages to age. Want to go?"

"How can I resist? Are we starting to build already?"

"Not yet; we're waiting for our master plan. But a friend of Deek's father has a load of lumber he will donate. He wants the lumber out of his way right now."

"You said Deek and some of the boys. Could you arrange it for just Deek?"

"That would be cheating," Signee teased.

"I'm not sure your methods work, Siggie ... I haven't called Deek or waited by his locker for a long time, and he hasn't even seemed to notice."

"But you get to see him every day while we work on the barn. Just keep working on friendship and having fun, and let romance come at some later date, when the time is right ... his choice."

"All right, but friendship isn't as much fun as making out."

"That depends on how you look at it ... the rewards in the end are bigger and more satisfying."

"Well I haven't anything to lose, since I was losing anyway. Bring on the plays ... I can't wait to entertain Deek and some of the guys. Saturday, here I come."

In the meantime, Signee was talking to Eric back and forth. The first time he called after Kolby had had time to get back and make his report, it was the usual early-in-the-morning chat.

"Sig?" came Eric's voice, loud and clear as the morning he was interrupting. "I'm mailing your plans today. Is everything going according to schedule?"

"Moving along just fine. I can't tell you how exciting this project is; I've already seen some good results with the young people. But ... I'm really glad you called."

"Why? Anything wrong?"

"Not if you aren't upset with me."

"Why should I be upset?"

"Well I wasn't very nice to your fix-it man. I'm afraid I was rude and ungrateful."

"You were? He didn't report that. I got the distinct impression he thought you were quite a girl."

"I don't understand that. I should have been nicer. But Eric, he tries to take everything over. I can't let him take it away from the kids; but still we really do need him, and we need you, too. Do you see what I'm going through?"

"I see, but don't worry about it. Kolby is a very talented guy; he is also very efficient. But as far as his feelings are concerned, he can take care of himself. I'll let you two fight it out. However, when you're ready for lights ... better give him his way. He's fantastic on lights, and he'll arrange them in ways no one else has ever thought of."

"I've got some boys that want to help with that ... some eager ones that want to learn about electricity."

"He'll work with them, just ask him."

"I'll try. And now, about Alta. How is she? She has only written once since she was here."

"She's doing pretty well, considering. Of course she has to stay down a lot."

"She what? Is she sick?"

"You mean she didn't tell you?"

"No. But can I guess? She's pregnant?"

"She thinks she might be. Now I've done it. She'll kill me. I know she wanted to write you all the details."

"Don't worry; I'll be completely surprised ... if I can wait that long to scream. Eric, I am so happy. Your miracle...."

"Yes! I think she'll be more content now. She's been so restless since she was out there with you."

"What did I do?"

"It wasn't you, but I think she still thinks there might be something between you and me."

"Didn't you tell her?"

"What can I tell her? There *is* something between you and me."

"Oh, Eric, be sensible ... especially at a time like this. I'm told women are really touchy when they're pregnant."

"I'm told the same thing. Don't worry, she'll be all right. All she needs to make her happy is a baby."

"She'll be a darling mother."

"I hope she doesn't give all her attention to the baby. Anyway, we're happy ... now you get yourself happy, and we'll be a big happy family."

"I'm happy with my theater."

"You can love a theater, but you can't cuddle up to it at night, or hold it in your arms and rock it."

"I'll wait for that. Thanks for calling, Eric. Now, that's a happy thought," said Signee as she hung up the phone and talked to no one in particular. Minta was just coming into the room.

"What's a happy thought?"

"My friend is having a baby, after all the waiting and doctors telling her never—she's pregnant."

"Which friend?"

"I can't tell you for a while, because I'm not supposed to know ... but I'm so happy for her. She's waited a long time and was so afraid she would never have a child. Minta, having a baby must be the most wonderful thing in the world ... if you are married and in love with your husband."

"And I can't know who?"

"Not yet, but I'll give you the details when she writes to me. The doctors were wrong—all wrong. A married lady, having a baby ... how wonderful. I'm so excited, you'd think it was me."

"I hope it isn't...." said Minta, making a bad joke. They both laughed and Signee hugged Minta.

"Someday, Minta, we'll be having our babies ... maybe both of us at the same time ... you'll be a young mother and I'll be somewhat older. That will be a wonderful time."

"Signee, I think I want to have a lot of children. I think having more children can reduce the odds of making so many mistakes on one."

Signee laughed. "Minta, that is the strangest reason for having a lot of children I've ever heard, but it sounds logical."

"I have other reasons, too. I've never had to baby-tend, or share with a sister, or anything neat like that."

"Good for you, Minta. I want lots of children, too. I've always planned on twelve."

"Twelve? You can't be serious. When I say a lot, I mean maybe four or five at the most. Twelve ... that's a lot of children."

"Certainly. That's why I can't just marry anybody. Twelve children will take a special father."

"That's important, isn't it? Do you think Deek will want a lot of children?"

"Sure thing ... he's been raised with lots of brothers and sisters, and he takes care of them a lot of times. Sometime, when the time is right, why don't you ask him?"

"I think I will. I wouldn't be afraid to have Deek's children."

"A very worthy goal, Minta ... keep it in mind and don't be

impatient. But remember, you'll need all the talents you can develop to stay up with those children. That's why schooling is important, and all the education you can get."

"I'm beginning to understand that. I've wasted a lot of time being spoiled and wanting my own way, haven't I, Siggie?"

"You're human. It's never too late to start. While Deek is on his mission, you'll have time to go to college and find out what some of your talents are."

"I do have to send him on a mission, don't I?"

"Do you want him to complete his goals? If he doesn't do the things he's wanted to do, he'll have a low self-image; and low self-images don't make very good husbands because they don't like themselves."

"I'll try to understand that."

"Just keep busy and be prayerful and you'll be guided. Now, how about that trip into the library?"

"Right. I'll see Deek then."

Chapter Eleven

It was a beautiful Saturday morning when Deek pulled the big truck up in front of Signee's house to pick up Minta. The weather was just chilly enough for a jacket and bright enough for sunglasses as they drove toward the city. Big Jeff went with them. Jeff was a tackle on the football team. Football was his only game; he didn't switch from one sport to another with the seasons as Deek did, but he and Deek were year-around friends. Big Jeff was always fun to have along because he had a dry wit and a brotherly, bashful attitude toward most girls. He was quiet as he sat beside the window. Minta, sitting between the two big team men, looked smaller than she really was.

"I think Siggie is trying to make an actress of me," said Minta, with an effort to make conversation.

"If Siggie decides you're going to be an actress, you'll be one. She's one determined lady." Deek smiled, visualizing Signee in his mind.

"She thinks you have acting ability too, Deek."

"I guess I'll try if she wants me to. She has a way of bringing out the best in...."

"In everybody, not just boys."

"Right, Minta ... in everybody ... even you, huh?"

"What you're trying to say, Deek, is that I was such a mess Siggie had to make me over, aren't you?"

"Not exactly, but improvement is good for us all. And Siggie is the one who brings out the improvements."

"I know how you feel about Siggie, Deek, but are we going to talk about her and her many accomplishments all the way to town?"

"Can't think of a better subject. Can you, Jeff?"

"Who, me?" asked Jeff, suddenly aware that they knew he was with them. "Well, I can't think of a better subject for conversation ... as far as I'm concerned."

"Now Jeff," Minta looked up at Jeff and twinkled her eyes at him, at the same time just touching his arm. "Jeff, I need somebody on my side. You will help me to change the subject, won't you?" She smiled coyly, aware that her efforts were bothering Big Jeff.

"I ... I ... I'm not taking anybody's side. I just came along to help.lift lumber. Don't pay any attention to me."

"But you will help me, won't you, Jeff?"

"Minta," cut in Deek, "don't waste your time trying to charm us. We are the original missionary prospects and we aren't going to let any girls batting their eyes pull us away from our goals."

"Who wants to take you away from goals? I'm not the serious type myself ... just call me a game girl."

"Yeah, Minta, we know."

"But Deek, I am. I've decided it will be a long time before I'm ready to get serious with anyone. Just call me one of the guys."

"New approach, huh? Well, one suggestion for the new you. If I were you, I'd be really careful about saying anything against Siggie when she's been so good to you."

"Me, talk against Siggie? When did I do that? Siggie and I are friends. She understands me."

"It's a good thing somebody does, and if anybody can it would be Siggie. You're lucky to be living with her."

"You immortalize her, Deek. It is obvious she is first in your thoughts. Be careful, or somebody might get the wrong idea."

"I don't care if they do. Now don't make a big deal out of that, Minta."

"I just react to you . . . just because I didn't want to talk about her all the way to town is no sign I'm saying anything against her."

"Minta, do we have to discuss this?"

"No . . . we don't have to discuss anything. We can sit here in universal silence, if that pleases you more."

The rest of the trip was stilted and awkward, each person trying to choose his words carefully. It was painful for Minta, and she was glad when Deek stopped the truck in front of the library and let Minta get out. Trying hard to be casual, she asked:

"What time will you be back to pick me up?"

"We'll be about two hours. Is that enough time for what Siggie asked you to do?"

"I'll make it be enough." Minta answered grudgingly with her lips in a tight line. "I'll be right here in two hours. I won't keep you waiting."

"This I've got to see. It seems like in the past, I have waited. . . ."

"Can't you ever forget the past, Deek? Do you always have to remember what was and not what is?"

"If it bothers you, I'll try to think of now . . . which bothers me."

"Good. I'm glad something bothers you."

It was hard for Minta to concentrate on plays at first when she went into the library. She had a strong desire to find a quiet place where she could be alone and just cry. But before she could settle on the idea, she'd found a whole section of plays with everything from farce to melodrama, with samples and addresses of where to send for more. Many plays had royalty fees that had to be paid before they could be performed. There were some without royalties. Minta tried to select a variety, and then she sat down by a table to read and wait for the boys to return. She wasn't very interested at first, but as the time ticked off she found herself deeply involved in the plays. The tightness she'd felt when she was with Deek began to slip away, and all she remembered was how much she cared about him. Almost every play brought her a vision of herself and Deek, and she began to relate to the emotion she read about. Signee was right, she decided; she had to get away from romance and concentrate on friendship so they wouldn't hurt each other all the time. She wanted to be rid of the feeling of fight and just enjoy Deek's friendship. And what else had Siggie said ... something about learning to pray when times were hard to take. "Pray even when you don't feel worthy ... pray the hardest then ... pray to become worthy, even pray about what to pray about." That was what she needed now to know how to get along with Deek. Then, as if still reading, she bowed her head and let her mind form the words her heart was feeling. After the short prayer she went on reading. When it was time to meet Deek, she went to sit on the front steps of the library, laden with a large stack of plays.

"Hello," she said cheerfully when she looked up to see Deek standing beside her.

"Hello. You're right on time. Did I keep you waiting?"

"Only a minute or two," she said and was aware they were both being noticeably polite to each other.

"We're parked around the block; do you mind walking a little?"

"I don't mind."

"We've got a big load of lumber that's hard to handle in this traffic."

"Fine," said Minta politely, and wondered what had happened to Deek. It had been a long time since he'd treated her with this much respect.

Together they walked to the truck, exchanging only a few remarks as they went. Then they drove home, and the three of them made only small talk. But the atmosphere was good, and Minta wondered if it was all pretending—and why? As they turned into the community of Green Village, Deek drove directly to Jeff's place first and let him off.

"Jeff, if you can get the guys we talked about, I'll meet you after dinner and we'll unload this stuff."

"We'll make it. Hope Mom has dinner ready on time."

Jeff said his goodbyes and Minta and Deek were on their way again, this time to Signee's house to drop Minta off. Minta sat there without words, almost afraid to speak, afraid she might break the spell that she was enjoying. But she didn't have to worry very long. Deek was the first to talk.

"Jeff is a good friend, Minta. He likes you, too."

110

"He does? I don't think Jeff and I have ever had much to say to each other."

"But he likes you, and he really raked me over today after you went into the library...."

"What for?"

"For the way I was treating you."

"Is that what changed you?"

"Yes. I suddenly realized I was taking out my frustrations on you, and that wasn't right."

"What frustrations?"

"I'm going through some decisions right now. It isn't easy to give up two years of your life to go on a mission."

"Then why do you do it?"

"It would be worse not to go. I know you don't understand; but like Jeff said, I could at least talk to you and we could be friends ... if you want to."

"Is friends all we'll ever be, Deek?"

"I don't know ... honestly. Friends is all I can be with anyone right now."

"Even Siggie? Are you just friends with her, too?"

"Oh, Minta, you are so dumb."

"That's what you think, isn't it? I'm too dumb to be good for you."

"No, that isn't what I mean. Look, this is our last year in high school together, and I like you, Minta. I really do."

"You do?" Minta turned smiling eyes to look at Deek.

"Yes, I do. I don't want to fight with you. I like working on this theater with you. You live with Siggie, and we should all be friends."

Minta's smile disappeared. "Siggie again."

"Now, don't be jealous of how I feel about Siggie. You can't change that, but I'm not thinking of marrying her."

"Are you thinking of marrying me? I'm sorry, I shouldn't have asked that."

"No, you shouldn't. If ever I want to ask you to marry me, I'll do it my own way. But Minta, I'm not going to leave a girl behind when I go on my mission. I don't want anybody waiting for me."

"What if I want to wait?"

"That's up to you. If you are here when I get home, then we'll see."

"Why don't you want me to wait? Why can't we have an understanding?"

"Because we could both change, and I don't want to hurt anyone."

"I'm hurt already. Deek, do you know you are the only guy that I can't go with when I want to?"

"I know. But Minta, some of the guys you go with aren't really good competition. We've been together a lot in the last two and a half years. We have some good memories I don't want to spoil. Now do you want to be friends, and maybe we could date sometimes ... at least we could get along ... or do we call it quits? I don't like being rude to you. Jeff was right; it isn't like me to be rude to girls."

"Does it have to be girls?"

"Yes, it does. I'm going with all the girls I want to go with in the next few months. I won't be dating for two whole years, and I like girls."

"So I've noticed."

"You don't have to be sarcastic. Either we're going to be friends and trust each other or not. Which will it be?"

Minta was thoughtful for a while; the silence seemed to close in around them. And Minta suddenly wanted to talk to Deek in a way she had never talked to anyone before.

"Deek, I'm going to try and be as honest with you as you have been with me. I'm not fooling you if I tell you I want to be your friend. You know how I feel, but I'm learning a little about not having my own way all the time. Siggie is helping me; she seems to think I'm worth it, and she says I have to send you on your mission and learn to be noble ... I don't know if I can do that, but I know I'd like to be like Siggie. I'm jealous of her, but I want to be like her. I'd like to be the kind of girl that a guy like you would want as a wife. I don't know how long I can stick to the rules she's trying to teach me; but I guess she's right, because here you are, talking to me and giving me hope, and I thought it was all over."

"You're pretty, Minta, and a lot of fun when you aren't trying to boss and get your own way. The way I see it, we could be friends. You can write to me if you want to, and whatever happens in the future ... we'll take it from there. But I won't

112

make out with you ... not one kiss ... I won't let you push me around and I won't stand you checking up on me. I won't check on you. We'll see if we can learn to trust each other, and if we can pass the tests."

"You sound like love is a course of study we take."

"I think it is ... just like life. That's what we are here for, to be tested and return to our Father in Heaven. Either we pass, or we don't."

"That's what's so hard to take about you, Deek. You are so smart and you know where you are going. I wish I knew where I was going."

"Set your goals, Minta. I'd like to say I hope you are still around ... single ... when I get home. But if you aren't, then I'll know it's for the best."

"I wish I was as patient as you are. All I can say, Deek, is that I'll be whatever you want me to be, the best I can. I'll take your friendship terms, because I haven't really any choice, and I'll try."

"Thanks, Minta. I'd like to date you sometimes."

"I'd like that, too."

"I'll call you."

"I'll be waiting ... but not too close to the phone."

"Good girl ... " said Deek with genuine enthusiasm, as he opened the truck door and went around to open the door on Minta's side. "And I'm sorry if I've been hard on you. We'll always be friends, huh?"

"Sure, Deek." Minta slid down from the high seat to stand beside him. He turned, and, taking her arm, he walked her to the door.

"I'll be calling you, Minta. And tell Siggie we got the lumber all right, huh?"

"Sure." She opened the house door, but turned back to look at him once more. "And Deek ... thanks for talking to me. I have a good feeling about us now ... better than I thought we could have."

"You'll see ... being friends is neat."

It was strange, the change that had come over her as she closed the door and leaned against it. Maybe she could wait, she was thinking. Maybe waiting for the gold at the end of the rainbow her father had always talked about would be worth the wait. Deek would always be worth waiting for; she knew that more clearly than she had ever known anything before. If only she could be the kind of girl he wanted her to be. She shut her eyes, remembering the look on Deek's face when he had told her she was pretty.

"Minta," came Signee's voice from somewhere in another room. "Minta, is that you?"

"I'm home, Siggie...." called Minta opening her eyes to reality again.

"I'm glad you're safe; I always worry a little about those top-heavy trucks." Signee appeared in the hall. "Your mother called and a boy ... the one we talked about, Barney Tremon, is looking for you."

"What did he want?"

"You ... he'll call back later tonight." Coming closer, Signee looked at her intently. "You look different. Something the matter?"

"Different, how?"

"Kinda soft and dreamy...."

"I feel soft and dreamy."

"Deek must have said something nice."

Minta nodded ever so slightly. "He did." She moved forward and put her arms around Signee. "Siggie, I love you, do you know that?"

"No, but I'm glad," said Signee and returned her hug. "Anything you want to talk about?"

"No, I just feel good. I'm trying to live by the rules you talked about, Siggie ... and I think they work."

"Of course they work. They aren't my rules, though ... they come filed under honesty and integrity of the Gospel in our lives ... if that isn't too much to handle."

"I'll make it," said Minta, and went up the stairs to her bedroom.

"Did you get the plays?" called Signee as she heard the door to her room open.

"I got them ... can we talk about that a little later?"

"Sure ... that and a lot of other things. I got a big package from Eric today."

"I'm going to study and do a little dreaming while I can. No matter who calls tonight, I don't want to be disturbed." The

114

door closed behind Minta, and Signee turned to go back into the kitchen. "She's pretty dreamy-eyed," said Signee to herself. "I hope I didn't leave something out of our conversation on how to use integrity to forward love."

Chapter Twelve

Deek Pendalton hit the shower after ball practice, smoothed his wet hair, dressed, and made it into Signee's room before she was ready to leave school.

"I'm here, Siggie. Now, what's the big surprise?"

"Ta ... da..." said Signee holding up a package she unrolled quickly. "Eric has sent the last plans, and we are on our way. Can you read blueprints, Deek?"

"Sure thing. I've been reading them for my father for a couple of years now...."

"Good. And this is a list of what we'll need to complete this much transformation. This first list is how we'll reinforce the second story, and Eric has even listed the steps of what to do first and next and how."

"Hey, pretty talented, huh?"

"More than I remember. I think maybe he had some help from Mr. Kolby Burke, who is also an accomplished designer. Kolby Burke will do our lighting system, and he should be here any day to install it himself. Is that all right with you and the boys, Deek?"

"All right with me."

"Well, I'm not sure about me; but I guess he'll do a good job. Eric thinks he's great. Now, the reason I called you. I thought you might be able to take this list and make some copies, and then give each guy a picture of what he is supposed to do. We'll work from the individual copies, and you work from the masters. All right?"

"Sounds very organized. You've got yourself a boy, Siggie... I'll get on it." He started toward the door, but stopped and turned back to talk some more. "I didn't know before that it can be so neat to build and create things. We're learning, and it's fun. Even when the guys complain."

"Thanks to you and your father's barn, Deek."

"No big deal. I like what I'm doing."

"I've learned to depend on you, Deek. And I want to thank you for making Minta so happy. She's actually singing in the shower these days. I don't know exactly what you said a few weeks ago when you took her to the library, but whatever it was, you inspired her."

"Siggie, you're the one to be congratulated. I thought she was gone, but now she's like her old self and more. If she turns out like you, I might marry her ... after my mission."

"She'll turn out her way. We all have to be ourselves, Deek."

"Yeah, but our better selves are better than our other selves."

"I guess you can put it that way." Signee laughed and Deek joined her as he took off down the hall. Signee picked up her handbag and the other set of blueprints and followed.

The boys went to work, and in the days that followed, Kolby Burke was as good as the word he'd given to Signee. One morning early, just like the first time, the doorbell rang and there he was leaning on the pillar outside, as if he were a permanent fixture.

"You're buzzin' right along, Siggie. You're ready for lights."

"I wish I could get a little light into my eyes without blinding myself so early in the morning. Mr. Kolby, don't you ever sleep in the mornings?"

"I can't get anything done staying in bed. I've come to borrow your car so I can get the lights in your drama barn today."

"All in one day?"

"I'll be working a few days, but I'll only need your car today."

"Oh, all right," Signee yawned in spite of herself. "I'll get the

118

keys, Mr., I mean Kolby."

When she came back with the keys, Kolby took them from her, smiling at her confusion.

"Sig, you have brown eyes. How can that be? I thought you had blue eyes."

"I'm sorry, Kol ... by, but this is too early in the morning to color my eyes for you. A little later, perhaps, when they are open all the way...." She was answering his questions, aware she was being a little goofy. But at the moment it didn't seem important; all she wanted to do was get him on his way.

"It's all right, don't apologize. I'm somewhat relieved, you see, all the spirited ladies in my family have brown eyes, and I couldn't understand your spirit with blue eyes. Now the whole thing is all cleared up."

"I'm so glad," she said automatically, as if they were having a perfectly sensible conversation. "You'll find my car in the garage. You won't mind if you have to get it out by yourself, will you?"

"I'll be glad to do that. You know, you must stay up too late with your students. I think you're too busy. Well, I'll be back in time to pick you up at school and give you a ride home. You get out by 4:30, don't you?"

"I get out at 3:30."

"Yes, but after cheerleaders and drama barn assignments it will be about 4:30 before you're ready, won't it?"

"Yes, I guess it will. How do you know so much about my schedule?"

"Sig, I am a very perceptive fellow. I'll have your car here by that time, or rather, I'll meet you at school."

His voice became dramatic at the end of his last sentence as he switched to a British accent. Signee, her eyes still not completely open, couldn't help smiling as he walked to the door, opened it, and was gone. Signee shook her head and went back to her bedroom to get ready for school.

But Kolby Burke didn't wait until 4:30 p.m. to see Signee again. It was just five minutes after noon when Signee sat down at a school lunchroom table about ready to cut into a tossed salad when Kolby appeared in the double door space. He stood there a minute, his feet apart, his arms deliberately hanging limp at his sides, but there was something about the muscles of his face that warned Signee as he strode across the room and stood opposite her on the other side of the table. Signee was sitting at the teachers' table; there were just the two women teachers and the rest of the occupants were men, including the football and basketball coaches. Kolby opened his mouth and closed it again, then turned to address the others at the table and spoke to them.

"Please excuse Sig. We have some talking to do."

The words were plain and simple enough, but there was something about the line of his mouth that warned Signee again. She didn't argue; she just stood up with an apologetic smile on her face for her friends and said:

"Shall we go to my room?"

Kolby didn't answer; he just stepped back to let her lead the way and then followed. Nothing was said until they were inside her classroom. She pulled up a chair for Kolby and then sat at her own desk.

"Yes, Kol." She used the familiar title he'd asked her to use. "What is it you want to discuss?"

For an answer, he took her set of blueprints that were ever present on her desk, rolled it out, set articles on each corner to hold it, and began to tap with his pointer finger in the middle of the blueprint.

"Who has been reading this blueprint?"

"We have some people who read blueprints."

"Where did these people learn to read blueprints?" His mouth was still tight.

"One of our boys has worked with his father, another has...." For some reason she couldn't understand, Signee began to feel threatened. "Look, Kolby, we've been following what Eric outlined step by step, and it has been working very well."

"Oh, it has, has it? Then why aren't the braces put at the specified points, and why don't they meet on 45 degree angles?" His voice was deliberate and low as he spit out the words, but as he continued it became stronger. "You have made a mess of my drawings, and your barn will not hold up. I refuse to put one single light in that place until we have it properly braced. What kind of carpenters have been working on the drama barn?"

"Your blueprints?" Signee turned off everything else he was

saying and caught only that. "These are your blueprints?"

"Of course ... what did you think?"

"I thought Eric...."

"Eric and I are friends. I owe him a favor, and so, very like Eric, he lets me pay him off by letting me help him out. Yes, I agreed to draw up the blueprints and put in the lights. Where is the list of step-by-step details?"

Still stunned, Signee opened her desk drawer and took out the list. Burke took it and unrolled it quickly, his eyes drinking in what was written.

"How could you follow these steps and make those..." he pointed in the direction of the barn, "mistakes?"

"You won't put in the lights?"

"How can I? When we jiggle those braces, everything could fall down. It has to be changed, of course."

"No!" Signee shouted through her confusion. "I don't want it changed. The kids have worked hard, it's their drama barn." She stopped as she called her theater the drama barn the way Kolby had referred to it twice. "They did it, and they loved doing it."

"Then they'll love fixing it. What kind of an example of building do they have? What right have you or anybody else to let them put together a sloppy mess?" He wasn't angry, just deliberate.

"It isn't sloppy, it is just...."

"Don't justify what you don't understand."

"I won't stand here and let you destroy their work!"

"I won't be standing here. I'll be working with them the way I should have been working with them from the first. But Eric thought I might hurt your feelings. Hurt feelings? When did hurt feelings have any voice when a building is at stake? I blame myself. I should have been here doing what Eric asked me to do, but my way, not his."

"You mean you have all the say? That isn't the way to help students learn."

"Students learn by watching things done right and helping them to be correctly built, not by blundering until the building falls down."

"I'm sorry," said Signee, her chin set. "I didn't know we were hurting *your* building. But I had the funny notion the building ... the drama barn," she deliberately used his name for the barn, "was our project, my project to be exact, a project I shared with my students ... a project they love and want to work on."

"They will work on it, but under my direction."

"Haven't I anything to say?"

"Of course ... start directing your plays. With a few extra blessings we might have the drama barn ready when your play is ready."

"I had a funny feeling," Signee went on saying as if talking to herself, "from the first time I saw you, that you'd try to take over."

"You were right. If I build a thing I do it right. You're kidding yourself if you think reconstruction details will hurt the kids; it is your ego that's hurt. But don't worry; you'll get over it when everything begins to work and your show is ready. Now, let's get hold of the guys, and you girls just get busy with some sandwiches and soup."

"Sandwiches and soup?"

"Hungry boys don't work very hard. If sandwiches and soup are too difficult, then bring anything you can fix. I want a crew of boys starting after school today and working through the week until Sunday morning."

"Sunday morning?"

"We won't work on Sunday. I have a Priesthood class to teach, so I'll need to fly back for that."

"Priesthood?"

"Yes, I hold the Priesthood," Kolby said with a smile. "Did you think they had given it to the women?"

"Oh ... " Signee felt her anger rise; and yet what was there to be angry about? She heaved a few sighs. "You are right, of course. I can see that you are right, but your deliberate calm is maddening. The least you could do is to give me the satisfaction of losing your cool."

"There's no use to lose your cool when you're right, and I make a practice of being right." He looked at Signee, his eyes penetrating her feelings. "You have no idea how bad your construction is. It won't take long to make the necessary corrections, and then the project can go forth. All right?"

"All right," was all she could think of to say After all, the problems were causing him problems more than anyone else, and he was facing the whole thing rather calmly.

"Don't worry, you'll make your deadline."

Signee turned quickly and looked at him. "How do you know about that?"

"I know everything about this whole project. I took your ideas and designed them into workable blueprints. I know your schedule and what you do with most of your time. Now, don't waste any more of your time or mine. I also know that even though you are stubborn, you are honest, and you won't let your ego interfere with what you want for this community." His voice lowered again and was disturbingly tender as he continued. "What you want is right. I admire your ambitions and your caring. Your dream is not unlike my own. I saw the value of drama on my mission, and I've thought about doing just what you are doing, but I wouldn't be good at your part. I haven't tried yet, but I just think I wouldn't be good at construction. So settle down, and let me help you and these kids put some action into this project. Together we can accomplish more than separately." He smiled broadly. "Where have you heard that before? And don't worry about your kids. I won't hurt them, I promise...."

His eyes were so intent and his smile so bright that Signee wondered why she wasn't angry with him, why she found herself drawn toward him, understanding more than she wanted to understand. The feeling frightened her, and she stepped back. He smiled even more broadly, as if he knew what she was thinking. Then he took her by the arm.

"See if you can get yourself excused for the rest of the day, and come and boss the job. I need your ideas."

"You need my...."

"Your ideas," he smiled. "I don't mind a lady foreman as long as she'll let me work the way I want to."

The work went forward just like Kolby had said it would, and Signee had to admit he knew how to handle boys. She and the girls did as he asked, and had food ready every day. Signee often stayed to watch the work just to see Kolby accomplish the things he wanted to accomplish. It was a fascinating experience, and when the week was over and the work finished, ready for painting details, she sighed with satisfaction and prepared to drive Kolby to meet his plane. He had stayed with Deek, and Signee couldn't help seeing the admiration Deek had for Kolby and his talents.

"I have to admit, Kolby, that you accomplished your goals and won the kids over in a way I hadn't expected."

"Of course. I love kids, too. Your Deek did most of the work, and all the organizing of the guys. I won him, and he took care of the rest."

"Why do you call Deek my Deek?"

"It's obvious he's in love with you ... his eyes light up whenever he has to ask you a question."

"Now, just a minute...."

"Too old for him, huh? Sure. But that doesn't keep him from loving you. It's really admiration for the teacher ... don't worry about it. Every kid needs an ideal; it will pull him through some rough spots when he's a long way from home. A good missionary needs an image of what he wants to find in a wife; and if that girl is a little older, he saves himself the heartache and just keeps the image. You should be flattered."

"Well, I am ... but I was afraid you didn't understand and that you'd heard some gossip."

"I don't listen to gossip. I've been on a mission, you know, and I've seen a lot of missionaries. I spent three years' special permission in Italy."

"What made you start the lighting business?"

"A dream of mine. I always wanted to do it, and so I did."

"How did you finance your lighting business? Your father?"

"My father died when I was a boy. I've had some good businessmen that had some faith in me, and they pushed me when I began to dream. So far I haven't lost them any money. I hope I never will. My dream isn't unlike your drama barn dream."

"You called it a drama barn several times. I think it fits."

"You may have the name if you wish ... just a couple of words put together."

"I'll ask the kids ... maybe we can officially name her the Drama Barn."

She realized he was taking over again, but for some reason she didn't resent it now. Yet she couldn't resist asking: "You always take over. Do you really think you're the only one with good ideas?"

"Of course not, but every show needs one director."

124

"And you're going to direct this show?"

"Only my part. I offered to help with the construction and put in your lights; the plays are up to you. You'll probably have to fix the parking lot, too." His statement took her by surprise.

"I'll what?"

Kolby quickly grabbed her arm and patted it while he spoke in an accent. "There there, lil' ol' gal ... don't you go a frettin'; daddy is gonna take care of youse." Then, before she could answer or ask any more questions, he brought her car to a stop, opened the door and got out. "I'll be coming back next week. I've left enough for the boys to do while I'm catching up at home." He took his overnight bag out of the trunk, then came back to hand her a few more words. "And Sig, you can cut down on the soup and sandwiches. I don't want you or those boys getting fat while I'm away."

That was all; then he was gone, racing toward the airport entrance. Signee backed her car out of the parking lot, turned around and drove home slowly.

"He's such a boss," she said to herself. "He's such a boss, and I don't know how to stop him from bossing me. I'll have to do something about that," she told herself in the rearview mirror; then she answered herself, "Yes, Signee, you'll have to do something. But what?"

Chapter Thirteen

While the drama and the drama barn progressed nicely, there was another problem Signee faced. She and Minta were close while having meals together every night, talking and doing things together. But when play rehearsals and different scheduling began to interfere with their time together, Signee felt Minta's attitude changing. The change came about more quickly because of Barney.

Barney had never stopped calling Minta from the time they had met. At first she had no desire to go with him, and his constant calls only flattered her. While she talked about Deek and worked with him on the drama barn, Minta hadn't thought of going with Barney. Then Deek's schedule changed, and he was away with the team on weekend trips; and with the extra rise in the price of gas, the extra bus that usually carried the cheerleaders and the pep club had to be cancelled. Minta felt the loss of seeing Deek. That was when she began responding to Barney's attention. He'd started coming around quite naturally, picking her up at school, meeting her after a late rehearsal ... Signee knew Minta was going through an attitude change; but she wasn't aware that the change was triggered mostly by

Barney's attention until Minta started grabbing a glass of orange juice with no thought of fixing breakfast for herself or Signee. When Signee became aware that it was getting to be a habit, she started fixing breakfast herself; but Minta wasn't interested.

"That's all?" asked Signee as Minta downed her orange juice in one gulp and started for the door.

"All ... enough. I'm gaining weight, and I've got to cut down." Leaving the door open, she ran back to pick up her books. "I'll see you tonight, Siggie, but I'll be late."

"How late?"

"Late! Does the exact time matter? I'm all grown up now, remember?"

"I remember. I remember, too, that I invited you to live with me, and I feel responsible to know where you are in case you need help."

"I won't need any help. No one is responsible for me. I do what I want. I always have."

"I see ..." said Signee, realizing this change in Minta had come about more rapidly than she had suspected. She wanted to call Minta back and talk to her but something warned her this wasn't the time. To her surprise, Minta came back again through the open door to face her.

"Siggie, I wish you wouldn't say 'I see' in that hurt way. You sound like my mother."

"Is this the way you treat your mother?"

"Anything wrong with what I said?"

"If there is, I can't put my finger on it ... it's something with your attitude, more than what you said. Are you angry with me, Minta?"

"You? No, of course not. Why should I be angry with the perfect Siggie?"

"Is that what you think? That I'm perfect?"

"Everyone else seems to think so."

"Shall I try to change, or is there something specific I can do? If I've hurt you, I'll...."

"All right, now who's making a big deal out of little hills?"

"Sorry. I thought you might like me caring about you."

"Care if you want. I'm on my way."

"Don't you want a ride to school?"

"No, I..." Suddenly Minta turned, walked back to the kitchen table and slammed her books down. "All right. I might just as well tell you. I don't need a ride to school because Barney is picking me up. I'll be late tonight because he is also picking me up again after school."

"Barney? The one who's been calling you? The one you weren't going to date because you were afraid he'd been around?"

"The same. I decided that was crazy. He's just a man, and I've always been able to handle ... most men. Maybe that's what's wrong with Deek; he's still a little boy bringing apples for the teacher."

"You and Deek have a fight?"

"Fight? No. I don't see him enough to have a fight. He's always too busy with the drama barn ... playing ball ... a thousand things."

"You've been busy too...."

"He never talks to me. I'm tired of work and bored, and I'm going out for a little fun."

"All right...." Signee walked forward, smiled and kissed Minta on the head. "You've been working hard, play practice, cheerleading.... I guess you're ready for time out. Be careful, and let me know if you're going to be too late." With that she turned and went to finish getting ready. Minta was puzzled.

"Are you serious?"

"Sure."

"You don't care if I go with Barney?"

"Like you said, you're all grown-up—grown-up enough to make your own decisions, and to live with the results. Besides, I wasn't the one who said Barney wasn't the right kind ... you said that."

"I know I did." Some of the tightness in Minta relaxed. She moved closer to Signee. "I really think I can handle him. I am lonely, Siggie. After all, I'm a girl and used to dating a lot. Cheerleading is getting a little old, and I'm sick of being with girls. I do what I have to for school activities, but ... Barney is good to me, and the nice thing about Barney is that he thinks I'm perfect."

"Don't take any chances, huh?"

Before Minta could reply, a horn sounded outside, and she

went toward the door. "I'll be careful, Siggie really I will."

"And Minta...." called Signee suddenly.

"Yes?"

"Tell your Mr. Barney that it's ill-mannered to honk for a girl. See if you can get him to come to the door next time."

"I'll see if I can." Minta smiled and was gone.

Signee, looking after her little friend, suddenly had a funny premonition that this was only the beginning of Barney Tremon, and her throat caught in a quick prayer that Minta might be protected.

Signee was little prepared for what followed—a series of almost steady dating for Minta and Barney. She did get him to come to the door when he picked her up at Signee's house, but too often he met her other places. When she missed a rehearsal to be with him, Signee knew it was time to talk.

"Has Barney become so important in your life that everything else has to go?"

"Siggie, really, you sound like Deek."

"Then Deek has talked to you, too?" They were standing outside Signee's English room, talking in the hall. Signee had stopped Minta when she saw her leaving in a hurry.

"Yes, he's talked to me ... finally. I think he's jealous, and I like that. If Barney can get Deek worried, I like that...." There was a smug little tightness across her lips, and she tipped her head upward with pride.

"Minta, you are foolish ... boys like Deek aren't jealous of boys like Barney. He's warning you, don't you know that? Warning you to stay away from Barney."

"Then why doesn't he call me? Why doesn't he take time for me? Does he expect me to sit home and do nothing?"

"Do nothing? You? With all your activities around this school and the play rehearsals, I wouldn't say you are doing nothing. And that's another thing ... the play ... "

"I'm ahead of everybody else on my memorizing. I get sick of waiting for our leading man to learn his lines."

"Some people have a harder time memorizing than you do, Minta."

"Then that gives me time for a few dates with Barney while I wait for him to catch up."

"Minta, you're going to blow it."

"Is that a prediction?"

"That's a warning. Oh, Minta ... don't take chances. I don't like what's happening to you since you started going with Barney."

"You can't blame everything on my dates with Barney."

"Can't you see I feel responsible...."

"Why don't you kick me out?"

"Of what? The play? Cheerleading, or my home?"

"All of them, if you want to. I guess you have the influence for all three, if you want to use your charm."

"None of this has anything to do with charm."

"I've got to go, Siggie. I'll be here in time for the last act if you want me to, but I can't see myself sitting around while you work on the dances and check out the stage crew. Besides, I don't like to be in competition when you're talking to Deek."

"Minta, you are all mixed up...."

"Is that a new discovery you just made?"

"No, but I thought we were making progress until you started dating Barney...."

"Sure, blame the whole thing on Barney ... see you later, Siggie."

"We'll have a talk tonight, Minta."

Signee looked at Minta seriously; there wasn't a smile creeping around the corners of her mouth now. Minta swallowed hard, but moved away fast, with a backward reply:

"Sure, Siggie ... we'll talk, and you be my judge."

Play rehearsal didn't go very well that evening, and there were more problems with the scenery that only Signee knew how to handle. She wished Kolby hadn't gone home, that this was one of his unexpected arrivals. She'd come to depend on Kolby more than she wanted to admit. It had been quite a while since his last visit; and, even though he'd left instructions for enough work for the boys, she missed him, missed discussing things with him. He was a man; maybe he'd have some ideas about how to handle Minta and Barney, and she made up her mind to talk to him about them.

Signee was tired, and even though Minta kept her word and made it in time for the last act rehearsal, she wasn't any happier with her attitude than she had been when they had talked earlier. To make matters worse, Barney hung around to watch the rehearsal, and seemed to have a bad effect on Minta's performance. He would have to stay away, Signee decided; that was another thing she had to talk to Minta about.

"I'll take her home, Miss Short," said Barney, coming forward as soon as the order to break was given.

"I have an empty car; she can go with me." Signee didn't want to sound bossy, but she wanted Minta home. Minta's attitude was rebellious, and that meant trouble ahead if Signee couldn't get through to her.

"I don't mind taking her. It isn't out of my way. Can I help you with anything here before we leave?" He asked the question, but there was no sincerity in his voice. He reached for Minta's hand as she came to join him.

"Are you good at scenery change?" Signee wanted to test him.

"No, I'm not too good at anything in the drama world. . . ." He looked at Minta. "Except entertaining the star."

"Quite a talent," said Signee, hoping her voice didn't sound too sarcastic.

"Well, we'll see you at your house . . . I'll get her in early."

"That would be a help."

Minta hadn't said anything, but Signee had watched her respond to Barney's attention. And suddenly the feeling inside her wasn't just a little premonition of pending danger any more but a whole star flush of warning signals. For a moment she wanted to run after Minta and pull her away from Barney, taking her home by force if necessary. But that wouldn't work, she knew that; Minta had her own agency, and force would only send her to Barney's arms for more sympathy.

It was close to two in the morning when Barney brought Minta home. Signee had taken her shower and curled up in a big chair by the door so she'd be there when Minta came in. She'd fallen asleep from exhaustion, and hadn't moved until the car wheels awakened her. She heard Minta walk up the sidewalk and open the front door; she pretended to be asleep until Minta was inside.

"Oh," Signee said, trying to stretch. "Minta? What time is it?"

"Too late for me to receive any welcome from you."

"Don't rebel, Minta. Sit beside me. Or, better still," Signee pulled herself up, out of the chair, "I'll come to your room while you get ready for bed. You haven't had much sleep lately, have you?"

"No, and you know why. Are you going to lecture me, Signee?"

"No, Minta...." she said, taking her hand and leading her to her bedroom. "That wouldn't help anything, would it?"

"I guess not. I'm used to lectures."

"That's what I thought." Signee sat down on the cedar chest at the foot of Minta's bed. "Remember when I told you, when you first came to visit me, that we had to be honest and tell each other how we feel?"

"I remember."

"Well, right now I feel like I'm not doing you any good. I'm worried about you, and feel I am not a good influence."

"Because of Barney?" Minta looked surprised.

"Because of the effect Barney has on you. I don't know Barney at all, except for the way you react when you are with him. I'm really worried about you, Minta. I thought you loved Deek, and...."

"I can't love Deek. He has his whole life already planned out, and I'm not part of it."

"How do you know? Aren't you willing to live for ... to be worthy of a guy like Deek?" Signee was getting angry now. "Minta, you can't expect to be the kind of a girl a boy like Deek will love if you can't sacrifice time enough to be his kind of person."

"I don't know what you're talking about," Minta shouted back.

"And I don't know how to explain," Signee got up and walked around the room. After a few laps, she took a deep breath and sat down again. Minta just stood there, as if waiting to be sentenced.

"All right, Minta. I think you'd better go back to your parents. I think that is the best place for you. I can't take the responsibility of what I feel is happening to you."

"What is happening to me?"

"I don't know. You rebel, you don't want to listen. You came here because you wanted help to straighten out your life; but when you rebel, I can't help you. Rebellion is from Satan, and I can't fight it."

"I knew it. . . ." Minta threw up her hands and plunked herself in the middle of the bed. "I just knew you were going to kick me out."

"I don't want to, Minta, but what can I do?"

Minta ran her hands through her hair a few times and then clamped them together. Her lips were a tight line. "All right, I'll be out of here tomorrow. But I won't go home to my parents."

"That's up to you. . . ." said Signee, getting up.

"You don't care where I go, do you?"

"I care, but you don't. And I can't make you."

"I'll stay with Barney." Her tone was defiant and stern.

"Stay with Barney, if you want to ... that's coming next, anyway." Signee bit her lip and walked away fast, going straight to her room. She opened the bed, kicked off her slippers, and got in. Just as she was ready to turn off the light, she looked up to see Minta standing at her door.

"Can I talk to you?" Her mood was the old Minta, as if she were two different people and could turn herself on and off. Signee nodded, and Minta came close to stand beside her bed. Looking down, she spoke quietly.

"Don't send me away, Siggie ... this is the only home I have ever known. You are the only person I've ever been able to talk to. I'll do whatever you want me to. If you tell me not to see Barney again, I won't. Just don't send me away." She dropped to her knees beside Signee's bed; there were tears in her eyes. Signee put her hand out and touched Minta's hair, while her armor melted.

"I love you, Minta. I don't want to dictate to you what to do with your life. But I can't stand aside and let you throw it away, either."

"I'll do whatever you say. I do love you and Deek, but you're awfully hard to live up to."

"You're not living up to us, but trying to change your habits to live up to your own ideals. You've chosen us as what you want in your life, and you can become whatever you think we are. You have to be patient while you learn, Minta."

"I know. I really hate to be patient. All my life I've made things happen. This waiting is a new game."

"Not a game, Minta." Signee's voice was gentle now, and very quiet as she stroked her little friend's hair. "Changing your life

134

is hard, but you have the desire, and you can accomplish anything you have a desire for. But you have to live by the rules. You're trying to change Deek into what you want him to be, and yet you love him for what he is."

"Then why can't he love me for what I am?"

"Maybe he will ... if you are still here when he comes home from his mission."

"His mission...." Minta hit the bed with her hand. "I hate his mission."

"But his mission is part of him. That's the rule ... you have to learn to love what he loves, if you love him. If you are here after his mission, that might be the missing link of what keeps him from loving you."

"I'll try, Signee, I'll try ... but don't ever leave me. Promise you won't ever leave me?"

"I'll always be with you in my heart and mind. But you have to govern your own actions; no one can be with you long enough to stop you from anything you want to do. There's always that one time, and the right circumstances ... you have to protect yourself by staying in the right places."

"Like with you and the drama barn, huh?" Her eyes and voice weren't sarcastic now, but pleading for understanding as a baby tries to understand discipline.

"By staying away from what pulls you away from your goals. You love acting, don't you? You're so natural, I thought maybe the drama barn could hold you until you get a taste of the goals you're working for."

"I do love acting, Siggie. It is so wonderful being on stage with the lights, living in that special world ... I think I could always be happy on stage."

"Not always ... you'll want all the normal things, too, just like I do...a husband to love you and lots of children—when you find someone strong enough to lead you."

"Deek is strong enough."

"He'll be even stronger when he gets home from his mission. Now go to sleep, Minta. When your physical body is tired, your spiritual body can't think. Late hours bring Satan closer. Goodnight, my Minta."

"You haven't called me that for a long time ... do you only call me that when I'm trying to be good?"

"What?"

"You called me 'my Minta.' You haven't done that for a long time."

"But you are my Minta," said Signee sleepily. "You'll always be my Minta. I'll always love you, even if I have to send you home."

"Will you send me home if I don't stop going with Barney?"

"No. That's your choice. I'll only send you home if I cause more rebellion in you ... when I feel I'm not a good influence."

"You couldn't not be a good influence ... and I'll try to be your Minta. I'll really try."

Chapter Fourteen

Signee, relieved that Minta had stopped dating Barney, pushed ahead on production for the first play to be presented in the drama barn. The barn wouldn't be completed entirely by the opening night, but the facilities would be the best they'd ever had. Even for rehearsal the drama barn gave the real feeling of drama. And improvements would go on for years; at least that was Signee's dream. Things began to move rapidly, and as dances began to be perfected and scenery painted, Signee was excited beyond her loftiest dreams. Yet she still worried about Minta. She wasn't quite sure just why.

Barney didn't give up easily. He called every day, and Signee was happy that Minta talked to him only a little while on the phone and wouldn't go out with him at all. Yet Minta was different, almost as if she were trying too hard in an unnatural way. Without letting her know how worried she was, Signee tried to get Minta to open up.

"How about breakfast, Minta? I've fixed an omelette and orange juice, just like eating breakfast out."

"What you're trying to say is that I'm a slob and let you do all the work." Minta stacked her books beside the door, ready to go.

Signee's face clouded. "Oh, please don't think that, Minta. Breakfast isn't that important to me. I didn't really eat breakfast until you started fixing it for me. But I've missed our talks, and well ... you've seemed sort of down, and I wanted to do something to cheer you up."

"I'm all right. I get tired easy. I'm sorry if I'm a bore ... no, maybe I'm not ... anyway, I don't know how to change me any more."

"Maybe you're trying to change yourself too much."

"You didn't seem to think so the last time we talked. You were ready to kick me out."

"Don't say that, Minta. I love you."

"Yeah, I know. You love everybody."

"Yes, I love a lot of people. But let me tell you how I feel about you."

"Don't bother; I don't think I could take it."

"Yes you can, because it's all wonderful. Why do you suppose I asked you to come and live with me?"

"Because I pushed my way in. I'm always pushing my way."

"No. I wanted you right away because you're a good person. Minta, you want good things in your life, but no one has shown you how to get them in the right way."

"It's too late for me to learn, Siggie, and yet I can't be happy with less. That sounds dumb, but it's true."

"It doesn't sound dumb. We're all like that. I'm like that. Once we've glimpsed something better, we aren't happy with less. I've wondered if that isn't the reason the prophets all claimed to have seen visions. They had to know what they were being guided to attain."

"Deek is my glimpse of what I want. But it's too late for Deek and me."

"Why do you say that?"

"Because Deek has to go on his mission, and I want to get married. Oh, I know, I've tried to tell myself I can wait, but I'm just kidding myself. I want to get married now."

"Aren't you visualizing marriage as an escape?"

"Perhaps. But I can't live the way I've lived at home for two years more."

"Hasn't the drama barn meant anything to you?"

"Yes, it has. I love being up on that stage, saying the lines, being a real person with real feelings. I wonder if my play-acting isn't more real than I am."

"It doesn't hurt to pretend to be something you want to become, as long as you're working to attain that goal for yourself in real life."

"I can't understand all that; but it's too late for me and Deek. I'll stay with the show, even after school's out, if you'll let me."

"Of course," said Signee automatically. But she was thinking of the first part of Minta's comments. "What do you mean, it's too late for you and Deek?"

"I mean it's too late. I should never have gone with Barney."

"Meaning?"

"Nothing, but Barney is lonely, the same way I am lonely. My heart goes out to him because I know what he's feeling."

"Too much sympathy, huh?"

Minta shrugged her shoulders. "He thinks he's in love with me. He knows how to make me feel special."

"Other boys have liked you, and they didn't bother you."

"I know, Siggie, but that was before I knew what it's like to love somebody who doesn't love you. Barney ... there's a certain emotion that goes with being with Barney. He makes me feel ... well, he makes me feel sexy, like it's part of a woman to feel sexy."

"Without benefit of clergy?"

"I told you, he hasn't talked about marriage, so drop your little puns. You sound like my mother."

"I was just kidding...."

"I know, but I don't feel very funny nowadays. Don't worry about me. I'm trying to find out if I can be like you and Deek. Maybe I can't; maybe I will have to settle for less."

"Barney is less?"

"Barney is definitely less. But I get tired of the struggle."

"Don't get tired too soon; you have all the rest of your life. If you marry less than your ideals, you'll have a long time to find out if you can live without your dream."

"I need some time...."

"All right ... and in the meantime, let's spend some time together."

"Now, when could we do that?"

"Right after the show, we'll take a trip to sunny California and lie on the beach. Would you like that?"

"Would you?"

"I'm looking forward to it. I haven't ever traveled very much, because I have always either lacked the money or the friend. Hopefully, we'll have both when the show is over "

They'd talked a little more, and Signee went off to her classes that day remembering the smile on Minta's face. The talk that had followed on the way to school had been lighter and full of the play. Yet, by morning, Signee had some new worries.

Early in the morning Eric called long distance.

"Sig," came Eric's familiar voice over the wire. Yet there was something unfamiliar about it, too, even when he only said her name.

"What's the matter, Eric?"

"It's Alta, Sig. I'm calling you from the hospital. I brought her in last night."

"Is it the baby?"

"Yes. They think it's a miscarriage. She's had to stay in bed most of the time, but even that hasn't helped."

"Can they save the baby?"

"Hasn't been long enough. Our baby will just be called a miscarriage." Eric's voice broke. "I don't know if she can take any more."

"She can take it if you can, Eric."

"Maybe that's part of the problem; I don't know if I can. I feel like I'm ready to give in...."

"And what?"

"How do I know? I feel like I'm ready to blow...."

"Eric, this doesn't sound like you."

"Don't worry, Sig ... I'll be all right. I just feel rotten and confused. Sig, she's asking for you. I guess we both need your strength now. You're Alta's family, and mine is too far away to help...."

"I'll come, Eric."

"I hate this, Sig. I know how busy you are with the barn and all, but I don't know what to do for Alta. I really don't."

"Just love her, Eric. I don't know what I can do either, but I'll come."

"Fly, will you? I'll have a taxi to pick you up at the airport."

"I'll fly, Eric."

There was a click, and the phone sounded the dial tone. With her mind in a whirl, she flew into action. She knew Deek and the guys would take over at the drama barn as far as the scenery went, and she had an assistant director and several substitute teachers. It was a matter of a few calls. Pulling an overnight bag off her shelf, she began packing as her mind made a list of all she had to do, including finding out what time her plane left. Minta ... she had to get in touch with Minta. Minta had gone to an early dance practice and had Signee's car.

An hour later, with all the calls made about her school work, she dialed the school and had them page Minta; when they located her in the gym, she called Signee. After Signee had explained that she was going to be with Eric and Alta, she asked Minta a favor.

"Minta, I don't know how long I'll be away. I don't want you to have to be here alone. Will you go home and visit your parents, just for this little while?"

"Siggie, let me stay at your place. I'll keep everything clean and eat up the food that will spoil if I don't stay."

"I can't let you do that. I would worry about you. Please promise me you'll go home, just until I get back."

"All right, if I have to. Don't stay away too long, Sig."

"I won't. I'll be back as soon as I can. Take care of the play and see that everybody memorizes their parts, all right?"

"All right, Sig."

Signee hung up and stood looking at the telephone, thinking. Suddenly she dialed Deek's home. He was just getting up. She explained what was happening, and then asked a favor of him, also.

"Deek, I'm worried about Minta. I've asked her to move home, but she doesn't want to. I don't want her here by herself. Is there a way you can get her there, help her or something?"

"Sure, Siggie, I'll take care of it. Sometimes she doesn't like what I say to her, but I'll see to it."

"Take care of her while I'm away, will you, Deek?"

"Sure, Siggie. Don't you worry. OK?"

"OK."

The plane landed, and Eric's taxi was waiting to take Signee to the hospital. But she was too late to talk to Alta.

"They've taken her to surgery," said Eric, his face showing lines of anxiety. "They couldn't wait any longer. I wanted you to see her before she went in."

"I'm sorry I didn't make it in time. I caught the first plane."

"There isn't anything you can do, but I thought she would feel better just seeing you."

"A miscarriage isn't so serious, is it, Eric?"

"The doctor says she mustn't even try to carry another for a long time, and probably never will be able to."

"But in time...."

"Sig, our only hope is adoption, and we've tried that route for so long. I can't put her through any more waiting."

"Have you any other choice?"

"No, we just don't know what to do anymore. Sig, she was so happy fixing up the baby's room, painting and making little clothes ... she was so ... happy ... " Eric's voice broke and he turned away.

"Eric," said Sig, putting her hand on his shoulder. "If we could see the end from the beginning, we could place ourselves in Heavenly Father's hands with less fuss."

"Sig, when I think of how many people have children every day that don't want them ... I wish I could feel it's right."

"Don't torture yourself, Eric. This is you, not other people, and for some reason this is your test. If you can believe this is part of your training...."

"For what?"

"How do I know? I'm thinking about a friend of Mother's. She and her husband are two of the finest people I've ever known, and they couldn't have any children either. Finally they adopted two, a boy and later a girl, just a few years apart, and they felt so blessed to have them. Then, when she was past the age most women can have children, she finally had one of her own."

"A modern Sariah, like in the Bible?"

"Sure ... and you know, she said she just knew she needed to know the value of children, of raising two before she had her own. There's a real closeness in that family."

"Look, Sig," said Eric, turning toward her with a sudden motion, "I know you're trying to help, but I don't need it. Alta is the one...I'll be all right if she's all right."

"All right, Eric ... I'll try to help her. When do you think I can see her?"

"The doctor will be coming out any minute now. Sig . . . please pray she is all right."

"I've already done that, at least a million times. You really love Alta, don't you?"

"Of course." He looked surprised. "Why did you ask me that? Alta always asks me that, too."

"I guess it's because of what you and I had together before you started dating Alta."

"I know . . . and I thought if we could have this baby, she might stop doubting herself, and me."

"She will, Eric."

A little later, Signee followed Eric into Alta's room, where she was recovering. Signee had wondered what to say, but she needn't have worried. When Alta opened her eyes, Signee went to her and they both wept together while Signee held her tight. Then, at last, Signee reached for a tissue; she wiped Alta's nose and face and then her own.

"Is there anything I can do for you, Alta?"

"I-I'm all right."

"I know you are, but isn't there something I can do for you? I would so like to help."

"Y-yes," said Alta, smiling through her tears. "Will you take care of the nursery at home for me? I don't want to have to put away all of those little things again."

"Yes, dear, I'll do that, and clean your house and get dinner for you, and...."

"No. I think the house is clean, and Eric can eat here with me. Fix yourself something, and put my baby...." she hesitated while her chin quivered again. Then she smiled. "There's a cedar chest in the nursery. Just fold the things we have out, and put the little animals and—will you do that, Sig?"

Signee nodded, kissed Alta, and made her way out of the room into the hall, leaving Alta with Eric. She wanted to be alone so she could cry without Alta listening.

Later, when Eric came out, her tears were over and she knew she could do whatever he asked her to do. She looked up at him from the couch by the window where she had waited. To her questioning eyes, Eric said:

"The doctor has given her a sedative. She'll sleep for a while."

"Can you get some sleep, Eric? I'll stay right here, and...."

"No, you go to our house the way she asked. I'll stay here." From his pocket he took his car keys and handed them to Signee. "Take my car, it's in the back parking lot; and here's the address." He handed her a card.

"What if you need your car?"

"I won't. I'm not going anywhere until Alta is out of danger. There's a key to the house on that ring, too."

Signee had never seen the home Alta and Eric had built, but it wasn't hard to find the address Eric gave her. The hard part was waiting inside. From the front door she could see the door to the nursery, and she dreaded going into that room. With a prayer in her heart, she finally made it. Everything in the room was so ready, everything to the last detail. The whole room was as if suspended in time, awaiting the little occupant who wouldn't be coming, at least not this time. Swallowing her tears, she went to work putting the little soft toys away, doing all she could to make it look like an ordinary room. But try as she would, it was still a nursery, a nursery waiting for a baby, as Eric and Alta were waiting. Then suddenly she couldn't stand looking at the small world anymore. She left the room, closing the door tightly. Trying not to cry, she looked for something else she might do to help. In the kitchen, she found last night's dinner still on the table. Signee began to rinse and put the dishes in the dishwasher.

Funny, she had never thought of Alta with her own darling house, decorated to look so much like the two of them together. Alta had always been quiet and rather alone; but Signee had never had a friend like Alta, so loyal and without any jealousy in her whole system. She had been the one person Signee could share success stories with, without worrying about jealousy or having them used against her or being part of the gossip. Dear Alta.... The phone rang, breaking into her thoughts and the quiet of the house. Signee hurried across the room to pick up the receiver.

"Sig?"

"Yes, Eric."

"Have you eaten yet?"

"I'm not very hungry."

"Then get yourself hungry, huh? I'm sending you a rescue

party to take you out to dinner."

"No, Eric, I don't feel like eating."

"I want you strong and healthy so you can let Alta and me lean on you. The doorbell will be ringing any minute. Have a good time, and I'll call you in the morning, or sooner if Alta gets over being sleepy. Hey, Sig?"

"Yes?"

"Thanks for coming. You don't know how it helps to know you are here."

"All right, Eric." She hung up, and the doorbell rang almost at the same moment. She hurried to open the door. There on the other side, leaning against the side of the door frame, as she had seen him do several times before, was Kolby. She was so excited to see him that she almost threw her arms around him; but she didn't. She just stood there, a lump of gratitude in her throat, and croaked:

"Kolby...."

"Sig ... you look terrible."

"Thanks a lot ... I could say the same about you ... but I won't."

He smiled. "I'm glad, I'm not a very good sport. Come on, Sig, I'm getting you out of here ... at least for a little while."

"Bless you, Kol, you must have been sent by the angels. Only they knew I needed you tonight."

Chapter Fifteen

Minta didn't move home right away as Signee had asked her to do. Busy every day with the play, and winding up the cheerleading season, she had been too busy to pack. Finally, it was Deek who offered to help her move her things.

"I'll be glad to come by and give you a hand," Deek suggested as they left play rehearsal one evening.

"How did you know I was moving?"

"Siggie called me about the barn before she left and just mentioned you might need some help."

"Siggie has nice ways of checking up on me. All right, Deek, I was thinking about sleeping home tonight ... if now isn't too late for you?"

"Football season is over; no sweat."

So together they had gone to Signee's house; and while Minta put a few things in a suitcase, Deek played the piano in the front room. Then he helped her lift her things out to his car.

"I didn't know you could play the piano so well, Deek."

"I just touch the ivories a bit ... a result of Mother insisting that I practice an hour before I could play football. Any more stuff for the car?"

"No. I'm not taking much; Siggie should be back pretty soon."

"Yeah, I hope so."

"Ah ... yes ... would you like me to fix you a cheese sandwich before we go?"

"No, don't bother. The kitchen is all clean."

"I can clean it again. We've got some cheese, and it might spoil."

"All right ... I'm starved."

Minta's eyes glowed, and she went to work. Deek sat at the kitchen table and watched.

"I didn't know I liked to cook, but I do. Siggie lets me do most of the cooking."

"You look good ... kinda domestic and cute."

"Well, thanks, Deek."

"You're welcome ... I think it's neat watching women in the kitchen, like watching an artist paint a picture ... you women get so involved in food."

"I guess it is an art. Siggie lets me do a lot of things I've never tried to do before."

"She's a good person ... there's only one Siggie."

"Yes, you've said that before."

"I know ... and don't get uptight. You think the same way about her as I do."

"Hardly. I'm a girl and you're a boy."

"Minta ... there you go, being dumb again."

"You always think I'm dumb. Well, it might be that I know more about these emotional things than you do."

"Where emotion is concerned, you win."

"What was that supposed to mean?"

"Whatever you want it to mean."

"Here," said Minta, opening the toastwicher and putting the sandwich on his plate.

"I'm not very hungry."

"I made that toastwich for you, and you'd better eat it."

"All right, I'll eat it."

In silence Deek ate his sandwich while Minta cleaned up, and in silence they locked up the house and went to the car. Deek gave her a ride to her place, helped carry her bags in, and left.

Without Signee to intercede, Deek and Minta didn't get along very well at rehearsals, either. They looked at each other, but nothing was said—until one night, when Barney dropped by

148

rehearsal just as they were finishing. Deek saw Barney come in and sit down in the back of the barn, and went to inform Minta. He had had every intention of trying to protect her as he'd promised Signee he would, but somehow the conversation had changed the whole idea.

"Minta, there's a big important man waiting to pick you up."

"I'm not a pick-up, tell him to go away."

Deek smiled. "I'll do that. Are you serious?"

"Go ahead. If you don't want me to go with him, I won't. I didn't ask him here."

"Glad to hear it. Your taste is improving. For a while there, I was wondering what was wrong with me, that I could really be interested in a girl who had such bad taste in men."

"Oh, I thought you were jealous."

"Of him? You've got to be kidding."

"What's wrong with him? He's good looking, drives a nice car, and he's crazy about me."

"That makes him exclusive?" Deek meant it as a compliment, but it came out sarcastically.

Minta was hurt and wanted to strike back.

"And I'm wondering what is so dumb about me, that I care if you are jealous or not."

"Minta, you jump at everything. I didn't mean ... oh what's the use?"

"No use at all. And don't bother to tell Barney I won't go with him. I just decided I will go."

"If that's the way you want it...." Deek looked at Minta with an even look, the hurt in his eyes cutting into her. She wanted to reach out to him; but before she could, he'd turned and walked away in long, even strides.

"Deek, I...." but Minta didn't get the rest of the words out. It was too late.

"There you are, Sweetness," said Barney, coming up beside her. "I've nearly gone nuts trying to find you. What's all this about not going with me? I've stayed away long enough ... no more, no matter what you say."

Still looking after Deek, Minta talked to Barney as if talking through a curtain. "Barney ... tell me, do you love me?"

"What? Sure I do, Sweetness, you've never doubted that, have you?" He leaned close to her. "Want to know who I dream about every night?"

"Me? Do you dream of me, Barney? Tell me, tell me the truth, no lies or lines tonight, Barney. I want to know how you feel."

"Oh, Sweetness ... will I tell you. Let me get you out of this place, and I won't just tell you, I'll show you. Come on, Sweetness."

"No, don't show me, Barney. Tell me."

"Like the other night? Like the last time? Come on, Sweetness. I'm cramped in here, but when we're alone ... Sweet, you won't be sorry."

"Won't I?" asked Minta, putting out her hand to him, still looking at the other side of the hall where Deek had disappeared.

"Just like before ... ?"

"I don't want to talk about it, Barney. Go away."

"What?"

"I told you, I've got play rehearsal, I won't go with you tonight. Not any more ... not ever."

"But Sweetness, you ... if you think I'm going to give up on you, you're wrong. I'll wait. I'll wait all night if I have to, but you're coming with me."

"No, not tonight, Barney. Not any more...."

"I'm not leaving you feeling this way. You're all discouraged and it's my job to keep you happy. I'll leave while you rehearse and I'll come back, all right?"

"No. Not tonight. This rehearsal will be a long one."

"I'll still be back."

"No, Barney ... now go away."

"Then I'll be here tomorrow."

"No...."

"And the next day, and the day after that ... you'll see I don't give up on the girl I love. You're special to me, Sweetness, and I won't give up. I warn you."

"Go away, Barney." Minta left him standing there and walked toward the stage. Barney turned and left, his irritation showing in every step he took as he walked out of the drama barn to his waiting car.

The rehearsal was torture that night for Minta. Deek was there, but he didn't really look at her all night. Minta had a hard time feeling her part, and the assistant director began to nag at her. When the whole thing was finally over, Minta left for home without wiping off her grease paint.

But home wasn't any better for Minta. When she'd called to tell her mother she would be coming home for a little while because Signee was away, Minta couldn't tell from her mother's tone of voice or her actions if she was glad or sorry to have her back. Minta knew if she hadn't promised Signee, that she would have turned right around and gone back to Signee's place, all alone. It was even worse when Barney found out she was home and began calling her.

"It's that boy again, Minta," said her mother. "He's called several times."

"What boy?"

"Minta, that boy who came home with you the day of your accident. Did he think I wouldn't know his voice?"

"I don't think he's trying to hide his voice, Mother. The truth is, I don't go with Barney any more. But he's very nice to me."

"But what do you know about his parents or where he comes from?"

"I know one thing, Mother. He didn't come from here with a lot of gossip hanging onto him, the way some people think about other people."

"Minta, he isn't good for you."

"How do you know that, Mother?"

"Well, I don't know. I just don't feel good around him." She went close to Minta and put her hand on hers. "Darling, I only know what's best for you. I don't know this boy, but I don't think he'll bring you any happiness. I can't really explain it . . . maybe just mother's intuition."

"When did you develop a mother's intuition, Mother?"

"Minta, please be kind and couth. This is your home and you are welcome, but it is obvious you find my counsel disagreeable, so I won't waste it on you. Minta, I'd hoped your time away from us had softened your rebellion, but I guess you are going right on being nasty about everything. Well, go ahead. But I warn you, Minta, this boy is not a good influence on you. He is not cultured; he will do you no good."

Minta knew she had hurt her mother, and she hadn't meant to; it was as if the words were pre-programmed and she couldn't change them and was powerless to stop them. Minta felt a lump form in her throat as she started to unpack and hang her things in her closet.

The next day, Minta didn't feel well and stayed home from school. That night she missed rehearsal; the following day Deek appeared at her door.

"Minta," he said when she opened the front door and invited him in to sit down, "Minta, you missed rehearsal, and this play has to go on. I promised Signee we would have it all memorized and ready for her final touches when she returned. We can't do much without you, when you are in so many scenes."

"Don't worry, I won't let your little Siggie's play down."

"Good, I'm glad to hear it. Now don't miss any more rehearsals."

"What if I'm sick?"

"You aren't, and you won't be unless you think that way."

"Just call you Dr. Deek, right?"

"As far as you're concerned, right. I am not the director of this show, Minta; but I made a promise to Siggie about you, and I'm keeping that promise. You, of all people, should feel an obligation for what she has done for you."

"Oh, I do ... truly, sir ... " Minta was being sarcastic again.

"Just as long as you get it straight, Minta. Now, I hope the show can go on."

Minta was at practice after Deek's visit, but after the show, when Barney appeared, she went with him. That was the beginning, and he was there every night after that. Minta suddenly needed attention, and Barney was always there, ready and eager to take her wherever she wanted to go. After that, the only time Minta saw Deek was on the set; and then there was always Barney, waiting at the door.

One night as she left, exhausted and tired of Deek finding things to pick at during rehearsal, she met Barney at the door. He quickly took her arm to pull her toward the car.

"Sweetness, I'm taking you to a midnight dinner."

"Where?"

"It's a surprise, but you'll love the place."

"All I care, Barney, is that you cheer me up. If you don't say something nice to me tonight, I think I'll kill myself."

"Hey, what's happened, Sweetness?"

"Nothing; killing myself is just a figure of speech. I won't do

152

that; I really won't."

"Come on, Sweetness ... I'll keep you happy ... I'll put my arms around you and let you cry on my shoulder, and then I'll kiss all your troubles away."

"I'll bet you will, Barney, I'll just bet you will," said Minta as she let Barney lead her to his car.

Chapter Sixteen

"Come on, Sig, I'm taking you out to a nice little place to have a quiet dinner," said Kolby, still standing in the doorway. "Get your coat or your lipstick or whatever you women get, and let's go."

"Kolby, I can't tell you how happy I am to see you. But I really don't feel like eating."

"But that's just the point. I want you to tell me, even if you don't feel like eating."

"Tell you what?"

"How happy you are to see me." His face lit up like a clown at the thought, and Signee couldn't help laughing. He laughed too, and Signee felt herself relaxing. He took hold of her hand. "Come on, tonight you don't have to do anything you don't want to, not even make decisions."

"I'd better wash my face and get the salt water off."

He nodded and sat down in the nearest chair while she ran to take care of the details of getting ready; and then they were off.

"I don't want to get too far away from a telephone. What if Alta needs me?"

"It's the modern day and age; there are phones all over town."

"Kolby, you are funny ... but I mean it."

"I know you do. I shall leave you at intervals and check with the hospital, and let you know what is going on." He lifted his hand as if being sworn in. "I promise, Your Honor." Then, taking her hand again, he guided her to his car, waiting below.

Kolby was wise. He took Signee to a small eating place where the waiters did the entertaining. The atmosphere was very picturesque, reminiscent of the old-fashioned beer gardens of the Roaring Twenties that served everything from finger foods to sandwiches, including sprouts and avocado. Kolby ordered dinner by the item, one thing at a time, teasing Signee about not wanting to eat and yet tempting her to try new, unique foods. As they laughed and enjoyed the music that played between barbershop quartets and vaudeville comedy characters, Kolby, true to his word, disappeared to use the telephone. When he didn't say anything upon his return, Signee knew everything was all right.

"Kolby, you're a lot of things I didn't know about," laughed Signee as he picked up a handful of sprouts he'd ordered beside his sandwich.

"Ya' mean ya didn't know I could eat sprouts in ma' fingers?" She nodded and laughed. "Well, fer goodness sak' I'ze good at all kinz of eatin'."

"You're a health food nut, Kolby."

"No, I'ze not ... I'ze an individual eata' ... the goin' theng...."

Kolby talked in several different dialects throughout the evening, and for each dialect he had corresponding head movements. He was a natural at mimic; and yet there was a dignity about him, a culture, she responded to. And all the time he held her hand tight in his, and made her feel protected and cared for. After dinner they drove around the city, and Signee found Kolby had another side.

"Right over there, to your left ... you see that big school?"

"The one that spreads up and out in rather a grotesque fashion?"

"Please ... you're talking about the school that learned me," said Kolby, aware that his forced bad grammar was symbolic of what he was saying. "Of course it was a smaller building, and, I would say, sported a little better plan of design. However, the growth around here made some changes."

156

"Did you really go to school there?"

"Of course. This is my hometown ... after elementary."

"Where did you go to elementary?"

"A community a few miles out of town, for a few years. My parents moved to the city when I entered that school, and then I moved back after junior high to live with Grandpa."

"Is this for real, or are you still kidding me?"

"Why Madam, this is all real."

"You're sure I can believe you, now?"

"Honest injun."

"Honest injun. That's what my father used to say."

"We Burkes go back a way, Madam."

"Why did you move out of town again?"

"After my parents died."

"Kolby, did they really?"

He was serious now, but his eyes twinkled when he looked at her. "They did. They were both killed in an airplane crash, and left me to Grandpa in their will ... a will of love."

"I'm sorry, Kolby."

"Don't be. Grandpa is a combination parent ... I guess I needed him."

"Do you remember your life with your parents very well?"

"Like yesterday. A memory as clean as that stays all your life."

"I'm sorry you've been alone."

"I haven't been alone. I don't feel sorry for anything that's happened to me; they've all been blessings. In a way, my parents have been with me more than other kids, especially when I was young. When I needed their help, I'd just call out to them, and somehow things would change for me. I've had a lot of love from the other side. And then Grandpa ... what a grand old fellow." Kolby's face lit up, and his words were so enthusiastic Signee couldn't help thinking he was as blessed as he said he was.

"Is your grandpa still alive?"

"Sure. He lives in his little house ... that's what we can do tomorrow, Sig. We'll go meet Grandpa. You won't know me until you know Grandpa. You do want to know me, don't you?" He looked at her directly, the twinkle in his eyes insistent.

"Yes, y-yes I do want to know you," said Sig, and knew she meant it more than she wanted to. "I'm finding out you're a whole different person than I thought you were."

"You've only seen my work side. I get mean when I work."

"I wouldn't say mean...."

"You wouldn't?"

"No." Sig shook her head thoughtfully, eyeing him.

"What would you say? Now, be careful before you answer. I don't want my self-image to take too big a tumble."

"I would say ... bossy ... yes, that's the word ... bossy."

"No, I'm not bossy. Just particular, a perfectionist. There's only one way to do a job, in my opinion ... and that's my way." They both laughed, and Kolby turned the car onto a street Signee recognized.

"Are we going home now?"

"Not home ... too far ... "

"Kolby ... you ... I mean, are you taking me to Alta's?"

"No, I'm taking you to Eric's house."

"All right ... all right ... but in any case, the evening is over."

"Not really. I want you to dream about the rest of it."

"Are you going to govern my dreams, too?"

"Not govern, but dominate. I want you to think of us and see how you like the idea."

Signee gasped and would have come back with a comment, but there was something about the way he tightened his grip on her hand that made her just sit there and enjoy the moment. Later, at the door, Kolby took her key and unlocked the door of the Langden house. As they stood outside and the door swung open, Signee found herself hesitating.

"Do you suppose everything is all right at the hospital?" she asked quietly.

"Last time I checked." He lifted Signee's chin. "Don't you worry. Alta is a tough girl, she isn't going to let any of this get her down. She doesn't need our sympathy, and we're not going to give her any, right?"

Signee looked at the closed door to the nursery and stepped into the house, her lips in a thin line. She looked up into Kolby's eyes. "All right, no sympathy. Just love."

"Good girl. That's all you can give a girl like Alta; that's all she needs."

"Kolby, I didn't know you had this kind of concept of life ... so positive, and...."

158

"But of course. Why did you think I was attracted to you in the first place?"

"You're attracted to me?"

"Of course. You're why I took the job."

"But you were so obnoxious. Excuse me, but you were."

"I still am. For instance, I have to talk to you about putting an apron on your stage to use a new kind of light I want to try out...."

"You what?"

"Yes, but not tonight. We'll talk about that another time."

"But why do I need an apron stage?"

"So I can use my lights. But we'll talk tomorrow."

"Why not now? I don't think an apron is practical."

"It is for my lights." He went on, "Don't worry; we'll discuss it after we go out tomorrow. I'll pick you up in the morning."

"I can't go, Kolby. What if Alta comes home or needs me at the hospital?"

"I'll check with the hospital, and when Alta is ready to come home, we'll both be here. In the meantime, I have a whole list of things wrong with me that you can get to work correcting."

"Why would you do that?"

"Because I've found the only people who get your attention are people with problems. Is that true, or just circumstantial?"

"Well, I ... why, it's circumstances."

"Wrong again ... I've been studying you. Now go to bed, rest, and I'll see you tomorrow."

"All right, Kolby, and thanks...."

"And Sig ... no tears tonight, all right?"

"All right."

Signee was at the hospital early the next morning. She expected to see Alta still wrung out and feeling bad. Instead, as she was ushered into her room by Eric, she found Alta sitting up, freshly showered, her make-up on, and smiling.

"Sig...." She put out her arms and Sig went to her again. time they didn't cry; they just embraced. Then Alta said, "Sig, we're going to adopt a baby."

"Good for you, Alta."

"We're going to find out about every agency and what we have to do to measure up. We don't care how many times they investigate, or what we have to do to shape up, but we're going to be on the top of the list of approved parents for adoption. It will take a long time, Sig ... but we're going to do it. Aren't we, Eric?"

Eric looked into his wife's shining face. "We really are. If the agencies thought we bugged them before, just wait this time. We're going to show them we're capable, eligible parents."

"You know, Sig, I'm going back to taking music lessons. If we're musically talented, that helps."

"Good. Eric, you sing a little and play the piano."

"I do. I think I'll practice again."

"I—" was all Signee could say, since the lump in her throat caught her voice; then she swallowed hard. "I am so proud of you two. You look wonderful, Alta. When can you go home?"

"Tomorrow, if my tests are all right today. They want to give me some blood. I'll need some extra blood, too, because I've got a lot of things to do."

"You'll stay a while, won't you, Sig?" Eric's eyes were serious, but his smile was bright.

"Well, if you want me."

"Do, Sig, please do. I want to show you my house and our city, and we can catch up on talk, and ... will you, Sig? Just for a little while?"

"Alta, I have to...." She watched Alta's brave smile get a little weak, and her eyes were so intent and pleading that she didn't have the heart to tell her of all the things she was worried about at home. Moving closer, she kissed Alta on the forehead. "Of course I will. I'll stay until you don't want me any more. I came to be with you, didn't I?"

"Oh, Sig ... I'll get my strength back really fast, I promise. You should have seen me get up this morning—I didn't even faint."

"That's good. Now, tell me what to do to get things ready for your homecoming."

"Pick up some things for salad, fresh vegetables. You know, prospective parents who wish to adopt are checked for good health. I don't want to put on extra pounds. And get some potatoes to bake, and some T-bone steaks ... Let's really celebrate." She turned to her husband. "Eric, why don't you invite Kolby? I hate to have him eat alone all the time."

"I'll invite him, Alta." Eric and Signee looked at each other, and a look of understanding passed between them. Alta saw them exchange the look.

"Now, what does that mean?"

"What, honey?" Eric tried to sound casual.

"That look ... between you two."

"Oh, that ... " said Eric. "That look said your matchmaking is a little late. Kolby is ahead of you ... he took Sig out to dinner last night."

"While I was here suffering, you two were out celebrating?" She was teasing.

"We checked with you every minute," said Sig. "You slept very well on those pills the doctor gave you. At least that was the report from your husband."

"Good. I'm glad. It was a good sleep, but now I'm kinda tired. Why do I get tired so easily?"

"Lack of blood, I suspect. Maybe that's why they're giving you some extra."

"Could be." Alta lay back on her pillow, suddenly exhausted.

"I'm going to get out of here, Alta. I'll do all the things you asked me. You get some sleep. Right?"

"R-right," said Alta sleepily, as the exhaustion joined the late-working sedative the doctor had given her earlier.

"Goodbye for now, Alta dear," said Signee, leaning over her to kiss her cheek again. "Don't you worry about anything; just get your strength back. You've been through so much, and you have such courage. Do you know how much I love you, Alta?" There was a slight nod to Alta's head as her eyes opened heavily.

"Sig," she asked softly.

"Yes, Alta."

"Sig, did you take care of our baby's little things?"

"Yes, Alta, I did." Sig felt herself shiver again, remembering the pretty room.

"Sig ... did you wrap them in tissue paper?"

"Not all of them; but I will, Alta."

"Thank you ... I want them to stay nice."

"She's out," said Eric as Alta's hand went limp in his. "She'll sleep again now." Tucking the sheet around her, he kissed his wife, and then took Signee's arm. They went out into the hall together.

"Everything all right?" asked a familiar voice, and Signee felt her face warm as she looked into Kolby's eyes.

"Good morning, Kol. How did you trace me?"

"Very simple. I got out my detective officer and the first question he asked was my clue. He asked how many people did you know in our city? I went in search of the other two." Kolby turned to Eric. "Is Alta on the mend?"

"She looks good."

"Great . . . now I'm going to take this girl off your hands for a while, Eric."

"Kol," interrupted Signee, "I have some things to do that I promised Alta."

"We'll do them, Sig . . . we'll do them together."

"Fine," said Eric. "Now I can have my own car, and you women won't tie it up." Smiling, he turned to Signee and took one of her hands in both of his. "You're neat, Sig . . . I still love you."

"Hey, hey . . . watch that, mister," said Kolby. "Tell it to your own wife, huh?" They all laughed, but Eric didn't let go of Signee's hand.

"I'm grateful, you know that, Sig, and I can't tell you how much it means that you are going to stay. I'm worried the most about when she comes home . . . there's a lot of dreams in that house, and they have to be adjusted thinking from now on."

"She'll have us all. Are you sure you are all right Eric?"

"I can at least be as brave as my wife . . . sure, I'll be all right. But I wonder how I'll feel as my wife throws me into developing my musical talent?"

Chapter Seventeen

"I don't want to take your time, Kol. If you have something to do while I take care of these few details, I can be ready about noon."

"No deal. I'll come along and make sure you do them right."

"But you don't know what I have to do."

"All the more reason I should check on how you are doing the job. Where to first?"

"Don't you have to work for a living?"

"Sometimes. But right now I'm trying to find out how much profit there is in being a dreamer."

"Are you a dreamer?"

"All my life, but I've had to schedule my dreaming along with the work I had to get done. You dream, too, don't you?"

"Maybe."

"Maybe? What about the drama barn? Now, there's a dream if I know a dream when I see one."

"You sound like you don't approve."

"Did I sound like that? I didn't mean to...." He was kidding her again.

"You meant every word of it ... I know you."

"Do you now?" There was something mysterious about his look. Before she could answer, he asked another question. "Where to first . . . you haven't told me where we're going first."

"I need to pick up some things at the grocery store and then go to Alta's house. Which one shall we do first?"

"Grocery store on the way, and then the house."

Together they parked in the parking lot and went grocery shopping; Kolby bought a few extra things because he found out he'd been invited to the homecoming meal. When they went to the checkstand to pay the bill, Kolby took out his wallet and wouldn't let Signee pay the bill.

"But Kolby, Eric expected me to buy the groceries, and then he'll reimburse me."

"Shh ... people will think we're married and you're supporting me."

"I don't think they will; we don't look married."

"How do you know? Have you ever been married?"

"No, but I'm sure people look different than we do when they're married."

"Maybe we're a little happier; some of them have weathered a few more storms. Maybe I shouldn't look so happy." He pulled a face and tried to look old and bored. Signee laughed.

"Please, lady, you're laughing at my moods. You just don't understand me." As the checkstand girl reached for their basket, he put a little more into his act. "And really, wife, I wish you would check out prices better. These prices ... at these prices, we'll be out of money before the week is over. Are you sure that grocery store across the street...."

The girl in the checkstand looked at him annoyed, and Sig, trying to keep from laughing, pulled his sleeve. "Please, dear...." The girl looked annoyed, and Sig mustered an embarrassed look.

"Dear...." continued Kolby, "are you sure you got me the right checkbook?" He pulled out his checkbook. "Oh, this isn't the right one ... there isn't any money in this account."

"What?" Sig was looking embarrassed for real this time, since the checkstand girl was showing her nervousness.

"No, you see...." Kolby pantomimed sitting at his desk, "Let's see. This is my right hand, the one I write with; and this is my left hand, the one I eat with. And this checkbook is from the

164

right drawer ... no ... " he shook his head wildly, and Sig noticed people were watching, and she tried not to laugh, Kolby was putting on his act so seriously. "No, you see, I didn't want the checkbook from the right-hand drawer because that's the one I write the business account on. I wanted the one from the left drawer, the one I write with my left hand.... That's the only one there's any money in. Oh, dear...." he looked thoughtful. The checkstand girl had stopped checking groceries, and in an impatient stance she waited. Kolby looked up at her and seriously asked, "Anything wrong, miss?"

"Sir," she said, taking a deep, disgusted breath, "it seems you have a problem. Shall I go on checking these groceries or not? There are no charge accounts in this store, you know."

"No charge accounts? Miss, how can you run a store with no charge accounts? Everything is charge accounts nowadays ... that's big business. Haven't you heard about Master Charge and Guaranteed Charge and...."

"Yes, sir ... do you have a Master Charge or...."

"No, miss, I haven't."

"Then do you want these groceries charged, or...."

"But you said you didn't have charge accounts here."

"That is right," the girl said, trying to control herself, worried about the customer waiting in line behind Kolby.

"Well, then, we can't charge, can we?"

"No sir, you can't."

Sig, afraid she couldn't hold a straight face any longer, reached over and pulled on Kolby's coat sleeve. He looked at her quickly. "Dear, don't rip my coat sleeve, coats cost money." Sig let go of his sleeve and put her hand to her throat to keep from laughing out loud. Seeing her, Kolby let a little grin slip around the corner of his mouth, but quickly wiped it off as he turned back to the girl. "Well?" He looked at the check girl and waited.

"Well, sir?" She was openly nervous now.

"Well ... I'm waiting. How long does it take to get groceries checked out in this store?"

"But sir," she said as she went on checking the items, "What about your problem?"

"What problem?"

"You know, sir ... how are you going to pay for these groceries?"

"Pay?"

"Yes sir ... the store policy is that...."

"Well, miss, if you'll just finish checking...." He took a roll of bills out of his pocket and peeled off a fifty dollar bill. The girl's eyes opened wide, and her chin dropped. Kolby smiled, "Miss ... under the circumstances, I guess we'll just have to pay cash."

Sig couldn't stand it any longer. She hurried out of the store, almost running, so she could climb in the car and laugh. Kolby, behind her, put on an expression of wonder as he looked after her, shoved the money and change back in his pocket, picked up the groceries and left, walking as if everything was common but he was a little disgusted that his wife had made such a spectacle of herself. Not until he opened the car, deposited the groceries and sat beside Sig, who was doubled up in laughter, did he release himself from the character he'd been playing and burst into laughter with Sig.

"Kol, you are crazy. What will people think?"

"Just what I wanted them to think. Did I embarrass you?"

"I hope I never see those people again."

"You probably won't."

"Are you like this all the time?"

"No, just sometimes when the mood hits me."

"And where did you get that roll of bills?"

Kol took the roll out of his pocket and handed it to her. She unrolled a few, and found that only a few bills on top were real. "Fake, they are fake. This is dangerous, Kol; somebody might shoot you for this roll of bills. Why do you carry them, anyway?"

He shrugged. "In my business, you never know when you'll need to impress somebody."

"But you don't usually try to impress anybody, at least before you've...."

"Oh, we don't try to impress the big boys, just the little guys that need a laugh."

They laughed again. "I can't believe you. Whatever you're doing for a living, you should be on the stage."

"I'm trying to get on your stage, but you keep me doing lights."

"I would rather star you in slapstick comedy ... you'd be a sensation in the drama barn."

166

"Yeah, I would ... will you be my leading lady?"

"I wouldn't dare. I couldn't keep a straight face."

"If I don't get the girl, I'm not going to take the part."

"And he's tempramental, too."

They'd reached the Langdon house. Kolby opened the car door for Sig and picked up the two sacks of groceries. She fumbled for the key to the front door while Kolby pretended to struggle under the weight of the two sacks. Once inside, Kolby helped Sig wash and put away the vegetables and other things they had bought. Then they both went into the little nursery together. Carefully, Sig took out the little things she'd put in the drawers and wrapped them in tissue paper. Kolby helped her until the last one was put away safely and the last drawer carefully shut. Then they stood there and looked around. Neither of them said anything. Then Kolby took Sig's hand in his and held it tight, and together they went through the door and closed it behind them. Kolby picked up Sig's sweater on a hanger in the front hall and put it over his arm as they locked up the house and got back into his car. As they drove away, the lump in Sig's throat wouldn't move, and when she stole a look at Kolby, his lips were tight and there were tears in his eyes.

They didn't talk for a while, and then Kolby said:

"We're getting a late start, but I want to drop by my studio and show you something." Sig nodded.

Making a few quick turns off the freeway and into a business section, Kolby finally stopped in front of a modern building. "This is where I work sometimes," he said, helping Sig out of the car.

"What do you do besides lights ... and comedy?"

"I have a few side things. I'm going to show you one now."

Inside the building, they went down a hall and into a studio with a skylight. There, Kolby led the way to a canvas that he uncovered.

"This was going to be your birthday present, but I don't know when it is."

"My birthday present?"

"If you want it. I'm not very good, but...." With the cover off, Kolby stood looking at his own painting. It was a large painting of an outdoor scene; it looked familiar. Sig gasped. "It's ... to use your word, Kol, fantastic. Isn't it a place I know?"

"Don't you recognize it?"

"Yes, but ... oh, ... no, it couldn't be...."

"Couldn't be what?"

"The mountains above the drama barn?"'

"Of course. I thought you'd never recognize it."

"I did right away, but I couldn't believe it. When did you paint this, or did you hire it done?"

"I should have hired it done, but I wanted to paint the scene the way I saw it in my mind. It's for you."

"For me or my barn?"

"Is there a difference?"

"Maybe not. Are you ridiculing my dream?"

"Why should I?" Kolby's voice was soft and low as he looked at Sig while she looked at the picture. "Your dream is one of the things I like best about you. One of the first things that attracted me to the project."

"You were attracted, then?"

"Of course. I don't do anything I don't want to do ... unless I have to...." he added with a wink, looking at Signee across the painting as he switched out the light above it. "That's all you get to see for now. We're late for a very special dinner engagement."

"I thought we were going to see your grandfather."

"You'll see...."

When they were in the car, driving again, Sig was still thinking about the painting.

"Where did you learn to paint?"

"A little old man in a wheelchair taught me the basic principles, and then I took a few lessons besides ... mostly it just takes time ... which I haven't very much of."

"I can't get over that painting."

"I'll bring it to you in Green Village when it's finished."

"Green Village seems a million miles away right now. I've almost forgotten all the problems I left unsolved there."

"About time. You've had too much to do for too long a time."

"I'm all right." Signee stretched and leaned back in the seat. "Where are we going, anyway? This is beautiful country." They were a little out of the city now, and the fields on each side of the road were green and spotted with houses.

"If you really want to know ... we are going visiting to my

little grandfather, like I told you. He hasn't seen a pretty girl for a long time."

"And you're taking me?"

"I don't see anyone else around."

"I just wanted to make sure. You haven't said I was pretty before."

He smiled as he glanced sideways at her. "The lady is vain," he said with a toss of his head.

They drove deeper into the country. Signee opened the windows and let the warming breeze blow through her hair, and couldn't help thinking that she had never felt like this before in her life, never felt so at ease with anyone as she had come to feel with Kolby. Breathing deeply for a few minutes, she thought of how glad she was that she had waited for a moment like this in her life, glad to know a man like Kolby who had so many sides. Then it startled her that she could think such thoughts when she hardly knew him. Closing the window, she sat up quickly.

"Now it's my turn to ask questions. Tell me about you and your little grandfather."

"You'll know everything I could tell you about him when you meet him ... which won't be very long now."

"How many years have you lived with him?"

"I was living in the city with my parents when they were killed. I had visited Grandfather a lot and he was a favorite person of mine, even before I went to live with him. He always had animals, and things to build, and tools to work with. After my parents were gone I went to stay with him all summer, and though I was lonely, he made it less lonely than most kids would be. He taught me that they were happy on the other side and that they loved me and would be sad if I was sad. I began to think of them just through the veil, watching me and being there when I needed them. Then Grandfather and I moved into the city so I could go to school. As soon as summer came we'd go back again. He cooked for me and sewed on buttons and mended my clothes and told me stories and wouldn't let me get bad grades. He did all that until I went on my mission."

"You said before that you went on a mission. Where did you go?"

"To Italy. I learned to love opera and art in Italy. Grandfather insisted on that ... I was to take advantage of the country and what it had to teach. He was right, of course. My grandfather is very wise."

"I like him already."

For answer, Kolby reached for Signee's hand again.

Signee waited by the door of the little house in anticipation as Kolby went ahead, calling to his grandfather as he went. He found him in his bedroom. Signee could hear them talk.

"Grandfather, I've brought her to meet you. Come on, Grandfather, you can't go to sleep yet. It isn't time for the chickens to go to sleep, so neither can you."

In a few minutes Kolby and his little grandfather appeared in the door. He looked almost as Signee had imagined he'd look, only he was shorter and his hair was very white; but he still had plenty of hair.

"Grandfather, this is Signee." Signee moved forward and took the hand the old man offered; she was surprised to feel how strong the small hand was.

"You are a pretty young lady," said Grandfather, looking carefully through the spectacles he wore over his nose. "I always knew Kolby would pick a pretty girl."

"Thank you, sir," said Signee, and felt her face warm with color.

As Kolby, Grandfather, and Signee put together a meal and served it on the old-fashioned kitchen table, Signee was aware that she was living a scene she would never top again in her life. The little old man was over eighty, and yet still firm on his feet. He talked with a sureness, even though his voice sometimes squeaked. As they set the table together, the old man had a story for every piece they put on the table. Signee enjoyed every story. After dinner, Kolby went to cut some wood and do a few chores to catch up the work his grandfather took so long to do. While he was out, Signee sat and talked to Grandfather. She had already learned to call him Grandfather.

"You seem much younger than your years, Grandfather." Signee pulled up a stool and sat at his feet.

"But I'm getting old. I was glad you were here to help with the dishes tonight. I'm too slow now. My Melissa wouldn't like me so slow."

"You've missed her for a long time, haven't you?"

170

"My Melissa and Kol's parents . . . yes, I've been ready to go and meet them for a long time, but I can't go until my job is finished."

"You know what your job is, then?"

"Oh, yes. The family assigned me to take care of Kolby until he found a wife. When he's married, then Melissa will let me join her. I hope she will. I haven't been as good as she was, but she'll know I've tried."

"I think you must have been pretty good to raise a grandson the way you've raised Kolby."

"He's a good youngster, and he'll make a good husband. He needs some children. He's my talented one . . . it will take a good girl to keep him on course. He has a way . . . a way of thinking too big and being too flighty."

"Maybe he isn't ready to settle down."

"No one is ready to settle down until he finds a good girl."

"Hasn't Kolby ever found a girl?"

"He's strange . . . he doesn't seem to like girls as much as electric lights and things like computers . . . but he likes you."

"Do you know that he likes me?"

"Of course. He probably doesn't know it yet, but I think you'll be the one to settle him down."

"I'm not sure. . . ."

"Not sure of what?" Kolby interrupted as he came in with a bucket of coal and a load of wood. "You probably won't need this now, Grandfather, the weather is warm; but just in case."

"All right. I sometimes sleep late, though. I sometimes sleep until the day warms up. I didn't used to do that. I've picked up some bad habits."

"You sure have, Grandfather, you are getting positively lazy. You would never let me do that."

"You don't get cold like I do. . . ."

"That's true. Are you cold a lot grandfather?"

"Yes. A sign I'm getting thin blood and my liver doesn't work."

"Grandfather, will you quit trying to diagnose your own illnesses?"

"I'm not ill. I'm not going to be ill. I just get cold, and maybe someday I'll just get cold enough to go to sleep."

"Don't you dare, Grandfather. This old world needs your

wisdom for a long time yet."

They talked some more, and Grandfather told a few more tales about the house and the trinkets within. Then it was time to leave, and Signee kissed the little man.

"Thank you, Grandfather. I hope you don't mind me calling you Grandfather...."

The old man shook his head and tenderly kissed her hand as she offered to say goodbye. "You'll come again?"

"I hope so. I really hope so."

Later, in the car, as Signee and Kolby hurried back to town to be there in time to meet Alta and Eric, Signee asked questions and talked about Kolby's life with his grandfather. Then, as they drove up the street where Eric and Alta lived, Signee touched Kolby's arm with her hand.

"I have to tell you, Kol..." He turned to look at her as he slowed to make a turn into the driveway. "I have to tell you, that I have never spent a more beautiful day in my life. I will never forget it. I've been aware of that all day."

"Of course you won't. I intend to see that you don't."

Chapter Eighteen

Signee flew home, with Kolby beside her, when Alta was feeling secure enough.

"Kolby, there's a new closeness between Eric and Alta. I'm glad I was here to see that."

"She has a way of leaning on him to make him feel important."

"Isn't she darling? She has her old confidence back. She was feeling pretty shaky for a while ... when she was trying to have a baby...."

"Hurts bring people closer together, haven't you noticed?"

Signee smiled. Her face felt warm, but she went on talking about Alta. "She's always cared more about making him happy than herself ... they'll make it, even if they do have to wait a long time for a baby."

"Sometimes those things come about fast. Who knows? But it's a good thing you're going home. You've been anxious, haven't you?"

"I was having a wonderful time, but I'm uneasy about Minta. I don't know why, really."

"Don't fret ... we're practically there, and you can check on your other problems."

"Is Minta a problem?"

"You tell me. I thought you were worried."

Arriving home didn't still Signee's fears about Minta. She called her as soon as she was inside the house, but Minta wasn't any place she called. Finally she called Deek. He'd just gotten home from school, and was on his way to rehearsal.

"Hi, Siggie," he said, before she could tell him who she was. "Man, am I glad you're home. Everybody's bugging out on everything. We need you to drive us, Siggie."

"What do you mean? Who is everybody?"

"Well, Minta mainly, and...."

"Where is Minta?"

"Who knows? She's been Miss Temperamental Star ever since you left. We've seen her for rehearsals, but her heart isn't in it ... and that boyfriend of hers is always waiting for her."

"You mean Barney?"

"That's the one."

"She's dating Barney?"

"She sure is, and all the time."

"I don't understand."

"Who does? Are you coming to rehearsal tonight, Siggie?"

"I'll be there."

"How about me picking you up?"

"No ball practice tonight?"

"We're hitting it hard tomorrow." There was a pause, and then Deek went on. "Siggie, I tried to keep my eyes on her like you said, but I guess I just don't understand women."

While Signee waited for Deek, she tried every number she could think of to locate Minta. She wasn't any place she tried. When Signee heard Deek's car, she put on her coat and went down to meet him. Deek held the car door for her.

"What's happened to old-fashioned ideas of waiting for the boy...."

"I stand corrected, Deek, but we've got to hurry," said Signee as she climbed in the car to sit beside Deek in the front seat.

"I've missed you, Siggie," said Deek when they were both seated and the car was on the way to rehearsal.

"That's nice to hear, Deek."

"No kiddin', Siggie, things just don't run right when you're gone. Not classes, not the Barn ... nothing. Especially not Minta."

"We'll try and get them back into shape now."

"I'm glad ... and I've got a surprise to tell you."

"What is it?"

"Nothing much...." He ducked his head. "I had my interview with the bishop Sunday."

"Oh, Deek...." Signee almost squealed with delight. "Your mission interview."

"No, not yet ... well in a way. I was interviewed to see if they want to make me an elder."

"And...?"

"And, I'm going to be ordained as soon as my birthday gets here, and it comes right after graduation."

"Deek, I didn't realize your birthday came so soon."

"I'm one of the older fellows, Siggie."

"I'm so happy for you."

"Me too. I won't have to wait around wondering what to do with myself while I wait."

"You'll almost have to get ready the day school is out."

"That's right. Do you think Minta will like the idea?"

"I don't know." She paused a moment and then went on, "You really do care about her, don't you?"

"I guess so ... well, you know a guy doesn't like to go so far away from home without thinking somebody is waiting ... at least halfway waiting ... What if I go to a foreign country, say, 6,000 miles away?"

"And what if you are sent that far away? How will you feel about that?"

Deek smiled and shrugged his shoulders in good humor. "If that's where I'm called, that's where I'll want to go."

"I thought you'd feel like that. And you want Minta to approve too?"

"I'd like her to care and write to me."

"Tell you what ... I'll invite her to dinner tonight and you can tell her then, all right?"

"Hey, Siggie, you're the greatest...."

"Sure...sure."

Deek drove up in front of the drama room to let Signee go in before pulling around back to park in the student parking lot.

Signee went inside to check her desk before going to the rehearsal room. She was thinking how glad she was that they didn't have to do all their practicing at school now, but that the dance could be in the Drama Barn while the speaking parts were practiced in the school's little theater. She remembered, too, that she hadn't warned Kolby that the dancers might be on stage. She smiled, thinking how he might react to that. Kolby still had a temper, even though he was well practiced in controlling it. Secretly she wished she might be there, hiding behind the curtain, to see if this would be the time he lost his cool. Signee started on the things piled on her desk while she waited for the cast to gather. Surely Minta would be there when they started rehearsal; she'd been so diligent before, when she lived at Signee's.

Signee went into the little theater stage to meet the cast, but Minta wasn't there. Something inside Signee began to churn. Minta had come so far; what had happened? Somehow she felt it was all tied up with her dating Barney.

"Cast call ... let's get on with the show, and give me an idea of how well you did while I was away."

Signee was surprised that the show was so far advanced; it was almost ready to pull everything together for final rehearsal. Not bad for the little while they had practiced, especially when they'd been passing finals and building a Drama Barn, too. It was good to be back with the kids; it was a good feeling to see some of the bit parts come alive with expression she hadn't expected.

"You're great!" Signee said at last, when time was up and the cast members were beginning to leave for other appointments. "We're going to have a very professional-looking show. Your parents will be proud of you, and the town will be proud of you. This will make a very exciting graduation gift from each of you to the others. See you tomorrow after school, all right?"

The cast filed out, each of them expressing their happiness at Signee's return. It was touching, and though no one could see them past her smile, there were tears in Signee's eyes. When everyone had gone but Deek, Signee picked up her handbag, locked the door, and accepted Deek's offer to drive her home again.

"Where is she, Deek?" Signee asked the question, and neither of them had to mention Minta's name. They both knew the other was worried.

"I don't know. She's been different ever since she started going with Barney ... I don't like him."

"We can't coddle her, Deek. We can only teach her true principles and let her govern herself."

"I've been saying that to myself, too. But if I'd asked her out a little more, or hadn't had that fight with her, maybe she wouldn't have gone with him."

"That's part of the test, Deek. We get what we live for, and sometimes it's too hard to wait for tomorrow."

"What do you know about this Barney, Signee?"

"Not very much. Minta hadn't been with him very much and had given him up before I left. If only I hadn't stayed so long."

"You can't let her have all of your time."

"She has so much to give, Deek ... but she hasn't learned to look forward, or to sacrifice, or to be a little lonely today for something better tomorrow. We've got to find her, Deek. I'm afraid for her, somehow, and yet I don't know why I feel this way."

"When I leave you at your house, I'll go look for her. I don't know where, but I will."

"Dinner is at six. If you haven't found her then, come and eat. All right?"

It wasn't too hard to put together a dinner; just thawing a few steaks, a salad, and an apple dessert, Signee even had time to take a shower and to put on some hostess slacks. She was looking fresh and shiny when she heard the front door open. She looked up to see Minta. The next minute they were hugging each other.

"I've missed you so, Signee ... you'll never know how much."

"I've missed you, too, but where have you been? We've been worried to pieces."

"I drove into the city today. I need my teeth fixed, and I went to get a check-up and an estimate. My father is going to die when he hears how expensive it is to get your teeth fixed these days."

"I wish I'd known; you'd have saved me a lot of worry."

"I'm sorry. Can I have my old room back?"

"Of course you can; and you're invited to dinner in a few

minutes. If you rush like mad, you'll just have time to shower."

"Who's coming?"

"It's a surprise. Just hurry. You'll like our guests, I promise."

"Guests?"

"Don't ask so many questions," laughed Signee. "Just hurry. I'll finish the dinner while you shower."

Long before Minta came down to dine with the group, Deek and Kolby had arrived, and were deep in conversation about football. Yet, when Minta appeared, they both looked up and stopped talking. Minta came happily downstairs, but when she saw Deek, she backed off.

"What are you doing here?" Minta said, as if she hadn't seen anyone else in the room.

"I was invited. What about you?" Deek's voice was a little edgy, too.

"Come on, you two," Signee said, taking over. "If you're having a quarrel, make it a truce for tonight. Kolby is here to report on our Drama Barn, and he's flying out of here right after dinner."

"Don't mind me," said Kolby. "I like a good fight."

"We aren't fighting, are we, Deek?"

"I'm not ... want to sit down?" he asked, looking at Minta on the stairway where she had stopped when she first saw him. Getting up, he stepped behind the chair next to him and pulled it away from the table, waiting for Minta.

"Now, why didn't I think of that?" said Kolby, standing up to hold Signee's chair. "If there's going to be a gentleman in the crowd, we'd better all follow the leader. Come on, Signee, sit in this chair I'm holding before I collapse."

"What makes you so tired?" she laughed, sitting down. "You've only been up since dawn, and will be up most of the night ... you're a tough guy; nothing gets you down...." She looked up over her shoulder as she sat down. "Except my kids working on the Drama Barn."

"For a single girl, you have the biggest family I've ever met."

"And I adore them all. Someday, when I get married, I'm going to have almost that many myself."

"All by yourself? That should be quite interesting."

"You know what I mean. Don't get clever."

"Do you know what she means?" asked Kolby, looking from

Deek to Minta. They laughed, and Signee and Kolby joined them. The tension was eased, and then Kolby added, "Where are you going to get a father for all these kids of your own?"

"I'm going to advertise for somebody rich."

"Deek, these women only care about money ... remember that."

"I think I will."

Kolby had a way, Signee had to admit, of keeping everyone part of what was going on. Dinner was served; they talked and laughed a lot, and Minta found herself looking into Deek's eyes often through the conversation. When dinner was over, Kolby planned the rest of their time together.

"Deek, I'm going to help Signee; my plane isn't ready to take off in time to get me out of the dishes. How about you and Minta making a fire? ... Just a small one. That fireplace in the other room does work, doesn't it, Signee?"

"Best fireplace my father ever built, and he's a good builder. You'll find the wood just outside the door, Deek."

"All settled," said Kolby, picking up his plate to stack others on it. "Now, you two have your own conversation, and stay out of the kitchen. I need to talk to Siggie."

"We've been dismissed," said Deek, standing up to hold Minta's chair. "Let's go build our fire." Minta got up, and they went toward the front room. Kolby winked at Signee as they disappeared into the kitchen.

"Deek, you don't mind Signee being alone with Kolby?" Minta asked the question as she slid to the floor on the rug in front of the fire, which Deek had finally coaxed into a flame.

"Why should I? I didn't like Kolby at first, but we've learned to work together. He's kinda flighty, trying to do everything at once, but I kinda like the guy."

"I thought you wouldn't like anybody that took Siggie's attention away from you."

"Come on, Minta ... we're not going to spend the rest of the evening finding subjects to quarrel about, are we?"

"I won't if you won't."

"Well, I won't, because I've got something to tell you."

"Tell me, then."

"Well, it's ... well, maybe you won't think it's so neat ... maybe...."

"Tell me."

"Well, I've had my interview with the bishop. They're going to make me an elder and then I'm going on my mission."

Minta looked at Deek, but she didn't answer right away, and he wondered what was racing through her quiet mind. Finally, when he couldn't stand it any longer, he said: "Well?"

"Well ... you're really going to go, aren't you?"

"Sure I'm going to go. Didn't you think I would?"

"Yes, I guess I always knew you would ... well ... congratulations, if that's what you want."

"It's what I want, Minta. Will you write to me?"

"I don't know ... maybe ... but don't count on it. I'm really not your type of girl, Deek."

"You always used to say you were."

"Yes, but I'm not waiting for two years. I've never been one to put off until tomorrow what I can have today." She held out her hand. "My best...." Deek took her hand in a shaking grip, but held on to it.

"How do you know you can't wait, Minta?"

"Because I've tried. Anyway, Barney is more my type. He wants the same things I do."

"You can't mean you're serious about that creep?" The words just poured out without Deek thinking; but once said, he was glad.

"Be a little careful of your language when you talk about my friends."

"If he's your friend, then I don't want you writing to me anyway."

"I said I wasn't your type. Why did you ask me to write, anyway? Were you asking me to wait for you?" For some reason Minta couldn't understand, she was near tears. She had been close to tears a lot lately; she'd cried a lot, too.

"I didn't ask you to wait. We might both change. I can't ask any girl to wait."

"No, just sit around and write. And maybe after two years, you'll come home, and if there's anything ... it's a man's world, isn't it?"

"Minta, you're making a big thing again. I thought you'd like to write to me ... we could be good friends. And if you find someone else, someone respectable...."

"I get it. Barney isn't your class."

"Is he yours?" Deek's voice was getting angry.

"Yes, he is ... I don't know...." Minta stood up and looked around like a captured animal looking for a place to escape. "It's hot and stuffy in this house. I've got to get out of here." She ran toward the door; Deek followed slowly. Minta didn't stop; she went through the door and out into the yard. Deek watched from the screen door. She just stood there, looking up, taking deep breaths. After a minute he followed her slowly.

"Minta ... what's the matter?" His voice was quiet.

"Nothing."

"You aren't acting like normal."

"What's normal, Deek Pendalton? What am I supposed to act like? I thought you might say I was making a big deal of everything again."

"I wasn't going to say that. I don't want to fight with you, Minta. We've had some good memories. Can't we enjoy this last little while as friends? Can't we forget about meaning more to each other than friends, and just...." He hesitated. She hadn't moved; she was still looking up at the sky. Deek took a deep breath. "I guess you're right; it's foolish to try to capture what we once had. It's crazy, but I've been thinking about us ever since I talked to the bishop. I remember the first dance I took you to. I was bashful and I felt so dumb, but you were the rich girl with the pretty clothes, and you made me feel good. I don't know how you did it, Minta, but you made me feel like I was somebody."

"You *were* somebody, Deek." Minta's words were softly spoken, hardly audible, even though she didn't look at Deek.

"Remember the dance we went to the end of that year, when my foot was in a cast from the game? I thought you wouldn't want to be with me then, but you made me feel like sitting out with me was more important than dancing with your other friends. You had a lot of boyfriends then."

"I didn't like them any more after I started going with you. You spoiled me for the rest. You were so mature, and had such high ideals, and suddenly ... what happened to us, Deek?"

"Nothing happened, Minta. I still feel the same way, but you suddenly wanted too much ... all of my time, and I wasn't ready to be just one girl's boyfriend. I wasn't ready to be anybody's boyfriend, not for real. Not romantic."

"I know, Deek. There's no use talking. Why don't we just say goodbye now?"

"Why? We've got the show to do, and our dance date, and...."

"You still want to do the show with me in it?"

"I'm going to do the show anyway, but I like seeing you in it. You're good at the part, Minta."

"It's fun...." She turned and started to walk. Deek fell in step beside her.

"Then you'll do the part? You'll come back to rehearsal?"

"Maybe...."

"Super." Deek reached out and took her hand the way he had when they first dated. "Hey, Minta, want to take off your shoes and race to the old tree stump down there?"

"Sure, why not?"

Minta kicked off her shoes, and they set the mark and started to run. The wind felt good on her face, and her feet hardly felt the chill of the damp grass. Deek laughed and kept just ahead of her, just to make sure she couldn't beat him at anything. Then, just before they reached the old tree stump, Minta turned her ankle and fell; she rolled over and over. Deek yelled and reached for her. He looked into her eyes, and she was laughing; he was so relieved that he laughed too. Then the laughter died away, and they were left looking into each other's faces, the moonlight lighting the whiteness of Minta's skin and the softness in her eyes. She was beautiful; Deek had always thought so. He reached for her hand in the dark, and she leaned closer. He smiled and didn't move. Somehow, he wanted to hold on to this moment.

"Deek," whispered Minta, "aren't you going to kiss me?"

"I'd like to, Minta, but I don't want you to misunderstand...."

"Deek ... just this once, for all the times you won't."

He leaned forward, and his lips met hers. She trembled a little, and Deek wondered if it was emotion or cold. He put his arm around her and drew her to him. She tucked her head under his chin, and he held her close.

"Thanks, Deek ... thanks...."

"You don't have to thank me; it's the other way around." He tried to make his remarks light.

"No, this one is for me. We'll be in the play together, Deek, and I'll take long walks with you just until school is over. And you won't kiss me any more, will you, Deek?"

"I won't dare, Minta, or I might not be ready for my mission."

She turned and looked up at him. "There'll be other reasons, too, Deek. I won't wait for you. I won't be here when you get back. All we'll ever have is a friendship, and just this little time. All right?" He nodded and stood up, pulling her to her feet beside him.

"But when I get back, Minta ... When I get back, we'll talk again."

"No, Deek ... it's already too late for us ... whether you go on a mission or not, it's already too late. But for this little while, I'm going to be selfish and learn how to be a friend."

"Great ... but you won't get rid of me that easy. You'll see."

Chapter Nineteen

For the next little while, Minta showed up for every rehearsal. And though Barney often came by to pick her up and kept calling her, Minta didn't go out with him. Minta had changed; Signee was aware of the change, but not of what had brought it about. She was moody, often tearful, and often spent hours in her room by herself. She and Deek talked during rehearsal; but to Signee, Minta wasn't her old self, and seemed to be avoiding Deek as well as other boys. She hardly went out at all.

"Do you feel all right, Minta?" asked Signee at breakfast one morning.

"Sure. Why? Do I look sick?" Minta seemed upset by the question.

"No, not really, except you seem pale. Maybe it's just lack of summer sun. Graduation is close now, and when school is out you can get back to sunbathing and water skiing, and then your color will come back."

"Sure. That's what I need, some good water skiing." Her voice was sarcastic, but when Signee asked her about that she just smiled. "Don't mind me; I'm just being dull of late."

"Save your sparkle for your part. You are a beautiful heroine."

"You say that to all your leading ladies."

"Only if they are special." Signee put her arm around Minta. "You are special to me, Minta. You're like the little sister I haven't ever had. There's a new something about you, a quietness I like."

"I think it's more like panic and fear."

"Panic and fear? Minta, are you serious?"

"Why? Can't I panic and fear?"

"Why should you? What about ... the part?"

"A ... sure, that's it ... the part."

"Don't worry, you're going to be wonderful. You're going to take this town by storm from the center of the new Drama Barn stage. Kolby will be here this weekend to put in the last of the electrical work. You know he arranged for new mikes for the sound system?"

"He's been doing a lot for this play, hasn't he?"

"He loves drama ... I think he'd like to have a juicy part himself, and he could play it, too. He's a comedian, and I don't know how many other kinds of an actor."

"Like playing the role of the lover?"

"Maybe."

"But only if you're the leading lady?"

"Minta...."

"You aren't going to deny that you are attracted to Kolby, are you? Signee, with all your goodness, let's be honest."

"All right, Minta, let's be honest. I like Kolby, and the more I know him the better I like him. He has strong qualities, and I can't push him around. He isn't particularly vulnerable where women are concerned, however, but he has lots of talents, and I think acting is one of them. Do you believe me?"

"If you say so."

"Minta, why did you think I wasn't telling you the truth just now about Kolby?"

"Maybe I was just hoping ... somebody should be happy ... somebody ought to be getting together and be in love."

"Dear Minta." Signee reached out to hold her hand. "It's very hard for you not to rush life, isn't it?"

Minta pulled her hand away. "That's so easy for you to say, I know. But I'm used to action in my life . . . I can't wait forever. And even if I did wait, Deek and I wouldn't make it."

"So that's it. Trouble with Deek."

"Not, that isn't it. Deek is sweet; he's the realest thing in my life. But he won't ever want me, and I'm not waiting for what isn't going to be."

"How do you know you won't make it?"

"Because I just know." Minta got up and started clearing the table, opening and closing the fridge with too much force.

"Tell me what's bothering you . . . you seem so troubled lately. I thought you were just being romantically quiet. I saw the stars in both yours and Deek's eyes the night he was here to dinner, so I thought. . . ."

"Well, you are wrong." Minta stopped and faced Signee. "Deek knows where he is going, and he doesn't make any mistakes. If he even acts like he's going to make a mistake, red lights begin to flash everywhere . . . his mission, his parents, people who believe in him, his little brothers, and you . . . Deek couldn't go wrong if he tried, and he isn't about to tie himself to a girl who has and does and is making mistakes all the time. That's it, and I don't want to talk about it any more. I've got a date with Barney tonight. I won't be here for dinner; Barney is picking me up when rehearsal is over." She turned abruptly and started to leave. Signee's next words stopped her.

"Does Deek know about your date tonight?"

"No, he doesn't know. Why should he? Deek is not my keeper."

"I didn't mean that, Minta. I just. . . ."

"You just . . . you just . . . " Suddenly breaking into sobs, she ran to her bedroom. Signee thought of going after her, and then decided she needed to be alone. Busying herself in the kitchen, she waited until Minta wanted to come out. When she did, the tears were gone and there was a flippant atmosphere about her.

"Ready for school?"

"Ready . . . washing tears away is a new form of removing makeup for me. I needed a new paint job. Shall I back out the car?"

That was all. The door of communication was closed, and Signee knew she would have to wait until it was opened again. Smiling, she put her arm around Minta, and pretended not to notice when she felt Minta stiffen under her touch.

"Come on, Minta, it's a beautiful day. Let's go to school."

That evening, while they were rehearsing, with Minta on stage and Deek changing scenery in the final stages of production before opening, Minta finished her last scene just a few minutes after Barney entered the Drama Barn. Deek saw him come in while Signee was working with him on the scenery. She could tell he was annoyed.

"I thought Minta had given him up," he grumbled under his breath, just audible enough for Signee to catch his meaning.

"She hasn't been with him for quite a while."

"I know. Why now?"

"Maybe you haven't been giving her enough attention," Signee teased, not wanting Deek to know how worried she was about Minta.

"I can't give her any attention at all, you should know that. You, of all people. With Minta, I give her any attention at all and she gobbles me up."

"Aren't you a big boy?"

"No. I'm not that big. I'm unstable and emotional when I let myself go. I made the mistake of kissing Minta the night we were at your house, and..."

"Deek, you don't have to explain to me."

"I want to explain it to you ... to someone. Then maybe I'll understand it myself."

"All right ... talk away."

"Oh, it's no big thing, except she wanted me to kiss her and I wanted to, and then I thought we could just go back to being friends and having fun and going for walks ... just this little while that I'm waiting for my mission call. But I can't. After I kissed her, I couldn't get her out of my mind. I can't even talk to her any more, or I start thinking about her instead of my mission. Siggie, I'm going on that mission, and nobody, not Minta especially, is going to keep me from it. I've got to have my mind on making money and preparing myself for my mission. As soon as this show is over, that's it ... nothing but mission preparation for me."

"I understand, Deek."

"Do you, Siggie? I don't and I can't explain it to Minta or myself, so I'm just staying away. I hate her going with Barney, but I can't stop her if that's what she wants. And I'm miserable thinking about them together, so I'm not going to think about that. Right now I'm not strong enough to be my brother's keeper, or even Minta's."

"You're wise, Deek. Don't worry; I'll try and look after Minta, if she'll let me."

"She probably won't ... if I know Minta, she's already racing ahead, putting her life into shape ... if not the right shape, then any she can manage. Oh, Siggie, she has such a need, and I'm not sure what for. But it drains me being around her ... so I'm not going to be around her any more. I don't want her writing to me, either. I asked her to, but I don't want her to write to me. What if I got that same feeling from her letters? I just can't be around Minta, not until my mission is over. But, Siggie..." he turned troubled eyes to look at Signee, pleading eyes, "Siggie, will you take care of her for me? And if she's having trouble ... help her, but don't let me know. I'll pray for her while I'm gone; that's all I can do. I guess that's being a coward, but really, I may look calm but I'm emotional."

Signee couldn't help smiling inside at his honesty. "Don't worry, Deek, I'll take care of her. You are right, and your mission has to come first. If anything else follows, ... yes, you are right."

A smile spread across Deek's face. "Siggie, I always said you're the marrying kind. If I could find a girl like you who would have me, I might not go on my mission."

"And that, Elder Deek Pendalton, is not the truth ... however, you have built my ego for the day. Now, pull that top row of lights down four inches, and we'll get on with the show. That row of lights has to hit the center of the stage from this angle."

"Yes, ma'am." Deek threw a piece of wire wrapping at Signee in a fun gesture, and went on with his work. Signee couldn't help thinking how he'd matured. Deek would be her boy forever. Her feelings for him were deep; he had touched her heart in a way she could only compare to what a son of her own might do.

Chapter Twenty

Minta's moodiness continued, and even though she practiced hard, she was often irritable and emotional. Sometimes her emotions seemed to bring on an illness, and she would actually get sick at her stomach which she tried to hide from Signee. But she wouldn't talk; and though Signee tried to open up a conversation she might feel comfortable with, the door of communication was closed, and all Signee could do was just to love her and pray for her. Then one night, just before the play's opening, and with graduation only a week off, she announced:

"I'll be leaving for the summer, Siggie."

"Where are you going, Minta? Don't you like it here?"

"That's not why. I like it here, but I need a change. Barney's going to take me to see his parents in the East."

"Is it serious between you and Barney?"

"Of course. I told you, he loves me and wants to marry me."

"And you're ready for marriage?"

"Siggie, there comes a time when you have to be ready." She shrugged her shoulders, and there was something about her attitude that made Signee begin to worry all over again. It was something so deep she wasn't ready to express it to Minta just yet, so she changed the subject and they started talking about the play. That was one subject Minta could always talk about.

"Minta, you are so natural on the stage. I hope you'll be in our production for the summer."

"Don't count on that, Siggie. I may stay away all summer."

"Minta, you aren't thinking of staying with Barney's parents that long, are you?"

"Why not?"

"Minta, that's dangerous, especially with a guy like Barney."

"What do you know about Barney?" Minta turned toward Signee with accusation in her eyes.

"Only what you've told me and I've observed. He is a very emotional man, Minta, and he's out to be your escort. And I don't think all his thoughts are pure."

"I don't need another pure boyfriend. I've had one Deek in my life, and that's enough. I'll be leaving after graduation, and so I want to tell you now ... thanks for all you've shared with me."

"I've profited by our sharing, Minta. But I'm worried about you. You act strangely lately. Is there anything wrong?"

"Nothing I can tell you. After I'm gone, you may have to explain to my parents, because I'm not going home to them until after I get back."

"Minta, I don't think you should do that. I know they'll blame me."

"Do you care more about being blamed than being my friend?"

"No, I don't, Minta, but friendship is not only a privilege but an obligation. I have to earn the right to your friendship, and helping you deceive your parents isn't part of my obligation to my love for you."

"Signee, you do put things so beautifully ... honestly, Sig, you should be the one taking part in the play."

The wall was up again, and Signee knew she couldn't get through; but she worried more than ever now. All day she thought about the hurt look in her eyes, and during the night she dreamed about Minta ... she was going away, and Siggie couldn't stop her. The dream suddenly turned into a nightmare.

It was the night of the play ... opening night. The show was to run three nights before graduation. Opening night was beautiful, packed with townspeople, friends, neighbors, and relatives. The music from the orchestra pit below the second stage level, picked up by the sound system Kolby had installed, sounded like a full orchestra.

"I like it, Kolby," said Signee as she met him behind stage where he was working on a few last-minute details.

"I knew you would," he smiled. "It's my best work, and all for you."

"Then I thank you."

"You'll have to do more than that."

"What?" Signee couldn't believe her ears and the intimacy in his tone.

"I intend to collect more than a thanks for all my work."

"Oh yes, money too ... you are right. I need to get a check signed."

"I wasn't thinking of money, Sig."

"Well," said Signee significantly, "then what are you thinking of?"

"A day of your time."

"What does that mean?" She smiled.

"I'm going to get you out of this town before you collapse. When the curtain closes for the last time on this show, I'm getting you out of this town."

"Are you taking me to meet the family, like Barney is taking Minta?"

"You've met my whole family. And what about Barney?"

"He's taking Minta away ... to meet his family."

"Don't let her go."

"Just like that?"

"Sure. Tell her she can't go. Surely, with all the other things you boss, you can manage that."

"You're saying I'm bossy?"

He smiled and nodded. "You can boss everything and everybody except me." He looked at her steadily, a smile creeping around the corners of his lips. "You'll never boss me, Sig. But I'll boss you ... like I said, I'm taking you away from here at the close of the play. So get things ready."

"And if I don't?" she teased, hoping he would insist.

"You'll only have this one chance to see what I've planned. I'll pick you up after the last show, and in less than an hour we'll be leaving."

"Aren't you going to tell me more than that as a basis for making up my mind?"

"Nope, that's it. You'll have to trust me ... or let me go."

"I can't let you go—not yet," she smiled.

"I know," he said happily. "I do a nice job of lights and theaters, don't I?"

"Do I have to admit that and increase your ego?"

"Sure—you *are* my ego."

At the end of the show on opening night, Minta found a bouquet of pink roses in her dressing room backstage. Barney had put in a card telling her he would pick her up after the show. There was another vase, and in it was a single red rose with baby's breath. The card was simple:

"I'm saving our walks for two years, but I want you to know you were great tonight. Love, Deek." Minta took the card and tucked it in her handbag while she ripped off her costume, cleaned her face, and went to meet Barney. There was a crowd outside her door—students, friends and well-wishers. Her mother and father were there. Minta was pleased, but she made her way through the crowd as fast as she could. She went out the back door and searched in the parking lot, which was in the middle of the field, for Barney's car. She found it and ran to it. Barney was inside, waiting for her.

"Did you see the performance?"

"Sure, Sweetness ... you think I'd miss seeing my best girl?"

Minta got in by herself and Barney leaned over to kiss her, holding her shoulders tight in his hands. Minta fought the desire to move away from him. "Where are we going, Barney? This is opening night. Make it someplace special, huh? I left the group for you."

"I like that, Sweetness ... and I've got something special planned." He started the motor and backed out. As they drove, to where Minta didn't even inquire, they talked.

"Barney, did you mean it when you said you loved me and wanted me with you always?"

"Sure, Sweetness." He reached over and pulled her to him with one arm. She moved away.

"Both hands on the wheel ... I've a few more questions to ask."

"Ask away."

"Do you want to marry me, Barney?"

He looked at her quickly. "We didn't talk about marriage ... I mean, did we?"

"I'm talking about it now. Do you want me to marry you? Just say yes or no."

Barney squirmed and twisted the steering wheel a little uncomfortably. "Well, sure, Sweetness ... sometime."

"Stop calling me Sweetness. My name is Minta. And what do you mean sometime?" Her voice was full of annoyance.

"All right, Sweetness ... Minta ... what's getting to you? Some reason you suddenly want to talk about marriage?"

"I want to do more than talk ... unless you don't mean what you said about wanting me."

"Sweet—Minta ... " He shrugged his shoulders. "Now, why would a girl want to be called Minta when she can be Sweetness?"

"Barney, don't evade my questions."

"Why don't you like Sweetness?"

"Because I think you've called other girls that."

"Oh ... well, maybe a few ... you aren't my only love. But you're my best...." He smiled and reached for her; she resisted.

"Barney, when you take me away after the show closes, after graduation, will you take me to get married?"

"Say, Sweetness, you really are intense tonight."

"You mean I'm making a big deal out of everything?"

"Yeah, in a few words. How can you tell?"

"I've been told that before."

"All right, then, relax. Let's not be too intense and spoil the whole evening."

"I'm talking about our lives."

"Not tonight ... it's a beautiful night, and I'm out with a lovely new star. I tell you, Minta, you were something out on that stage."

"Then you'll marry me right away?"

"S-sure, if that's what you want. But maybe you'd better tell me what's behind this sudden proposal. Last time we talked, you were getting rid of me, as I remember."

"I know ... I was moody. I've thought it over, and...."

"And you've been sick lately?"

"Yes. As if you didn't know."

"I thought you were smarter than that."

"Oh, now it comes out. You know I'm not smart, I'm not that kind of girl, I didn't plan on anything like this ever happening to me."

"But you did, and don't tell me you didn't like it." He reached over to her to touch her face with his hand.

"I was lonely, Barney. You were so nice, and . . . Barney, do you think we can be happy together? Please tell me we can."

"We have as good a chance as anyone. Come here, Minta." He pulled her over on his shoulder, his arm around her. "I do think you're it for me. . . ."

"Then we'll be married right away, before you ever. . . ."

"Now, don't get excited. We need to talk. In the meantime, cuddle up."

Minta tried to relax while her head dropped on his shoulder. She wanted to cry, she wanted to die. If only . . . but the only part of her life she cared about was gone, and she knew it. "We will be happy, Barney."

"Sure . . . sure. We can make a good weekend of it, and then when we're through talking and making plans, we can decide about marriage."

"Then?" Minta sat up and stiffened. "Barney, I'm not going on another date with you until we get married. Can't you see I'm worried?"

He was quiet a minute, and when he spoke his voice was low and serious. "Minta, are you sure? Maybe it's . . . I mean once . . . it's hardly . . . "

"It's possible. Believe me, I didn't think that either. But I'm sure. I went into the city to see a doctor . . . I know. We've got to be married."

"I didn't know. . . ."

"You do now."

"I don't mean that."

"What do you mean?"

"That I didn't know you were so young . . . so new at making love."

"You talk like you're an old hand."

"I'm not a baby, Minta." He was quiet while she tried to visualize what he was saying. He went on after a while. "Minta, I think you should know . . . I've been married."

196

"Been, or are?..." Somehow, the words just came out without pre-thinking them.

"Well, if you must know, I'm getting a divorce...."

"Getting a divorce? Why didn't you tell me?"

"Because you wouldn't have gone with me. I didn't want to lose you."

"And now what?"

"It isn't so awful ... it's easier now ... I mean, nowadays you don't have to have babies until you're ready. Marriage is hard enough when you finish school, but before it ... Do you want to be without money all your life?"

"Money? What has that to do with our problem?"

"A lot ... Maybe you aren't used to worrying about money, but I'm not the daughter of your father."

"I'm not afraid to struggle."

"I am. But don't worry. Maybe your father will help us, huh?"

"Help us? Help us get you a divorce?"

"No ... I'm not sure about that. We've talked about a divorce, and I think I can get one, if I can afford it."

"Barney am I hearing right? You expect my father to support us, and get you a divorce? What a fool I've been." "You think that you have to be a fool to be in love?"

"With you, yes."

"Then we're getting off to a great start, aren't we?"

They drove in silence a while. Minta sat stiffly, as if in shock; she didn't even want to cry. Then Barney changed his tone and put his arm out to her again. She pushed him away.

"Look, Minta ... don't get things so out of proportion. You don't have to have this...."

"That's what I thought you said. Are you trying to tell me about abortion?"

"Well, it isn't uncommon nowadays."

"You keep talking about nowadays ... what kind of a girl do you think I am?" She was angry now, so angry she couldn't feel the fright or the hurt any more. "You sound like this is common to you. How many girls you know have had abortions?"

"Now, Minta...."

"Don't 'now, Minta' me. Tell me. I want to know just how blind I've been. Give me the whole story."

"You're not in the mood to be reasonable."

"I'll say I'm not. Never mind telling me any of your stories; just take me home. Where are we, anyway?" She looked around; the lights of the city were behind them. "Where are you taking me?"

"You wanted to celebrate. I thought we'd go to this house my friend owns. It's beautiful; we can...."

"Pretend we are married, with all the rights and privileges and no license?"

"Well, I thought...."

"No ... you aren't going to think for me again. Turn this car around and take me home."

"Be reasonable, Minta. We can work this out. I do love you."

"You don't know what love means. I was stupid ever to go out with you. Oh, how stupid can I get?"

"All right ... all right. If you want me to, I'll marry you. We'll have a mock ceremony. My wife is out of the country right now ... she's with her parents in Europe ... she won't make a fuss ... when she gets back, we'll...."

"Is that your last offer?" Minta was shaking now, angry, hurt, hating Barney and herself. She had hated him ever since he'd talked her into making love; but now he made her sick just to look at him. Her words were coming out in puffs of anger.

"Well, what do you want me to do? I've made every suggestion I know. I'm trying to do the right thing. I really do love you."

"You call that love? Take me home; take me home right now." She took hold of the door handle. "Take me home, or I'll jump out of this car right now." She pulled the handle, and Barney grabbed her just as the door flew open and he hit the brakes. Minta flew forward, hitting her head on the windshield, then she fell backward. By the time Barney got the car stopped, she lay quietly against the seat, blood oozing from her head and running down her face.

"Minta, Minta ... speak to me ... are you all right? You little idiot, why did you do that? Minta...." With his handkerchief, Barney made a pad and pushed it against the spot where the blood was coming from under her hair. Minta groaned. "You're not dead, you're not dead ... I'll get you to the hospital, Minta ... hang on, Sweet ... I'll get you there."

Barney swung the car around and headed back. As he drove,

Minta began to mumble, and he breathed a little easier.

"You're going to be all right, honey ... really you are. Keep talking, you're just stunned. You've got to be all right. Keep talking."

"Deek ... Deek ... I'm sorry ... I'm ... I'm sorry ... talk ... yes, yes ... Deek ... oh, Deek...." Unconsciously, Minta reached out and took hold of Barney's arm in a tight grip. "Pl-please ... forgive me, Deek...."

Barney stepped on the gas. The lights of the city loomed ahead; the hospital was close.

Chapter Twenty-One

"Selfish to the end, aren't you, Minta?" said Deek as he faced her in her dressing room, where she was throwing things in a bag.

"Yes, that's me, selfish to the end...have it your way." Minta set her chin and went on packing the things she'd left around the dressing room during the last days of rehearsal.

"After all Siggie's done for you, you're going to run off and let her down. Do you know what she's gone through for this Drama Barn?"

"I'm not hurting your precious Siggie's Drama Barn, and she has an understudy just dying to take my part. Don't worry; the show will go on."

"Without you ... and with a half-trained understudy; you know she doesn't really know the part."

"Then she can learn it. Look...." Minta stood up her full height and looked at Deek. "There isn't anything you can say to get me on that stage ... ever again. I'm blowing this town, I'm getting out, and...."

"Go on, then. I always knew you didn't have what it takes. A disappointment in a boyfriend you'd set your mind on, a blow on the head, and you turn against your friends and everything you could have been."

"You said it . . . could have been. Now get out of this dressing room, and out of my life."

"I will; you won't have to ask again. Signee told me to leave you alone. I should have listened. I just thought you might do it for me . . . but I was wrong."

"Yes, you were wrong. And don't ever ask me to do anything for anybody again. From now on, I'm taking care of me. I'll think for myself, and won't depend on anybody else, ever. . . ."

"You'll find it hard to think for yourself and make any decisions at all without a heart. Wax cold . . . that's you. And I thought I knew you." Deek turned and walked out of the room, slamming the door behind him. Tears started in Minta's eyes as she watched him go.

"Heart, what do you know about heart, you, you . . . you missionary!" she yelled, throwing a bottle of make-up across the room, hitting the door where Deek had disappeared. She went back to her packing and was almost through when the door opened again. Fear showed in Minta's eyes as she looked up, expecting to see Deek, afraid he would come back to cut her up with more words. But it was Signee who walked in.

"I have the car outside, Minta. Is there anything I can help you with?"

"No," was all Minta said, and she went on packing. But just the sight of Signee had calmed her some. Signee didn't say anything; she just began picking up things. Finally, Minta threw her hairbrush in her handbag and looked at Signee.

"Don't you ever get tired of being a nice person?"

"I didn't know I was being nice," Signee said quietly, and went on picking up things.

"Oh, you're nice, all right. You should be hating me and yelling and throwing things. But not you. Siggie, aren't you ever normal?"

"I've had my normal times, the way you describe, but that's when I've got the problem."

"Just what do you mean by that?"

"I mean I know there's something wrong. That blow on the head wasn't that bad; and besides today wasn't the beginning of this outburst of emotion. You haven't been thinking straight for quite a while now. You still want to run out on graduation, too?"

"Yes. Why should I stay for graduation? It won't change anything."

"What do you want to change? If it's the play, you don't have to run away to get out of it."

"I'm leaving this town and everything in it."

"And not telling your parents?"

"What have they ever done for me?"

"Well, for one thing...." Signee's voice was quiet and soft, "they gave you birth."

At the sound of the word "birth," Minta felt her reflexes jump. She was quiet for a minute, then she came back fighting again. "Yes, they did that. But I hardly think they should be congratulated, when they take a good look at how I turned out. Birth for my mother probably wasn't a good idea."

"Minta, Minta, you're so cold. Can't you tell me? What's changed your plans?"

"Nothing's changed. I'm just leaving with Barney a little sooner, that's all. Can I help it if he finds me so attractive that...."

"Minta," said Signee, reaching out to touch her arm. "Don't."

"Don't what?"

"Don't make up things to tell me. If you don't want to tell the truth, at least don't make up stories. If you don't want to talk, I'll understand."

"What do you mean? I told you I was going to Barney's place after the show closed; and now I'm just going early, that's all."

"Minta, you aren't going anywhere with Barney."

"What makes you think that?"

"Because Kolby called his dorm this morning to ask him about the accident, and he's gone."

"Gone where?"

"No one knows. He checked out of his dorm this morning early, and didn't even leave a forwarding address. Kolby is trying to find out what's going on right now."

Minta sank into a chair. "Well, what do you know? I might have guessed."

"Might have guessed what?"

"Nothing ... well, now you know," said Minta, resuming the

packing process, finishing with a lipstick she threw in her purse and snapped it shut. Picking up her suitcase, she started toward the door. "Well, you're rid of us both, then, aren't you, Siggie?"

"Minta, I wasn't trying to get rid of either of you. Kolby is trying to locate Barney right now because he left with a hundred dollars that belongs to one of the guys he lived with. I think his name is Samuel ... he was helping Kolby with sound, and was to take the plane this morning back to work, but his money was gone. Barney had been so eager to share his room...."

"Yes, Barney is always eager to share."

"Minta, forget Barney. You don't love him, do you?"

"It's dangerous to love Barney. No, I don't love him. Well, it isn't your problem. Tell Kolby I'm sorry about the money. Maybe I can give it back."

"You didn't take the money."

"No, I didn't take the money. Well, see you, Siggie ... don't take any weak roommates after I'm gone, will you?" She opened the door, and hesitated.

"Minta...."

"Yes?"

"Minta, are you going to have a baby?"

Minta turned, dropped her suitcases, and looked at Signee a moment as if she might let down. Then she shrugged her shoulders. "Pretty smart, aren't you? You were right all the time, weren't you, Siggie? You told me, didn't you? Now you can brag to all your friends and tell them you have a perfect example of...." Signee walked to Minta and interrupted her as she led her back into the room to the dressing-table bench.

"I have a friend I love very much, and I won't let even you say bad things about her. Sit down, Minta. I want to talk to you."

"But I don't want to talk to you," said Minta, trying to stop her bottom lip from quivering. "You don't understand. I've got to get out of here."

"Where are you going, Minta?"

"Oh, I ... I don't know...." she looked at Signee, and suddenly the quivering lip wouldn't hold any more. She took a deep breath that ended in a sob from somewhere inside her. Signee put her arms around her; Minta burst into tears and threw her arms around Signee's neck. She sobbed and sobbed, and her breath came in little squeaks as if the hurt inside couldn't get out, as if it were too big to escape. Signee just held her tight and stroked her hair with the palm of her hand.

"Go ahead, Minta, cry ... cry all you want, cry it out ... you aren't alone, Minta; you don't have to be tough and strong right now. Just cry, don't try to be brave or act like you don't care ... just cry for now...."

Minta did cry, until Signee's shoulder was wet and Minta's face swollen into red puffs. When the sobs finally subsided enough for her to get her breath, she gasped:

"Oh, Siggie, what am I going to do?"

"We'll find a way ... don't worry. You're all tight inside, and worn out. You need some sleep right now, some rest."

"I can't rest, Siggie ... how can I rest?..."

"Come on, we're going home right now."

"I'm going away ... I've got to go away." Minta's voice rose again.

"All right, if that's what you want, come and get in the car. You ran all the way here this morning; that wasn't good for you, and after that cut on your head."

"I had to run ... I couldn't sleep or think or feel ... I had to run ... don't you understand?"

"Yes, Minta, I understand you had to run. Now come with me, and get in the car. You have to finish packing the things at our house anyway, so let's go there for right now."

Signee led her, almost like she was sleep-walking, from the dressing room and into the car. When they got home, she helped her out of the car and took her inside. There she helped her take her jacket off.

"Minta, I want you to get into a bubble bath...."

"I can't ... I can't ... I've got to go...."

"We'll figure all that out as soon as you've had a bath and some sleep."

"Promise?"

"I promise. Now, get in the tub. I'll run your water."

"Siggie? You won't tell Deek, will you?"

"No, Minta, I won't tell Deek."

The phone rang a dozen times while Minta took her bath. In between settling problems on the phone about the play, Signee made some warm soup; and when Minta came out of the bathroom, all warm and flushed, Signee put her into bed and fed her the soup while she talked.

"Siggie, I have to get away and think. I've got to think. Siggie, I don't want to run out on the show, but I've got to think what to do."

"I know, honey, I know. We'll both think. You sleep; and then if you want to go away somewhere, we'll find a place."

"Will we, Siggie? Oh, Siggie, I love you." Minta was in tears again; but this time they were pathetic tears, not the harsh, tearing tears she had coughed out before. Signee eased her back onto a pillow, and in a minute she was asleep.

Minta slept most of the day, and by the time she woke up the afternoon was beginning to fade into evening. When she first opened her eyes, like a child she yelled for Signee, who came running.

"Well, you had quite a sleep. Do you feel better?"

"I think so." Minta pushed the covers back and sat up. "Now I've got to get dressed and get out of here."

"All right. I've thought of a place you can go. I have an aunt who lives in a little town just a few miles from here. She lives all alone. I called her; she is going to be away, and she said I could use her house. I told her I had a friend who had been ill and needed to think. After all, movie stars often need to get away."

"Oh, Siggie, the play ... I'm so terrible..."

"Don't worry about that. We'll handle that some way. Your understudy has been working, and I think I know most of the part. The important thing is getting you well."

"I'm well; I just can't face people."

"You won't have to. I have to get to the Drama Barn now, but Kolby is coming by and he'll give you a ride."

"Did you tell him?"

"Of course not. He knows you need some rest, that bump on the head ... don't worry, he won't ask any questions. He'll take you to my aunt's place, and you can be all alone there ... and if you want me to be with you, I'll come after the show."

"Oh, Siggie, you are so good to everybody."

"No, I'm not. I just want to save my best actress from having a nervous breakdown."

"I'll make it up to you some way, really I will."

"I know you will. We'll see how you feel tomorrow. I'll call. If you want me tonight, call the theater and leave word."

"All right."

"Do you feel better now?"

"Yes, I do."

"All right, I'm going to leave and see what I can do with the show for tonight. Stay right here till Kolby comes."

Signee left and drove her car to the theater. Away from Minta, she began to worry about the play. It would be rough to pull it together, even if she could stand behind the curtains and cue. But she didn't know how rough it would be until she got to the theater and found out how many problems they had. The understudy was also a dancer, and the dancers would have to change a lot. They dug in, all of them. Signee told them only that Minta was ill, that her accident was worse than they expected, and they seemed to accept the explanation. A half hour before the curtain was to open, Signee was ready to call off the whole show. Nothing was working, and the understudy was so shook up she didn't know how she could go on. Signee called the cast together.

"We have a choice," she explained. "We can try a show with an explanation to the audience; or we can call it off and take another day and put it together."

"Is there a chance Minta will be better by tomorrow?"

Someone had asked the question; Signee didn't know who. But there was no mistaking the answer. It came from Deek.

"Not a chance ... her illness is permanent. It's called thinking of Minta only."

"That's not true, Deek," said Signee in defense. "Minta is ill. I just left her, and she isn't well enough to take this part."

"I vote we call it off," someone said.

"And work harder all day tomorrow? Will you all be willing?"

The answer was positive, and Signee went to check with the box office. It would be bad, but for anyone who couldn't attend the day after graduation, they could refund the money ... it would run into graduation problems on the practice. Everything was whirling around in Signee's head when the door opened, and there stood Kolby with Minta on his arm.

"Well, why aren't we ready?" Kolby said with a smile.

"Oh, Minta, I've never been so glad to see anybody in my life," said Signee, hugging her. "Are you sure you're all right?"

"Of course. Haven't you heard? The show must go on." Minta went to her dressing room, and Kolby stood there smiling at Signee.

"How did you do it?" Signee put her hands on her hips and looked at Kolby.

"I told you, I know about show business and actresses . . . I know all about everything."

"Everything?"

"Everything I need to know to handle you. You didn't think I would let Minta spoil my surprise when the show closes, did you?"

"Persistent, aren't you?"

"I always know what I'm doing . . . didn't I tell you that? Now, you'd better get things rearranged back, so you won't mess up my lighting effects for tonight. Lady, you have cost me so much money I can't believe you." Reaching over he held her hand a minute and the shine in his eyes made her want to hang on to him. But all she said was:

"I've cost you so much money?"

"Sure. I've been taking off a lot of working hours for this Drama Barn of yours. To say nothing of escorting your leading lady around. Let me see, how many hours have I invested in you now?" She smiled; he dropped her hand. He made his way to the ladder to climb up for the lights while Signee made her way backstage. The crowd would start to come anytime.

"Sig. . . ." called Kolby, just before she stepped through the curtain.

"Yes?"

"Just for the record . . . I got that hundred dollars back."

"How?"

"Tell you after the show. You'll find the story quite interesting."

Chapter Twenty-Two

Minta's second performance on the stage of the Drama Barn was even better than her first. To Signee's surprise, she put herself into the part as if she had lived it all her life. The orchestra seemed to take their cues from her, and the music was outstanding, as if they had rehearsed to top her mood in each scene. In the serious moments on stage, you could hear a proverbial pin drop in the audience, and the comedy scenes filled the old barn with laughter. Signee was so pleased, so happy, that tears of joy ran down her face through scene after scene. When the show was over, she went backstage and was the first to enter Minta's dressing room.

"You did it, you did it ... you were an angel out there."

"Thanks, Siggie. If I've made it with you, that's the most I'll ask for."

"Coming home with me, Minta?"

"I'm counting on it, Siggie. How soon can we leave here?"

"I'll get with the stage manager, we'll button up the set, and I'll meet you in twenty minutes ... barely enough time for you to get rid of the crowd outside your door."

Signee left Minta in the arms of her friends and went to talk to the stage manager. But the first person she saw on stage was Kolby.

"We saved the show this time, didn't we?"

"You did it, Kolby. You did it. I give you full credit."

"I'll take you out for a quick meal tonight, and let you sing my praises. But only if you ask nicely."

"I would ask nicely, too, but I can't go tonight."

"But I saved your star. Have a heart, Sig."

"Because you saved my star, I can't eat with you."

"What kind of justice is that? I'll throw her back."

"All I have is gratitude. All right, Kolby?"

"All right ... who has a problem they are dying to get rid of tonight? As if I didn't know. Minta, huh?"

"How did you guess?"

"It's been Minta for a long time, hasn't it? Ever since she came to live with you, huh?"

"How do you know about Minta and when she came to live with me?"

"I have my private detectives, and I get information from Eric."

"Eric is like a private detective."

"Aren't you ever going to let these kids run their own lives?"

"As soon as they grasp a few concepts. It's the method of growing up that hurts."

"All right. I'll leave town without dinner, as usual. But I'll be back tomorrow night. You haven't forgotten tomorrow is closing and our date, have you?"

"I haven't forgotten, but I hate to see the show close."

"Because, Mr. Kolby," he mimicked talking to himself, "the leading lady needs this part right now."

"How much did Minta tell you, Kolby?" Signee switched out the upper barn lights and walked toward Kolby.

"Not a thing; not one blasted thing."

"Then how did you get her here?"

"I used common sense; and don't pry into any more of my secrets. I appealed to her love for you ... simple."

"Oh, Kolby, I don't know when to believe you and when not to."

"Believe me all the time; you'll never go wrong."

"Then you're really flying out tonight?"

"Taking the last plane ... I've got to get some work done on my own job. But I could be intrigued for a dinner, late, if you change your mind."

"Not tonight. I've got a friend waiting, so...." She turned to go, and then remembered. "What about the hundred dollars? You were going to tell me."

"You said you'd tell me after the show."

"You can ask favors, but I can't, huh?"

"Kol ... if you don't tell me, I'll ... " She lifted a prop stool as if she might throw it.

"I didn't say which show."

Kolby turned and looked at her, a big smile across his face. "Uh-huh ... you'll what?"

"Well, I'll...." She let her arm and the stool drop.

He shook his head. "You'll never boss me, Sig. If you need me, I'll be there; but you'll never boss me. Just like I told you before."

"So you aren't going to tell me about the money?" Signee knew it wouldn't do any good to try and push Kolby, so she turned to leave again. "All right."

"Wait a minute." He reached out, took her arm, and pulled her back. "I think you might need this when you talk tonight."

"And after you tell me, will you button this place up? I've talked too long and I want to get Minta home."

"Always giving me work, huh? All right, Director, what can a poor insignificant stagehand do?"

"If you ever become insignificant, I'll let you know."

"A few crumbs of praise from Her Majesty? I knew you'd love me. That's what I said to myself: 'She'll love you.'"

"Come on, Kol ... the story."

"All right, Sig—the story. When I went to check on Barney checking out, I started with his apartment. It was news to his friend that he was leaving. But his friend has such a suspicious mind ... must come from living with Barney."

"The story."

"Don't be impatient. I'm detailing this on purpose; I like having you around. Anyway, it seems that big car Barney has been driving really belongs to his roommate, and he's been paying his roommate rent to drive it. However, he isn't too good at paying ... only renting ... so his friend pushed him and insisted he pay up, since he was planning a weekend away. He was planning a weekend away with Minta, wasn't he?"

"I don't know the details; there have been some changes. She did talk about after closing ... I'll find out. Kolby, you are something. Here I am, telling you things I have no right telling you. What kind of friend am I, anyway?"

"It's all right, Sig. If you're interested in her, that makes me interested, too. She's lucky if she's called it off with this Barney character; he's a loser. Anyway, when he was pushed to pay, he did. The roommate doesn't know where he got the money, and was shocked that he did. But he paid up with this one hundred dollars, so Barney knew his roommate had it. So, when he decided to blow, he took it with him. As soon as I mentioned that Barney had checked out, his roommate looked for his money, and it was gone. With Barney."

"So how did you get it back?"

"The roommate ... he knew a few places Barney might go, and we caught him taking a bus out of town. He had the money on him."

"Why didn't you stop Barney, too?"

"What for?"

"He'd asked Minta to ... never mind. I'll talk to her first. Thanks, Kolby; thanks so much. See you tomorrow night." She turned and moved fast, talking as she went. "There was a smell of burning in the left wing. Have you checked those connections?"

"More work ... what about mine?"

"You don't want the place to burn up tomorrow night, do you?"

"Yeah," he called, "but after the show." She didn't hear him; she'd disappeared behind the stage. Kolby climbed back up his ladder.

Inside Minta's dressing room, there were still kids hanging around. As Signee entered, Deek had pushed his way ahead to stand beside her.

"You came through like a storybook heroine ... and you did a good job. I'm proud of you." He took one of her hands in both of his.

Minta smiled and looked up into Deek's face. She was serious. "Thanks, Deek, and good luck on your mission. I'm glad you're going, truly."

"Thanks, Minta . . . but don't push me out too soon. We have a little time yet. And then there's the dance—maybe we could go together once more."

"No, thanks, but I'll remember you asked. Just in case we don't see each other again. . . ."

"You going somewhere?"

"Yes. A vacation. . . ."

"Sure, every star needs a vacation after a show. Isn't that true, guys?" He looked at the crowd. They responded. "Sure, I know about these things. I go to the movies."

"There was laughter, and no one but Signee seemed to notice that Minta didn't laugh. Then it was all over; the kids cleared out, the lights were cut in the building, and Signee and Minta sat side by side in Signee's car. They talked about the show until they got home, and then Minta went to her room.

"When you're ready for bed I'll tuck you in, Minta . . . if you want me to. Just call out."

Signee took a shower, and her mind was full of questions about Minta. Once her fears were realized and she'd asked Minta the main question, hurt had welled up inside her. But Minta had needed so much she couldn't think about how she felt; and then the show needed her attention. But there was a sickness inside, a deep concern, and . . . guilt. Yes, she admitted to herself, there was a guilt on her part, that this could have happened right under her eyes. Minta wasn't bad; Minta was just eager for life. There were so many questions she needed answers to, but maybe Minta wouldn't want to answer. If she didn't. . . .

"If Minta doesn't want to tell me, I won't ask," she said aloud in the shower.

Turning off the water, Signee slipped into a towel robe, picked up a small towel to dry her hair, and sat down in front of her mirror. She had her hair half blown dry, when over the top of the blower she heard Minta call. Signee went to answer, and found Minta in bed looking over the top of the sheets like a little child. Signee stood looking down at her. Minta smiled, and then the smile turned to desperation.

"Siggie . . . what am I going to do?"

"We'll find a way. We'll discuss it and find a way. We'll pray, and. . . ."

"Pray? Me? You think Heavenly Father will listen to me now?"

"Do you think He won't?"

"After the dumb things I've done? Oh, Siggie, how could I have been so stupid?" Minta turned her face away, and the tears came again.

"Come on, Sweetie...."

"Don't call me that," Minta screamed, as she curled up in a ball as if in pain. Signee grabbed her in her arms. Minta screamed again, "Don't call me that, don't ever call me that."

"I won't, I won't...but why, what did I say?"

"Sweetness. Sweetness ... that's what Barney always said. He always called me Sweetness... I hate that, I'll always hate that."

"All right, now I know ... I'll never say it ... don't cry, Minta. Don't cry. We'll talk."

"I can't, don't you see I can't?" She opened her mouth just long enough to push out the words, and then went on crying—a cry that was more like inside pain.

"Can't, can't what?"

Minta looked up, her eyes streaming with tears, a look of fear, hurt and desperation in her face. "I can't, Siggie ... I can't ever stop crying. I can't pray, or t-talk ... Oh, Siggie, what have I done to my life?"

Signee held her tight and kissed her hair, and prayed desperately inside herself. "Oh Father, help me to help her, help me to say and do the right things. What can I do, Father? Help Minta, help us...." While her heart wrung out the words in empathy for Minta, Signee just went on holding her, rocking her back and forth as she sat there on her bed, rocked her like a baby and prayed harder than she had ever prayed. No, there had been other times she had prayed for herself and for Jimmy; for Eric and Alta; and there had been other desperate times in her life, when her mother was ill, when ... but those had passed. Heavenly Father had helped her then, and He would help her now; she knew it. She began to talk positively to her Heavenly Father in her mind as she rocked Minta. "You'll show us the way, Father, you always have. Minta has been foolish, she has made a big mistake. But help us turn this mistake into experience; show us how to go on from here, to see the light of

214

what we can become in goodness as we make up for past wrongs. Help me to help Minta." Reaching for a tissue, she put it in Minta's hands. The sobbing had lessened.

"Are you tired enough to sleep? Shall we talk in the morning?"

"I don't think I'll ever ... s-sleep again. I can't sleep, I haven't for a lot of nights now ... I can't remember how many."

"Then we'll talk. I'll make you a cup of warm soup, and...."

"I don't want anything."

"Minta you have to go on living. What you've done is a ... a big mistake ... and ... "

"A big mistake! You sound like I just spilled a glass of milk at breakfast. Don't you understand? My whole life is over. Everything I ever wanted is lost ... gone...."

"Minta!" Signee almost shouted at her. "All right ... all right ... It's a terrible mistake, and it will affect the rest of your life. You have to face that and go on from here."

"I don't want to. I just want to die."

"Oh, stop it, Minta." Signee was getting disgusted.

"I do want to die, don't you believe that?" Her eyes were wide with mounting hysteria. Signee put her face close to hers and yelled, something Minta had never heard her do before.

"I do believe that ... but unfortunately we can't die when we want to, either." Shocked, Minta momentarily was quiet, staring at Signee. Signee let her voice drop to a low tone, full of patience and understanding. She took hold of Minta's hand and straightened the pillow under her head with the other. "Minta, yesterday ... a few yesterdays ago, you were a little girl. You had the brightness of life before you, and your choices were in your hands. You made one of those choices, for what reason I don't know. But you made a choice, and you have to live with that choice. I'll help you all I can; but you have to decide, and you'll have to live with this choice, also. But you can live, and you can get your life together again. It will be very very hard, but you won't be alone ... I promise. All right?"

Minta nodded, still looking at Signee.

"All right, now let's take a look at what choices you have, and what will fit into what you want to do. Is there any chance of marriage?"

Minta shook her head.

"No chance at all? I know you were thinking of it, and ... the baby is Barney's, isn't it? You don't have to tell me if you don't want to."

"It's Barney ... " She rolled her head from side to side. "I wish it wasn't ... I wish...."

"The time for wishing is over. You don't want to marry Barney at all, do you? Then why...." Signee stopped. "I'm sorry; I don't mean to pry."

"I want you to know." Minta started talking quietly, as if she were really making an effort to control her emotions. "Siggie, I didn't deliberately become this kind of a person. I thought I loved Barney; I needed someone; I felt so alone. He was good to me, he had a way of keeping his arm around me wherever we went. I felt protected and loved. I had tried to be the kind of person you and Deek wanted me to be, but I was so tired of trying ... I thought I could never do it ... I can see a lot of things now that I couldn't see before. Deek was going away, and I knew I wasn't good enough for him. Living at home was so bad while you were away ... Barney said he loved me, over and over, and he said he needed me and was lonely, too. And he said I needed to be fulfilled ... that no woman would be happy until she is fulfilled...."

"He told you just enough truth to get you to believe in him. A woman isn't fulfilled until she is loved; but when there is no obligation of marriage, then...."

"Then the girl is left to face her badness, and he goes...."

"Is that what you're trying to say, Minta? That he's gone and left you?"

"Kolby said he'd left."

"But I thought he might just have gone to make arrangements...."

"Barney would only make arrangements for more of the same," said Minta bitterly. "He not only didn't ever intend to marry me; he can't. Barney already has a wife. He told me last night."

"Oh, Minta."

"I thought he'd take me away and marry me when he knew, but he just wanted another weekend. Even when he knew, all he thought about was getting me to give in again ... once more before he left. I hate him, I hate him ... I'm glad he can't marry me, because then I might feel obligated to marry him, and I don't want to marry him or ever see him again."

"He has to be stopped. We'll tell the bishop, and let him take it from here."

"What do you mean, tell the bishop?"

"Minta, you are a member of the church; and whenever anything like this, a moral sin, is committed, we are given the commandment to tell the bishop. It's for your good and help. He'll help you."

"I don't want anyone to know. I won't tell anyone."

"Didn't we say you'd grown up now? You can't keep a thing like this a secret. Talk to the bishop, Minta, and to your parents. I'll be with you...."

"My parents? I can never tell my parents. I can hear my mother right now ... and how would she face her club? Father would have to resign as principal ... they would hate me. I can't do that to them."

"But you have done it; and once you face it and confess to the right people, it will be easier."

"I won't. I won't do that."

Signee sighed. "Then what do you want to do?"

"Like Barney said, I don't have to have this baby. I don't want this baby."

"Is that what Barney said?"

Signee was suddenly frightened. "You wouldn't! Minta, you won't do that. Promise me you won't even think of that!"

"Why not? Everybody is having abortions these days..."

"Minta...." Signee took her by the shoulders and shook her a little, trying to get her attention. "Minta, you don't understand ... you would never get over that. Making a bigger mistake isn't going to rid you of the first one. Grow up, Minta ... you can't go on making mistake after mistake. You have to start back. Why do you think I tried to keep you from getting into this mess ... the one you're in right now? Why do you think I dared interfere with your dating life? Because I knew you were headed toward this, and I tried to stop you ... tried to teach you...."

"Go on and say you told me so."

"What good will that do? But are you going on and on? You've got to start back to clean living, or you can't stand the pain ... the hurt ... the inside scars that will never leave. Promise me you won't think of ever doing anything to take the baby's life or your own. I can help you if you'll let me, but I can't keep you from these things. I know ... I've tried before."

"What do you mean, you've tried before?"

"It's like history repeating ... oh, Minta, you have no idea of the pain, the spiritual ache, the mental suffering...."

"Right now, I'm concerned about the physical ... and my parents. I've got to think of them."

"We will Minta ... we will...."

"Oh, Siggie ... there's no way out. It's all such a mess ... such a mess...." Minta burst into tears again; rolling from side to side in her confusion and hurt, she sobbed and screamed in turn. "There's no way out, what a mess I've made of my life...."

Chapter Twenty-Three

Curtain time on the last night of the Drama Barn's first play, and Signee made her way to Minta's dressing room. Minta had been ill when she awakened. Signee had stayed beside her until she was asleep, and they hadn't tried to talk any more. But when Minta tried to come to the breakfast Signee had prepared, she turned green and ran for the bathroom. Signee had talked her into staying home in bed to prepare herself for the show. But Signee was worried. When she got home from school Minta was up, dressed, and looking as if nothing had happened; and though Signee was grateful, still there was an attitude, a don't-care, don't-bother-me attitude, that worried her.

"Ready for our star," said Signee, as she opened the door and looked in.

"Come in and shut the door," shouted Minta. Signee followed the order.

"Anything happen, Minta?"

"Yes, I'm sick. I can't go on."

"If you don't go on, what excuse will you give? Do you want everyone to know?"

"Only you can tell them." There was a nastiness in Minta's

tone.

"I brought you an eggnog and a small pill to settle your stomach," replied Signee, ignoring Minta's outburst. "It's a pill the doctor gave me when I had the dry heaves ... perfectly harmless, but should help temporarily."

"I don't want an eggnog. It sounds terrible."

"I know, but you'll need some strength. Drink it like a good girl."

"I don't want it." Minta turned and threw her brush on the table. Signee began to burn inside.

"You think I'm going to make you go out on that stage, Minta. You are acting like a child and don't deserve any help or understanding. You are really showing your colors, aren't you? Go ahead, act like a spoiled baby and let everyone know what you are. I'm tired of spending time on you. I thought you wanted help, but you don't. You want to feel sorry for yourself. Well, go ahead. Take off that costume."

"It's curtain time. Just what do you think you are going to do?"

"I'll do the part myself, if I have to ... this show goes on. This theater wasn't created for dramatic spoiled girls who only want to feel sorry for themselves. This is a blessing for those who want to learn and develop their talents, and right now I'm sick of you. It takes courage to go out there and face that audience when you don't feel like it ... but if you don't, it will be a long time before you ever face anybody again, especially yourself. So you just go ahead and throw away your opportunity ... I'll go find your understudy, who will be more than happy to have a chance. And what she can't do, I will do myself." Angrily, Signee turned to leave. There was a knock on the door, and someone yelled "curtain time." Signee jerked the door open, but shut it again as Minta yelled.

"Signee ... don't leave me."

Signee stopped, took a deep breath, and just stood there, her back to Minta.

"All right, you win. You care more about your show than you care about me. But I'll do it ... if you just won't leave me alone."

Signee turned and came back, put her arms around Minta and kissed her on the cheek. "I won't leave you, Minta, unless you push me away. I mean what I said; I won't stay and let you use me to cover up your hurts. Go on stage; you'll feel just a little better about yourself after the show." She handed her the eggnog. "I'll go out for the opening prayer, and see you in the wings before you go on."

"And you'll be here after the show? You promise you'll be with me? What about Kolby? He'll be around, and Deek...."

"I'll be with you, Minta. I promise."

The curtains opened, and Minta went into her part like she had been an actress all her life. Signee knew what she was going through, but at least for the playtime she was able to keep her feelings of guilt and hurt out of her voice. There was a special awe that came over the audience when Minta performed; she was even better on stage than Signee had predicted. She had promised to be with Minta even as she remembered Kolby's promise to show her a special surprise after the last performance. For some reason, she was uneasy about telling Kolby she would have to break that date. It was near the end of the play when he finally caught her backstage; he'd been late getting to the Barn and had made it just in time to shoot the first scene, so Signee hadn't seen him then.

"This is the night. I'll meet you by the box office after we've put the set to bed." He was on the way up the ladder to the loft and didn't stop. Signee called after him:

"Wait ... I can't, not tonight."

He looked at her over the top step of the ladder. "What does that mean? Look ... we've got a date." He pointed his finger at her.

"Be there ... or you'll miss out." He was smiling, but Signee had a feeling he was serious.

"Really, Kolby, I can't ... please understand."

He gave her a look she couldn't quite figure out, and then his head disappeared over the top of the ladder.

After curtain calls, Signee gave the orders to strike the set while Kolby wrapped up the lights and locked up the controls. Then Signee went to pick up Minta. As they walked through the rows of benches, there was Kolby by the box office.

"You're a little late ... the light crew moves faster."

"And very systematic. You didn't miss a cue."

"We aim to please. My car is just outside."

"Your car?"

"I drove this time. Come on, ladies...."

"I told you, Kolby... I can't tonight. And I have my car, too."

"Minta can take it home, can't she?"

Minta looked nervous; Signee turned to her. "Minta, unlock the car and drive it around front while I talk to Kolby, all right?"

"You won't be long, will you, Siggie?"

"I won't be long."

"You meant what you said?" Kolby asked the question before she had a chance to say anything at all.

"I wish I didn't mean it, but I can't leave Minta tonight, really I can't."

"Sig, tonight is important to me. It's important to you, too; but if you don't know that, I guess I'll just have to let you go."

"Can't it be another time?"

"Are you going through life doing for everybody else? Won't you ever take time for your own life ... or what you want?"

"I will...."

"No, I don't think you will. But maybe that's what makes you you."

Kolby looked at her for a long minute, then turned and left her standing there. A shiver went through Signee's body as she watched him go. Kolby had become a dear part of her life and she wanted to reach out and bring him back or run after him and not look back. But somewhere behind her a familiar horn honked, and Signee went to answer it.

The talk on the way home was mostly about the play. Minta was still high from the excitement of the sweet part she'd played and the response of the audience during the show and after. It wasn't until she got in the house that she began to feel ill again.

"I'm not going through with this, Signee. There's one thing Barney was right about. An abortion is the only way. Don't you talk me out of it, Siggie. I'm not going to hurt a lot of innocent people. This is my mistake, and I'll take the consequences. Didn't you say I should learn to pay...."

"Not that way! Hurt innocent people? What about the baby?"

"I haven't seen the baby. For me it doesn't exist."

"But it does exist and because of you. And not seeing it isn't reason enough to deny its existence. Minta, you can't, you just can't. I've got to make you see."

"I won't. I've made up my mind. If you won't help me, I'll find someone who will, because I'm going to get rid of this baby."

"I will never help you ... take your clothes and get out of this house. I won't be a party to such a thing."

"You said I had to decide."

"I won't help you that way ... ever, ever. Go on, get out of here. I mean it, Minta. If you're that kind of girl, I don't want to have anything to do with you. A mistake is one thing, and killing an innocent child is another. No ... no."

Signee ran from the room and from Minta, because she didn't want to say out loud the things she was thinking. She turned on a hot shower in her bathroom and got into it, and she was thinking: "Oh, why did I ever get into this? Why did I ever let Minta come and stay with me, and why did I let Kolby leave without me tonight?" Suddenly she wanted to talk to Kolby more than anyone else. Somehow she had to find him and talk to him. Minta's parents had to know. That would be hard, but nothing was as hard as what Jimmy had.... Signee was thinking about Jimmy as she snuggled into her furry robe and slippers and went to the kitchen to make a warm drink. As she passed through the living room, Minta was sitting in front of the gas log fire. She looked up as Signee came in.

"I'm sorry, Siggie ... I didn't mean to go against anything. I just thought ... please, help me. You tell me what to do. I'm so unstable I want to cry one minute, and the next I'm fighting."

Signee walked over and sat down in front of the fire opposite Minta. She started to talk.

"Remember how I told you about Eric and me? Remember that I told you I wasn't home when he returned from his mission?"

"I remember, Siggie."

"Well, I didn't tell you where I was. I was with Jimmy. I had gone with him to meet his parents. I loved Jimmy. I might have married him, but I met him too late. Jimmy was a convert to the church, had been in it only a little while when I met him. He was eager to learn, and a person of integrity. I loved Jimmy almost as soon as I met him. He felt the same way about me, and he took me to meet his parents. While we were there, I met a girl Jimmy had gone with in high school. She called him one night while we were there, and told him she had to see him. He went to meet her, because her parents had told him how ill she had been and that she'd had a nervous breakdown, and they thought Jimmy might help if he talked to her, since his name was the one she had called over and over in her illness. When Jimmy came home from seeing her, he was different. He took me home the next day, and on the way he told me. He told me, and together we cried. I can see the pain on his face even now—the hurt inside him—"

"'My Sig,' he said. 'You'll never marry me now. And even if you would, I'd never let you. I've made some serious mistakes. I told you that ... before I found the Gospel ... and the girl I went to see last night is part of my mistake.'"

"Then he told me how he'd gone with this girl through high school and how the crowd he was part of all played with immorality. How he'd been with her at a party one night when they all got drunk, and he ended up sleeping with her. He hadn't remembered, even; he was that drunk.

"'I left soon after that, Sig,' He told me, 'to take a job with a lumber outfit in Idaho. That was when I found out about the church...I haven't been home since. I didn't know, I really didn't ... but I've put that girl through hell, and she's been all alone. You see, she was pregnant with my baby and didn't tell me. She was scared, so she had an abortion. Now she can't live with it ... night and day the thought is with her. She thinks marrying me will make her feel right again.'

"Minta, I talked to Jimmy after I got over the shock. But he was a good person, and he left me and went to her, to marry her. It was a good thing, because that would always have been between us. He tried to make it right, but it didn't work. She had another baby after they were married ... and then I heard she committed suicide. She couldn't live with what she had done."

"He was a fool to marry her. Maybe it wasn't even his baby."

"Jimmy and I both thought of that. But he was with her, and he couldn't prove anyone else was. Besides, he felt so guilty he had to try and make up for what he had done. But he couldn't bring back the child she'd aborted, and she wouldn't ever let him forget that she'd had an abortion because of him. Jimmy was just one case. So many can make you think it's all right, but no one tells you how you'll suffer mentally as well as physically. There are so many ways to make up, without hurting that unborn baby. At least, giving birth, you begin to make up for your guilt."

"But what can I do? There isn't anyone to marry me. Isn't it worse to bring a baby into a mixed-up world without a father, to have to live with the mistake of his mother all the days of her life ... or her mother? I don't even know if I'm carrying a girl or a boy." Minta put her hands on her stomach. "Oh, Siggie, I can't believe it ... I've always wanted children, and I would like to have this baby. If only ...."

"And you don't want to take a chance of hurting yourself so that you might not ever have any more. Some people can't have...." Suddenly, Signee was thinking of Alta. "Minta ... I have a solution ... if you want to. You can have your baby and give it a good home ... if you want to."

"What do you mean?"

"Have your baby, and give it up for adoption to good people. Make sure your baby has a good life and a good family."

"You mean give my baby to strangers?"

"We can handle it through the church. The bishop will get in touch with a social worker. They have homes for unwed mothers, where you go and live and all the expenses are taken care of and you don't have to let others know ... not people who might hurt you with foolish gossip ... and then give it for adoption into a Mormon home where it will be raised and sealed to parents in the temple."

"I couldn't give my baby to strangers."

"A minute ago you didn't want your baby to live—now you can't give it up to strangers?"

"I'm all mixed up."

"I know. Minta, let me tell you the procedure as much as I understand it. First, we go to the bishop...."

"No, I won't do that."

"Minta, listen first and then decide. If you are going to try and make up for your mistake, let's do it right. There's less hurt when you follow the right way. First to the bishop, and talk to him. He'll get in touch with a social worker...."

"A social worker? What am I, a case number?"

Signee paused and looked at Minta, then said very quietly but firmly, "You've made a bad mistake. You'll need help, and there are professionals who can help you. In this case I'm sure it will be a social worker, one who can find you a place to live. All expenses will be taken care of. You won't even have to have money from your parents, if you don't want to. If you go away to a house for unwed mothers, with good people who are members of the church, then when your baby is born the social worker will take care of all the details. You'll be away from here, people will think you're away to work for the summer or on vacation, and your parents won't even have to tell anyone if they don't want to. Your baby will be given to parents who are waiting for a baby, parents who have waited and waited and who can't have children. . . ." Signee's mind was thinking of Eric and Alta and the little room ... a light began to form in her mind. But she didn't dare tell Minta; she knew enough to know it was part of the rules that the parents and mother didn't meet.

"Oh, Siggie, how can I go through with all this?"

Signee came out of her thoughts and put her hand on Minta's arm. "It won't be easy, but it will be better than suffering inside all the rest of your life. When you do what is best for the baby you are on the way back to forgiving yourself.

"Minta, there is one comfort in all of this. You can make a couple happy who can't have children of their own. Won't it make you feel better to know you have made another father and mother. . . ."

"It's hard to think of that right now."

"Minta, they will be eternally grateful."

"Maybe I can do it, Siggie. Will you go with me to see the bishop?"

"I will be with you whenever you need me."

"My parents, Siggie, that's what I'm dreading. . . ."

"But if you can do it all now, you won't have the fear of them finding out later."

"I can just hear Mother ... she'll never forgive me."

"You might be surprised. But no matter what, can you ever look at them again if you don't face them now? You won't be alone."

"What would I ever do without you, Siggie?"

"Then you'll do it?"

"I haven't any other choice, really. But I'm going to hate being sick, and all that pain, and ... Siggie, I've heard terrible things about having a baby."

226

"My mother always said the pains of birth are the kind that don't stay with you."

"Well, at least I will give my baby his or her chance on earth, won't I? I wonder what my baby is?

Minta got up and went toward the bathroom. She was calmer now than she had been in a long time. "It seems I'm going to have to learn patience the hard way ... and to think I couldn't wait two years for Deek. How I would like that chance now. I've got an idea I'm going to learn about loneliness the hard way, too."

"But there will be some satisfaction in knowing you are making up, and doing what's right under the circumstances."

"Yeah ... Siggie?"

Signee looked up from where she still curled by the fire. "Yes, Minta."

"Siggie, what about the dance?"

"Why don't you go, Minta? Enjoy this last little while. You've worked for good grades, and deserve to be with your class. You still look lovely; your figure hasn't changed yet."

"Maybe I'll get to say goodbye to Deek ... for the last time."

"Maybe you will, Minta."

"Siggie?"

"Yes, Minta?"

"After I have the baby, will you let me come home and work with you in your Drama Barn?"

"Of course, Minta. You have a real talent. In fact, I'll give you some parts to read that you can be memorizing while you're away."

"Thanks, Siggie ... I'm sorry you couldn't go with Kolby tonight, but I don't know what I'd have done if you had. Sorry I'm so much trouble, Siggie."

"I love you, Minta."

"I love you, Siggie...."

Signee didn't move, but a few tears fell into her lap as she bit her lip and said a prayer of gratitude. At least for now, she'd been able to get Minta to see the light of right ... right in the face of such disaster. She could be forgiven; Minta could make up for her mistake. Somewhere she'd read in the scriptures that sins, though they be scarlet, could be washed as white as the snow. Somewhere....

Chapter Twenty-Four

To convince Minta she should have her baby had been difficult. But carrying out the plan wasn't easy, either.

"Are you sure we have to tell the bishop, Siggie?"

Minta pulled back in rebellion, shame filling her whole body.

"You'll feel better when the bishop talks to you, and when you get someone schooled in these things to make arrangements. We also have to tell the bishop about Barney. Barney is a member of the church, and he needs to be stopped . . . he needs to be investigated. We don't even know if he's telling the truth. The bishop will know what to do. You'll see; when you've told the bishop and begin to make amends, when he forgives you, it will help you forgive yourself."

"Will I ever? Siggie, will I ever forgive myself? Will I ever like me again?"

"When you've done all you can to make up for what you've done. When you've changed your life and become the person you want to become. The bishop will help you."

"Will you come in with me? I know I shouldn't ask it; I should start standing on my own. But. . . ."

"I don't mind, Minta. You'll stand on your own as soon as you learn how. Maybe the bishop won't let me come in with you, but I'll be close. We'll do whatever he says, all right?"

"Without you, I wouldn't know what to do."

So an appointment was made, and together they went to see the bishop. There was more crying, but when it was over Minta began to face herself. She'd made a start toward changing her attitude. There were still nights of tears, when Signee heard her crying alone in her room; but by morning she was smiling again. Signee couldn't help feeling a little sad to see her have to grow up so fast, to hurt so much when she was so young. But each time she made a right decision, it made her stronger for the next one.

"Siggie, I'm going to tell my parents. I'm not looking forward to that session, but I'm going to tell them."

"Do you think they will accept your decisions?"

"I don't know, but they are my parents, and they deserve the right to throw a fit, if that's what they want to do. I have to start with them, Siggie. If I had learned to get along with them sooner, maybe none of this would have happened to me."

"Bless you, Minta," said Signee, kissing her on the forehead. "You're going to make it; I know you are. Shall I go with you to see your parents?"

"No; this is my turn alone."

"I don't mind."

"No. You see, they might try to say it all happened because of my living here, because of things that were said in the past...."

"That's true, Minta. My presence might do you more harm than good. You see, I didn't ever tell people about Jimmy. I just let them think, and some of their thoughts weren't good."

"I can understand that now. But I want you to know, Siggie, that if I ever amount to anything in my life, it will be because of you. I love you very much."

"I love you, too, Minta. But when you're handing out credits, remember the two ahead of friendship."

"I know ... my parents ... they gave me life." Minta put her hands across her body where new life was forming. "I wonder what my mother went through to bring me into this world? I wish I hadn't failed her. I hate to hurt her, but I know I've got to tell her. The bishop said he would help me if I had trouble. Well, here goes ... can I take your car for a little while?"

"Sure ... and I'm as close as the telephone. I'll be right here."

Signee watched as Minta got into the car and drove away. Then, as the tears started, tears of gratitude that Minta was learning to face herself and her problem, Signee went to her room to say a prayer.

The afternoon was gone when Minta finally came home, and Signee could tell by the look on her face that the meeting had been a rough one. But she looked up and smiled as Minta came in.

"Are you all right? Has anything changed?"

Minta shook her head, her lips tight. Then, putting her hand over her mouth, she ran for the bathroom. Signee pretended to ignore her illness, but when she came out of the bathroom she had warm soup and a toasted sandwich with dill pickles waiting. Minta looked at the food and sat down at the table.

"Dill pickles, huh? Anyone would think I'm having a baby."

They both laughed until Minta's laughter dissolved into tears.

"I cry all the time, Siggie. Do you suppose tears can wash away sins?"

"I think they help. Heavenly Father said a broken heart for wrongdoing, or something like that ... you'll make it."

"I found out something new about my parents today, Signee. I found out they really do care about me. A funny way of caring, maybe, but ... you know what Mother said?"

"Tell me if you want to."

"She said she wondered if I could stand this traumatic experience of having a baby, that maybe an abortion would be easier for me. You know, Siggie, in some ways my mother is younger than I am. How glad I am that I talked to you and the bishop first! But they do care. Father said he would pay all the bills, and Mother will send me dresses and books to read. They weren't as angry as I thought they would be ... just hurt. There was a hurt on their faces ... someday, I want to do something to make them proud of me, to make up for what I am doing to them now."

"You will, Minta ... you will."

"Siggie ... do you suppose Mother thought of the abortion to spare me, or her?"

"She doesn't understand ... and public opinion has always

meant a lot to her way of life. We can't blame her; she has never been very active in the church."

"I'm glad you said that, Siggie, because when she suggested abortion tonight, inside I began to hate her. But then I remembered I'm making the mistake. How can I blame her for any she has made?"

"When we forgive others, it helps us to forgive ourselves. I'm glad they are willing to help you."

"A favor, huh, Siggie? I know I've asked for so many, but one more?"

"What, Minta?"

"Promise me you'll never tell Deek. I can't stand it if he has to know."

"I won't tell him, Minta. But if he finds out some other way, what then?"

"If he asks me, I'll tell him the truth. But he won't. I'm going away, and he won't have to know ... oh, please, he won't have to know."

"Someday, we'll all know about everything. But maybe we'll have more understanding then." Signee was thoughtful, then she smiled at Minta, "Don't worry, I won't tell him. I promise."

"He was so nice to me at the dance, did I tell you?"

"No, you said very little about the dance."

"I didn't feel very good. But when I danced with Deek, he talked about how I was in the play, and when the dance was over he just said he'd see me around. It was just sort of special, like he always said when he dropped me off after a game, like tomorrow was another day ... I'm glad it was that way. I'll be gone when he leaves on his mission. Before he comes home I can be back, starting a new life, working in the Drama Barn, helping other kids the way you've tried to help me. Maybe I'll learn better by helping others ... do you think so?"

"I think so. Minta, setting goals is the best thing you can do to get your new life going. Set goals and fill them one after another. Now, we'd better get you ready to go with Miss Parker. She's very nice."

"How do you know? Have you met her?"

"Uh ... the Bishop said she was very nice." Signee hoped Minta hadn't heard the hesitation in her voice. She didn't think it wise to tell her that she had met Miss Parker; nor did she think

Minta should know she had talked with the bishop alone. Ever since she had thought about Minta having a baby, and having to give it up for adoption, she had thought about Alta and Eric. Yet who could tell if they could get the baby, or if it would be healthy? There were so many if's, and yet she was so concerned about Alta that she had asked the Bishop. He had put her in touch with Miss Parker.

"Miss Short, it wouldn't be a good idea to place the baby outside of the agency. There are many reasons...."

"Like?"

"Well, the agency will take care of the mother, her bills and health, and finding her a place. They will also take care of the health of the baby. They match baby and parents."

"But what if a girl wanted to give her baby to someone she knows?"

"She can do that, of course, but there are problems."

"What kind of problems?"

"The mother knows where the baby is; and later in life, if she changes her mind after she's married, that can cause a lot of trouble for the new parents as well as the mother. It's much more successful for all involved if she goes through the agency and makes a clean break."

"I can see the wisdom of that."

"Especially when the mother is young and emotional, and when she needs to forgive herself for her mistakes and start over. If she knows where the baby is, she will want to visit; and if the new parents aren't treating her just right, she will fret... you can see."

"Yes, Miss Parker, I can see."

So Signee hadn't told Minta about Alta and Eric ... she only knew that Alta had a miscarriage. And more and more she could see the wisdom of the agency.

When the details were all complete, it was Miss Parker who arranged for a place for Minta to stay in a Mormon home for unwed mothers, a home far enough away that she wouldn't have to worry about what was going on in Green Village, and the townspeople wouldn't have to worry about her. Signee took her to meet Miss Parker and told her goodbye. Then the long months of writing to Minta began. Signee decided she would do all she could to see that Minta wasn't too lonely, that she had encouragement for the future and knew that she was loved. And it was through their letters that Signee felt an even greater change in Minta, felt her mature and learn to live with her mistakes, and find patience in building her future.

As time passed, Signee was also learning about loneliness. The house was so empty with Minta and Kolby both gone. She hadn't seen Kolby since the night the show had closed, and she began to realize just how much she'd needed him and was missing him. She couldn't figure out why he hadn't called or written, though he'd told her he wasn't the writing kind. But she wondered what she had done to offend him to the point that he had vanished so completely.

School, cheerleaders, drama, and letter-writing had become Signee's way of life. New young people moving in and old ones moving out; letters to write to Alta and Eric; her parents away and soon to be coming home; Minta and Deek. It was a summer to write.

Deek left on his mission after Minta went away, and Signee had gone to his farewell talk in church. Deek, handsome, happy, and on his way to complete the goal he had looked forward to all his life. She was so proud to have been a part of his life; and his tenderness with her as she went to see him off, the way he held her hand and looked into her eyes, let her know that he, too, felt the bond of true friendship between them.

"Siggie ... you'd better be here when I get back. It wouldn't be home without you, Siggie. You keep those plays going ... right?"

"Right, Deek. I'll keep our Drama Barn producing plays and people ... I'll try to put them into your footsteps."

"You do that ... and I'll make mine big footsteps to follow while I'm on my mission. Tell Minta I've missed her; and send me her address, huh?"

"I'll try."

Signee felt a twinge at the deception, but thought it was better to let him think what he wanted to think. Then Deek was gone.

One morning near the end of the summer, when she was finishing her letters, she thought about writing to Eric and Alta to find out about Kolby. But before the thought had time to materialize, her doorbell rang. And there he was, smiling as if there had never been a lapse of time.

"Don't you ever get dressed in the morning?" he said, leaning on the side of the door as he smiled at her. "Do you always start the day in a robe?"

"A robe a day ... that's me. Kolby Burke, where have you been?"

"Through an adventure you would have loved ... but you let me go without you."

"I thought you'd ask me again."

"One chance to a girlfriend ... that's my platform to sell myself. Either you buy or you don't."

"I'll buy...."

"You'll have to take me on faith, all right?"

"I...."

"Yes or no?"

"Yes, you idiot. Yes. I've missed you. And you'd better not leave me again."

"Any problem girls hanging around?" He poked his head in the door and looked around.

"Not a one...."

"Now you're going to have time for you?"

"I'm sick of me. I've had too much time for me."

"Then take time for me."

He laughed, and she laughed with him. She put out her hands, and he took them and pulled her inside, and they laughed again, like two silly kids. They held hands and laughed at nothing and everything. Like climbing to the top of a floating cloud, they seemed to lift each other, and neither of them could explain why. Finally, Kolby wiped his smile off and tried a serious, gruff voice on her.

"I am here to take you away on my flying machine. Pack a bag with a change of clothes, and turn your responsibilities over to a dozen other people. We're off on an adventure. I'm giving you a second chance at my surprise ... only this one isn't the same one. And if you miss this one, there won't be another. I'll give you three hours to make all your excuses and arrangements, and I'll be back." Kolby finished as he strode toward the door.

"You're serious, aren't you?" she asked, not wanting him to leave.

"Have you ever doubted that?"

"Yes ... no ... I mean...."

"Get yourself ready ... I'm taking you with me."

"How far, and for how long?"

"Don't you trust me? Faith, remember?"

"I remember."

"I'll see you."

Chapter Twenty-Five

"I've never done anything this crazy in my life," said Signee as she got into Kolby's car. He threw her bag into the trunk. "It is your car, isn't it? You aren't renting it from your roommate for a hundred dollars?" She was teasing, and Kolby responded by looking at her over his make-believe glasses and using a dramatically wise tone.

"My dear, little as it is, this car is mine."

"Little as it is? It must cost a fortune in gas."

"A small one ... but it runs, and has enough power to get me where I want to go."

"Four-wheel drive?"

"That's where I want to go."

"You are frightening me. I might need a chaperone."

"You just might," he said, roaring the motor as he backed out. "Did you leave word with anyone about where you'll be?"

"Why: Are you trying to cover our trail?"

"That, too ... but I want to make sure there's someone to rescue us if we don't get back."

"I should have left notes all over the house. Shall I go back?"

"Don't bother. I've taken care of all that."

"How?"

"Don't worry ... faith...."

"Can't I even ask where we are going now?"

"I guess that question is in order. But maybe I'd better wait until we're out of town, so you can't jump out of the car."

"That serious, huh?"

He looked at her out of the corner of his eye; there was a twinkle in his look that made her tingle. He twisted his head in a positive way. "That serious ... I thought you knew."

"Knew what?"

"That I've always wanted to capture you and ride off into the sunset."

"On a white steed?"

"I thought of that, but steeds these days are so slow ... Really, Sig, you've studied too much literature. Nowadays we use jeeps."

She looked at the heavy car, a few years old but luxuriously equipped. "This is a jeep?"

"No, but it works like one. I've been fixing it up."

"You do the craziest things. I thought your field was electricity."

"It is ... but I have a few sidelines that tie in."

"Like what?"

"I like art. Someday, we're going to tour Europe and haunt the art museums. I may even turn out to be a painter, if I ever get rich enough. I'm not talking, my dear, about that kind that daubs on brick or wood; but an artist, one that can fashion a face or sketch a city of some renown." He was dramatic again, and Signee laughed.

"Is that the way you're going to make your living?"

"Why?" He asked the question quickly. "Can't you struggle with an artist?"

"I can if he can afford me."

"Oh, mercenary, huh? Well, relax. That isn't the way I'm going to make a living; that's the way I'm going to spend my fortune after I make it. You have to be wealthy to struggle in the arts these days. First, I have to build my electronics factory."

"That's what you're doing?"

"Of course. Now stop asking questions, and get out that basket of food on the back seat. I'm starving."

Signee reached for the basket and lifted it over the seat. *That* was the beginning. They ate and talked and laughed, and she couldn't really tell when Kolby was serious and when he was kidding. But the atmosphere around him was enchanting. She felt alive, more alive than she had ever felt before; and she trusted him completely even with all his teasing and foolish talk.

"We live in a wonderful age, Sig ... we're on the verge of homes that will be run by computers. Our children will learn their math on a screen in the playroom. They can pick up a foreign language by color, and wake up to symphony music they won't even have to turn on."

"You are going to be rich, aren't you?"

"Reasonably ... enough to supply all our needs, and...."

"I wish I knew when you are telling the truth."

"About our electronic world, or our children?"

Signee looked up at him questioningly. There was a dear note in his voice that made her shake, as Kolby only went on sparkling ... that was the only word that came into her mind when she looked at him. He sparkled from somewhere within, like a light turned on inside him that came through his eyes and his words.

"Tell me a little about them both."

"Well, our children will be...."

"No, start on the electronic world. Talking about the children confuses me."

"Children are supposed to be confusing."

"No, I mean ... oh, just talk about our electronic world."

"I'm going to help build it. Would you like to be part of the operation?"

"Will I be part of the operation?"

Kolby shook his head, "You do ask the most leading questions."

"But you don't answer my questions, leading or not."

"All in good time. You'll see."

"When?"

He leaned forward and looked ahead, as if straining to see what wasn't there yet. "Any minute now ... you'll see a cut-off road on your right; we'll take it."

"To where?"

"It's just a little road that leads to a metal structure ... it's the beginning of an electronics plant. Inside the plant is the beginning of a company that will supply electronic equipment to an electronic world."

"What kind of electronic equipment?"

"Remember the lighting system we installed in your Drama Barn?"

"Yes."

"In the structure you will see, we will build panels of lights, high-intensity, that can be installed in drama barns, little theaters, wards, and cultural halls, that can be dropped in after the building is completed, can be portable or permanent, and be run by one well-trained man from the audience."

"Really? Lights make the show. Why, you wouldn't need scenery, or...."

"You've got it. And while we're perfecting that, we'll install computer systems for businesses and begin with home computers ... it's a world of wonder. I'm going to spend my life improving communication the electronic way, and ... oh, there's the road."

They turned onto the side road, which was hardly visible until they were practically on it. And, just as Kolby had promised, the metal structure came into view. Signee looked at the structure rising in front of them, and then at Kolby again. There was the sparkle again, that light inside him that came alive. On an impulse, she asked another question.

"Kolby, why haven't you ever married?"

"Because I couldn't find a girl who could live with me. I'm a dreamer; I chase rainbows. I'm not stable...."

"But you are. You took charge of...."

"Wait a minute, Sig." Kolby pulled off the road and parked his car on the edge of a hill overlooking the structure below. From where he parked, they could see the city just beyond the metal structure. "I want you to get a clear picture from up here, and then I'll take you inside. I'm not kidding you now ... I haven't wanted to be married because I didn't want a woman holding me down. My dreams are wild, and I have to fulfill them. I won't have much money for a long time. If I don't make my dream this time, if I'm stupid with the business end of my dream, then I may go broke and have to start over. But I won't give up ... I'll

240

never give up. I want to be part of the inventions that make life more beautiful, and I want financial security so that I can follow my art, and serve Heavenly Father whenever I'm called."

"You mean a mission ... another mission?"

"To whatever I'm called. You see, on my mission I got a taste of service and living by the spirit, and I knew the Gospel would always be my whole life. These other things have to fit in."

"Other things, like children and a wife?"

"Children and a wife will be part of my dream, and they'll have to go along with it. I have never allowed myself to fall in love, because I didn't want to share my dream or let anything tarnish it."

"So that's why you did the lights on the Drama Barn?"

"What do you mean?"

"You were experimenting; you were putting ideas together."

"Sure. If they work on a small scale, they'll work on a full, high-intensity scale. But that wasn't my main reason for taking the lighting job."

"What *was* your main reason?"

He turned and looked at her again, and she was frightened by the sparkle this time.

"I wanted to meet you. You are a girl with a dream—or maybe the modern word is goal. I've been reading literature, too."

"You came deliberately to get to know..."

He nodded. "To get to know you. I've put together some plans for my life, and I had to find someone who fit into them."

"And I passed the test?

"You passed. You almost outran me."

"What do you mean by that?"

"I resented your giving Minta the attention I wanted you to give me. Minta, the play ... Deek. When I left your Drama Barn that night, I meant never to return."

"Then why did you?"

"Because you were suddenly the main part of my dream. I couldn't visualize anything without you. Now, that's one for the books, isn't it?"

"I missed you too, Kolby. I have never missed anyone so much."

He turned to face her, his eyes full of the light she had seen in his sparkle of laughter. But this light was steady without the help of laughter. "I've changed my mind," he said abruptly, just as Signee thought he was going to take her in his arms.

"You've what?"

"I've changed my mind. I'm not going to show you all the stuff I'd planned. I'm going to take you home and marry you."

"But Kolby..."

He started the car and backed up to where he'd taken the cut-off road. "Don't argue with me, Signee ... I'll tell you about everything on the way back, but I can't be out here alone with you."

"Why not?"

"Because I'm a hot-blooded American boy, and I'd better marry you first and *then* show you the plant. Besides, I don't want to ruin your reputation—our future children have to live with us."

Chapter Twenty-Six

The ring Kolby brought with him the next time he came to see Signee was a diamond, a beautiful quality stone set high on a plain gold band.

"I can't really afford that, but we have to keep up appearances," he said as he slipped it on her finger. Signee laughed at his humor and squealed with delight as she ran to look at her finger in the mirror. Kolby followed her to stand behind her and smile down, even though his voice was full of practical sounds like a husband would make. "You have some qualities like other girls."

"Which ones? You mean I'm a female."

"I'll say you are and vain too ... looking at your diamond in the mirror. Can't you see it on your hand?"

"Not the way I want to see it. Kol, I can't wait until my family gets here to show them my ring."

"Are you only going to show your ring? I go with that piece of polished hard carbon...."

"They'll never believe it's real."

"The diamond?"

"Of course the diamond. I'll show them the diamond first,

you might frighten them." She was teasing him again.

"They'll have to get used to *me* if they want the diamond in the family."

"They'll want my diamond in our family," said Sig, turning around and holding up her hand. "Here, kiss it on."

"You mean kiss the ring?"

"Of course, you know I read literature, it's an old tradition of some country or another ... come on, kiss it on."

Lifting her hand Kolby kissed the ring and then kissed her, making her tingle all over. She wanted to laugh and cry at the same time. Then Kolby let her go reluctantly but went on talking as if the emotion hadn't touched him.

"I'm leaving everything in your hands," he said swallowing hard. "Get the wedding on ... and hurry it up, will you? I've got a lot of work to do and I don't like being alone."

"The folks will be home soon and then it won't take long."

"I'll call you every night and remind you. Then if you have any problems we can solve them over the phone before they get too big."

With those words Kolby had gone back to his work and Signee prepared the house for the home-coming of her parents and for the first time in her life she knew what complete happiness was. She trusted Kolby in everything he said and did, and she knew at last she had found a man with the strength and convictions she could follow without reservation. In the time span that followed he often warned her over and over that he didn't have much money and that her life with him would be a struggle, but Signee was happy at the thought they would be struggling together and the idea of ever being afraid of anything with Kolby beside her just wouldn't take root. And even though he said he didn't have much money, he always seemed to manage to have enough for whatever he needed.

In the beautiful summer months that followed Signee planned her wedding, worked on her trousseau, wrote to Minta and Deek and was thrilled when her family at last arrived home from their sabbatical leave in Europe. Now she would have help to finish the wedding details. She was delighted and found herself enjoying the most exciting time in her life.

There was only one blight on her new-found life. Minta was close to delivery and Signee knew the birth of the baby would be

244

running a race with her wedding. She was almost glad Minta couldn't attend the wedding because she didn't want to flaunt her happiness in the face of little Minta, who was struggling to overcome so much hurt. But she wanted to be with Minta when she needed her to and Signee felt she might have to choose between Minta and the wedding details. Then dramatically, just a few days before the wedding, she got a call.

"Minta has been taken to the hospital," said Miss Parker. "She's asking for you."

"Is she all right? I mean are there any complications?"

"Nothing definite, but she is calling for you."

"I'll come. Please tell Minta that I'll come."

Signee hung up a minute and then dialed Kolby's number. He wasn't home. Disappointed, she hung up and ran to put a few things into a carry-on for the plane. She wondered how long before she would be coming home. She hated leaving without talking to Kolby, but she decided it would be better to call him from the hospital than wait to try him again later. It was strange, she was thinking as she left word with her mother where to call her, how much she had learned to depend on Kolby for so much in such a short time. Then miraculously, just as she was leaving the telephone rang and it was Kolby.

"How did you know I needed you?" she asked and told him everything.

"Will you need me, Sig?" was all he said when she'd finished the explanation.

"I'll always need you," she answered, trying to swallow past the lump in her throat.

"Then I'll be there."

"No, darling . . . you don't need to come, not this time. You go ahead and finish your work so we can get married on schedule. I'll be all right this time and Minta might not like us both mothering her. But call, Kolby, please call."

"I'll call Sig . . . I'll call. . . ."

Feeling teary-eyed with gratitude, Signee hung up and once again felt a surge of assuredness that at last, after all the years of wondering, she had really found someone strong enough for her to lean on and turn to for help when she had decisions to make.

While Signee waited to board the plane she called Minta's

parents to see if they would like to be with her. They weren't home, they'd gone on a business trip, the secretary reported, Signee felt a wave of sympathy for Minta who was so alone that her parents didn't feel it necessary to be close to her at a time of such heartbreaking suffering.

The delivery of Minta's small daughter wasn't an easy one and Signee was glad to be with Minta, to hold her hand and whisper comfort to her when she was frightened. As Minta cried out in pain she dug her nails into Signee's arm and then she'd apologize for the trouble she was causing. It was unlike the old Minta to be considerate of others. Signee couldn't help noticing how much Minta had changed, she was becoming a lady.

As Minta twisted with pain and the perspiration stood out on her body, Signee held her hand and prayed to keep from crying. She couldn't help thinking about Kolby and how much she wanted him to be with her when they had their children, not alone like little Minta. And as she thought, she held on to Minta even tighter and tried not to think of what she was going through and how she'd feel when she couldn't keep the baby she was risking her life to give birth to.

At last when Minta was so worn out she couldn't yell any more, when they had put her quietly to sleep to rest and had taken her little daughter to the nursery to be bathed, Signee went into a small room off the hall close by and broke into tears. Away from having to lend Minta strength, she was able to shed all the tears that had been welling up inside her for the sweet courageous girl who had just become a mother to lose her child. Yet she was so proud of Minta, so impressed with her willingness to sacrifice and give birth ... somehow she knew she'd be strong enough now to complete the repentance that would eventually give her back a life that was better than the one she had known before.

"Is she beautiful?" asked Minta a few hours later, when Signee looked up from the chair beside her bed to see Minta open her eyes.

"I don't know, honey, they haven't let me see her. She's still being watched, but the doctor came by and said she was just perfect and that you could see her any minute now."

"Please ... ring for the nurse, Siggie."

246

"Do you feel up to it?"

"Yes," said Minta moving in bed to show she was awake and able. "Oh...." she said as a pain caught her, and she lay back on her pillow again.

"Do you hurt?"

"I'm fine."

"The doctor said you were very cooperative and as near as he can check you out, you are right as right and will be able to get up today."

"Can I see my...." Minta began but was cut off as the door opened. A nurse signaled Signee it was time to leave, and placed a small bundle in Minta's arms.

Signee stepped into the hall and waited. The nurse came out and apologized.

"I'm sorry, it's the rule...."

"I understand," said Signee. "The baby is all right, isn't she?"

"Ten fingers and ten toes ... as the saying goes. Mother and baby doing fine."

"Thanks for telling me." Then as the nurse moved away Signee asked, "Is this the only time...." she couldn't bring herself to finish the question. The nurse understood and nodded.

"Yes, this is the only time she will ever see her baby."

"I see...." said Signee and turned to walk toward the window so she wouldn't cry in front of the nurse, then turned back to ask another question. "Will the new parents pick her up when she is thirty-six hours old?"

"Yes, that is the rule," said the nurse and walked rapidly away.

As Signee left the floor she was trying not to cry any more. She needed to be strong for Minta, but when she stepped off the elevator and found Kolby waiting beside the open door on the first floor, the tears burst forth as he put his arms around her.

"Here ... that's not my girl...." He started to try lightness but ended up just holding her tight until the tears began to subside. Then he led her quietly to a chair just outside the waiting room.

"Well, I must have touched the shower button," he said seriously.

"You did, Kol, and it's electronically controlled to be very sensitive where Minta is concerned. How did you know I needed you?"

"I thought you might need a cushioned arm around you."

"Dear cushioned arm," she said touching his muscle. "You'll never know how much. Oh, Kol, it is so sad to see how brave she is and how much she's going through . . . and to know she can never have that baby. . . ."

"That's a tough one. Heavenly Father will give her some special blessings for doing the right thing . . . after the hurt has passed."

"I hope so . . . I do hope so, Kol."

"If He doesn't deal kindly with her . . . well, He'd better take a good look at our Minta's problems or I'll just have to talk to him personally."

It was a silly statement, as if he really meant to talk to Heavenly Father personally, as if they could talk face to face. Signee realized with Kol, that was the way it was . . . his own personal Heavenly Father. She felt comfort in that.

"Do you have to stay here long?"

"No, I just have to say goodbye. I've done all I can for Minta right now. I do hope the couple who gets little Min is a worthy . . . Oh, Kol, don't you wish it was Eric and Alta? How I wish they could. . . ."

"Come on, Sig, you know what Miss Parker said . . . and it would be hard, especially with Minta, to know where her baby is . . . she wouldn't be able to stay away."

"I know," said Signee, "but it would be so. . . ."

"Go on, check out with Minta and we'll be on our way. You've got a wedding to go to."

"I know. . . ." she smiled, "but I wish I could do something to cheer Minta up, something to ease her hurt. . . ."

"Maybe she'd like to visit Grandfather," said Kolby looking serious.

In spite of herself, Signee laughed. "Kolby, there's no one like you. Can you just imagine how hard it would be for Minta to visit a stranger, feeling like she does? Especially a man?"

"Grandfather isn't a stranger, and I've always been glad he's a man."

"Well, good for you . . . now stop trying to make me laugh. I'm really concerned about Minta. When she's up and back at work

248

in the Drama Barn, I think she will be fine; she can take some classes at college, and meet some new people, and help kids. But right now, it's going to be really hard for her."

"I think you might be underestimating your Minta, Sig. She's toughened up these last months."

"She really has come a long way. But I feel so...."

That wasn't the end of their communication with Minta; there was more to come. But on arriving home, Signee had a call that cheered her up. It was from Eric, and Alta was on the extension.

"Sig, we won't be able to come to your wedding,"said Eric. And Alta added, "That's right, Sig."

"Well you don't sound heartbroken. What are you two up to?"

"You tell her," said Alta. "All right," said Eric, and proceeded. "Well, Sig, you see ... the long months of waiting are over ... we are being smiled upon."

"Can't you guess?" said Alta, too happy to contain herself.

"You aren't? Not after all this time...."

"I'm not going to have a baby...." said Alta.

"She's getting one," put in Eric.

"Tell ... tell me all!" said Sig, using the words she and Alta had always used when they were in school together.

"Our bishop called this morning," said Eric.

"He's been working with a social worker in our behalf ... he's kept it quiet because he knows how long we've waited, and he didn't want us to be disappointed again."

"But we can pick her up tomorrow...." added Eric "So, you see, no wedding...."

"Some excuse for not coming," said Signee, unable to keep her happiness for them out of her voice.

"It's taken a long time, but we were lucky this time...."

The rest of the conversation was mostly just happiness, and Signee hung up thinking Heavenly Father had really answered her prayers and brought happiness to her two friends. The news came in time to ease the hurt of knowing that Minta was giving her baby away while Alta and Eric didn't have one. She smiled, and spent a long time on her knees that night.

It was about midnight when the phone rang again. This time it was Miss Parker.

"Miss Short, this is Miss Parker. I'm probably out of line doing this ... but I thought you might like to know that Minta is having quite a time. I'm afraid she's going to keep her baby, in spite of the odds."

"But she can't keep her baby ... she can't ever find her way back alone, and her parents will literally disown her."

"I know. We've talked about all that, but she seems determined. I feel sorry for her; she doesn't really know how hard it will be to raise a baby alone."

"And the baby ... what about the baby?"

"I know, Miss Short ... well, I just thought you should know."

"Is she asking for me?"

"No, I think she's determined to do this by herself."

"I'll come anyway."

Signee hung up and called Kolby. He came right over.

"She can't do this, Kol," said Signee, grateful that she and Kol were sharing this together. "She'll wreck her whole life, and that baby's ... I've got to go to her."

"Right now?"

"If I don't she may do something crazy like getting out of there, and we might never find her. Minta is strong-willed, and when her thinking gets mixed up you can't tell what she'll do. She's been level-headed for the first time in her life; but with all the emotion, and being weak from giving birth...."

"In fact, I think she's a little weak to be taking off."

"What shall I do, Kol?"

"What you have to. Will it help if you're with her?"

"I don't know. She usually talks to me, and when she talks she gets sensible."

"All right, let's go."

"Will you come with me? Oh, Kol, what did I ever do without you?"

"I'm puzzled about that myself. But I'm here now, and I won't go away. You're dangerous, Sig. With your emotional values, somebody could rip you off."

She laughed. Kol could always make her laugh; and somehow, when she laughed she relaxed.

Chapter Twenty-Seven

"I know what you're here for, Siggie, and it won't do you any good," said Minta when she saw Signee standing inside her room. She and the baby had come home from the hospital early; the nurses had been helping her at first, but now Minta stood up by herself, determination showing in every muscle. She was in the house where she'd stayed during her pregnancy, packing what few things she had.

"Minta, how can you do this?"

"How can I do this?" Minta shouted. "How can I *not* do this? She's my daughter; she looks like me. She is the only thing in this whole world that belongs just to me."

"And with the ownership you are going to ruin the lives of her new parents, your life, and her life."

"I'm going to love her and take care of her. No one can love her as much as I do."

"Is that right? What kind of a love is it when you care more about your own feelings than the feelings of your child?"

"What would you know about it? You haven't ever had a baby. Sig, I have borne her body, I have felt her grow within me. I have lived with her for nine months, and she's mine. I can't give her up; I can't. Even though I want to, even though I know maybe her life with other parents might be happier, I can't give her up. Heavenly Father would never forgive me if I gave up my own child."

"Not unless you are giving her up to a better life."

"How can she have a better life with someone who isn't her real mother? No ... no, no, no ... I'm going to keep her, and nothing you can say will make any difference. I know I said I would give her up, but I've changed my mind. I have a right to do that; that's why I don't have to sign the final papers until she's born. I've changed my mind. Now leave me alone."

There was no use arguing; Signee could tell that. The old Minta of pre-baby days had returned. Signee sat down on the edge of the bed resignedly.

"All right, Minta. You're going to keep her. All right ... are you going to take her home to your parents?"

"No ... I can't do that, and you know it. Do you think I would submit her to Mother and her club? Besides, they wouldn't let me come home. I got a very nice wire today: 'Congratulations, dear, it's almost over. We're wiring you some money so you can take a little trip somewhere to make you feel better before you come home. P.S. Buy some new clothes. Love, Mother and Father.' You see, they want to make sure there are no tell-tale bulges in my figure, and that I'm wearing the proper clothes. No, I can't take her to that."

"All right. Where, then?"

"I'll get a job. Maybe my parents will lend me enough money to last until I get a good job."

"When they find out you're keeping the baby?"

"How will they find out?"

"How will you hide it?"

"Oh, Siggie ... it will work out. Aren't you always saying that?"

"I think my saying is ... don't worry, we'll find a way."

"All right ... all right ... now that you've said your speech, get out of here."

"All right, Minta. I'll go."

Signee got up and walked toward the door, wondering what was going to happen to Minta, knowing how stubborn she could be, praying she would know what to say and do.

"Siggie...."

"Yes, Minta."

"Oh, Siggie, don't be mad at me. Siggie, have you seen her? She is so lovely; she is the most wonderful thing on this earth, and she's mine. Don't ask me to give her up. I would do anything for you, Siggie, but don't ask me to give her up." Her voice was pleading and gentle now.

Signee shook her head and didn't turn around. "I won't, Minta ... I won't. That isn't my decision to make."

"Don't you think I will love her? Don't you think I will be a good mother?"

Signee turned around, her eyes full of tears. She walked back and kissed Minta, as she had so often. "I think you will be a very good mother, Minta. I know you will love your daughter; I'm not worried about that."

"Then don't worry about anything."

"I have to. I have to worry about the baby. How will you take care of her, Minta? Who will take care of her while you work? If there was anyone you loved that would marry you ... if you had help...."

"You love me, Siggie. You'll tend her for me, won't you?"

"Of course. And you'll announce to the world your mistake, and your baby will have to live with it all of her life. She is so innocent, Minta. Why punish her?"

"But I'm not punishing her. I need her ... I'll love her ... Siggie, you could take her, adopt her if you want to. And when I'm married, when I find a good father for her, I could adopt her back and move away, and...."

Signee turned sad eyes to look at Minta. "Yes, I could do that. And you can toss her from one to another, and break all our hearts ... yours, mine, her waiting parents' and hers. Do you think you can look at her day by day, and watch her go through the trials a broken home can give her, and not hate yourself? And, hating yourself, do you think you won't take it out on her? Sure, she's sweet and lovely now, and you'll cherish her even after working hours. But when she grows up unstable, mixed up because of being tossed around, and knows what you have done to her ... how will you love her then?"

"I can't give her up...." Minta began to cry, sinking back on the bed, trembling with weakness and emotion. Signee went to her.

"Oh, Minta, think. Think how difficult it will be for you. Think how hard it will be to start a new life, to change your pattern of living when you have a baby you aren't physically or financially able to take care of."

"*You* think, Siggie . . . think how empty my arms will be. Think how my heart will hurt every day of my life without her."

"I am thinking, Minta. It won't be easy; it will be the hardest thing you have ever done in your life. But you've come through some really rough things already, and with flying colors. I'm thinking of that; and I'm also thinking of two people who are waiting for her, two people that can't have any children of their own. They are somewhere right now, waiting." Signee was thinking of the happiness she'd heard in Eric's and Alta's voice. "I'm thinking of their empty arms, too," she went on. "I'm thinking of a little, new, well-equipped nursery, with diapers and teddy bears, just waiting for a new little baby girl to fill it, and the hearts of those two parents, who will give her a happy, normal life, and will take her to the temple to be sealed to them for time and all eternity."

"You care more about parents you don't know than you care about me!"

Minta was striking back. Signee knew she didn't believe what she said, but she had to let her think things out. Signee's voice was quiet, understanding, and tender.

"Yes, I'm thinking of my friends—my friends who have just adopted their first child. You should have heard their joy. And I'm thinking of you. But most, I'm thinking about your daughter. Only you can decide what you want for your baby. I'll love you and help you any way you decide. But this is the moment. You can't change your mind tomorrow or the next day, or when your daughter begins to give you problems. This is for always." Signee took Minta's hand and kissed her cheek.

"Signee, I want to think of her, too. I want her to be loved, and I want to do something for her . . . to bathe her and feed her, and. . . ."

"And stand over a sickbed sometimes? And get up in the night after working all day? I know, Minta . . . but don't you see? You *have* done something for your daughter. You gave her life; you gave her her chance on earth; no one can ever take that away from you. Only you have been able to give her a mortal body. In all the eternities to come, she will always be grateful. If now you decide to also give her a normal life, no matter what the cost to yourself, she will be grateful for that, too. And Minta, you are so pretty; you will have other children someday, when you have filled your life full of good things and found that one special person. You know, it helps to make up for our mistakes when we try to set things right. That's part of repenting ... to make up to those we have sinned against."

"You mean this is my mistake, and my daughter shouldn't have to pay for it?"

"That's the way I see it. No one can say what is right for you; no one can see the future except Heavenly Father. All I want you to do is be sure you see the baby's side as well as yours, and then be very prayerful before you make up your mind. You will be blessed for loving your daughter, and I know it is harder to give her up than to keep her ... right now. I can't decide for you. I'll always love you, Minta, but I know I shouldn't interfere with your life. You have to make your decisions and live with the blessings or consequences. Be prayerful, little Minta. I'm going now. I can't help you—I just came back because I thought you might need me. I'll go home, and I'll do whatever you want me to do to help you."

"You're going back today?"

"I have to, Minta. My wedding is only a few days off, and I have so much to do. Kolby has been very patient."

"Oh yes, your wedding. I wish I could see you married."

"You can come if you want to; you're invited."

"My parents would love that ... and so would all the other gossips in town. It will take me a while to get my tummy in shape."

"Whatever you want...."

Minta stood there. Signee knew she was about to cry, so she left quickly.

Chapter Twenty-Eight

"I've made up my mind," said Minta, sitting beside her bed and putting on her shoes. She was dressed, her hair combed, and she was wearing makeup which gave her face a rose color.

"And do you need some help?"

"Only moral support."

"You've got it. Kolby is outside."

"Will you drive me back to the hospital?"

"You're going to take your baby?"

"No, I'm going to see her once more."

"Minta...."

"Don't talk about it, Sig. If I do this thing, it will take every bit of courage we both have. I want her, Sig...." Minta's lip quivered. "But I haven't earned the right ... not yet ... to have a baby. You first have to have a husband ... I haven't earned that right."

Signee wanted to take Minta in her arms, but she knew this wasn't the time.

"I'm pretty weak, Siggie ... I keep flopping back to my old emotional ways, don't I?"

"Each time you're strong makes you stronger for the next

time."

"I hope so...." She looked up at Signee, and the look in her eyes cut deep into Signee as she said, "Your Kolby is a super person, isn't he?"

Sig nodded. "Truly super, Minta."

"Like my Deek?"

"Like your Deek."

"And Deek might have been my Deek, if I hadn't blown it."

"There are other Deeks around, and we don't know how Deek will feel when he comes home."

"Oh, I could never find another Deek. And I couldn't ever have this one, even if he wanted me. I would always feel so unworthy."

"Not if you change your life and make up for your mistakes."

"With his code of ethics, he could never forgive what I've done. I wouldn't ask him to."

"Maybe not. You've done a lot of growing up though, and there are men who have also done some growing up. Deek will do a lot of growing up on his mission. Only time will answer those questions ... time, and what you do with your life. You mustn't be impatient."

"No, impatience got me where I am today. I'll do my best to learn. I guess there will be a lot of times when I flop back ... just like I did this morning. After you left, I walked back to the hospital."

"All that way?"

"Three blocks isn't very far; I felt my strength come back. When I got there, I went in and looked at my daughter for a long time. She was so small, and so perfect ... and while I looked at her, I found myself praying ... and your words kept coming back to me. You are right, you know. I can never give her anything but confusion with my love. I called Miss Parker, and she has arranged to handle everything ... after I say goodbye."

"Minta...."

"Siggie, don't say you're proud of me ... I can't stand your sympathy right now. Will you please just drive me to the hospital, and then from there to a plane?"

"Whatever we can do to help you."

The scene in the hospital was a heartbreaking picture. Minta picked up her little baby and walked to the room off the nursery, where she sat in a chair and held her and rocked back and forth. Signee, watching, held tight to Kolby's arm. They heard Minta humming a little song, and saw her put her finger inside the grasp of the tiny hand. Then she was quiet, looked up and closed her eyes; Signee thought she must be praying. The tears dripped from under her eyelids and rolled down her face onto the blanket around her little daughter. Then Minta kissed the baby and held her over her shoulder, putting her cheek against the baby's cheek. Then, for a minute, she looked as if she was talking to the baby quietly in her ear. Then Minta wiped her eyes and took the baby back to the nurse. Releasing her tenderly, she went to meet Kolby and Signee.

"Can you wait just a minute more? I want to talk to Miss Parker." Signee looked at Kolby; he nodded. Minta went to the other end of the hall, through a glass door, and they saw Miss Parker come to meet her. She was gone longer than they expected; then she reappeared, and came to them again.

"I'm ready now. Thank you for waiting."

Silently, Kolby opened the door and let the two girls go ahead. They didn't say anything until they were in the car, and Minta told them which airport she wanted to go to.

"Where are you going, Minta?"

"I'm flying to California. My parents are paying the bills on a two weeks' stay in the Disneyland Hotel while I swim, sun, and get my figure back. I told you."

"Yes, but not where. You will write, won't you, Minta?"

"Without you to write to, I would die . . . I just said goodbye to the only other person. . . ." Her voice broke, and she was quiet.

"You can write to me, too, Minta," Kolby added with his usual effort at humor. They all smiled, but they weren't ready for laughter.

"Want to know what I said to my little daughter?" Without waiting for an answer, Minta went on, "I told her I had said a prayer about her new parents, and I knew they were good, and that Miss Parker had promised they would be parents who would take her to the temple and make her theirs through all eternity. I told her she was going to have a real family, and I knew she would be happy and live a good life. It's funny, isn't it, that I didn't realize what is important in life until I had my daughter?"

Signee reached for Minta's hand, and just held it. Minta didn't seem to notice, but started talking again.

"Then I went to meet Miss Parker, and I asked her to wait while I wrote a letter to my daughter." She looked at Signee now, as if feeling a need to explain. "I want her to have the letter in case she ever wonders about why I gave her up." She looked out the front window again, as if still living the words she had written. "In the letter I told her how much I loved her, and how hard it is to give her to somebody else, but that I love her so much I want her to have a beautiful life with a father and a mother. I thanked her that I had the honor of preparing her little earthly body, and I promised her I would try to live so she won't be ashamed of me when we meet somewhere in the eternities." She looked at Signee again, as if for approval. "I had to let her know I love her, that I didn't give her away because I didn't love her. It's terrible to think you aren't wanted or loved. I always thought my parents didn't love me, that I was just a problem to them. Now I know they do love me . . . in their own way. Siggie, I had to let her know."

"Of course you did," was all Signee could say, as she held her hand tighter. Minta didn't seem to notice; it was if she was numb.

They arrived at the airport, and Kolby got out of the car and helped Minta with her luggage. They stood together, the three of them, while Minta waited for her ticket and to have her luggage checked.

"I want to put my thinking back together while I sun my skin, Siggie, but I'll be home in a little while. You can tell my parents I'll write to them, if you will. You know, Siggie, I wish I had known what I know now before I ever started dating Barney. He didn't ever think of me the way he said he did, and he was wrong when he said we wouldn't hurt anybody else."

Signee couldn't trust herself to talk. She just put her arm around Minta as they walked to the waiting room. And suddenly the sun came out, filling the whole room through the big glass wall; and the light was as if, symbolically, Heaven was sending a blessing to warm their hearts. No one said anything; they just responded, feeling better because of the light. Then Minta slipped out of the circle of Signee's arm.

"Goodbye for a little while, Siggie . . . Kol, please take care of her. She's pretty special."

"You're pretty special yourself," said Kolby, as he put his arm around Minta and gave her a hug.

"Oh, go have a wedding," said Minta, and hurried toward the boarding room.

"We'd better make sure she gets where she's going," said Kolby, who had been the one most anxious to leave a minute earlier.

"She knows where she's going. She'll find her way now."

Minta talked to the ticket man beside the sliding doors, and then ran back to Signee and Kolby.

"My plane leaves in fifteen minutes. You two don't need to wait around any more. I'm strong as can be, and I'll soon be buying me some new clothes, and . . . and Sig, . . . don't you dare give my directing job to anybody else. You said I could have it."

"You can have it, Minta."

"I'm going to like working with kids . . . look what it got you!" She blew a kiss to Kolby, waved to Signee, and ran to catch her plane.

"Come on, Sig, I'm going to see to it that you are a bride before another Minta comes into your life. Too many Mintas can turn you into an old lady before I get a chance to make you a wife."

Together they turned and ran toward the car.

They drove all night. When they got home, Kolby dropped Signee at her home and promised to meet her the next day by noon. Signee showered and fell into bed. She slept soundly for the first time since Minta's baby had been born. The next morning, she was aware of the bustle of the family and the phone ringing . . . it was good to have a family again. She'd put a pillow over her ears in order to sleep a little longer; but as the family went on their way and the house was quiet again, she rolled out of bed and into the shower. She'd have to rush to be ready in time when Kolby came by for her . . . they had a lot of last-minute details to arrange for their wedding.

"Good morning, dear," said her mother cheerfully as she appeared in the kitchen and went to the fridge for her juice. "Eric called last night."

"Eric? What's the matter? Is it Alta?"

"He didn't say. He wanted to talk to you, but I had the feeling it wasn't good news."

"Oh, what has happened? I hope Alta is all right. I'll call him."

She drank her juice, put her glass in the dishwasher, kissed her mother, and stepped into the bathroom to put some finishing touches on her hair. She heard Kolby's car outside. Looking at her watch, she raced to the telephone and dialed Eric's number. She got him at home.

"Eric? What's the matter?"

"Sig? Is that you?"

"Yes. Mother said you called, and you didn't sound too happy. But you sound all right now. What's up?"

"Well, last night I called because I was as low as a guy can get."

"Why?"

"I was worried about Alta. You know, she's had hopes and disappointments so often with this baby thing...."

"What's happened? Didn't you get the baby?"

"We did ... a beautiful little daughter ... Alta is walking on air."

"Oh, Eric. I'm so happy. You really have her?"

"We do ... beautiful as ... so beautiful, there is nothing to compare."

"Tell Alta I love her, and I forgive her for not coming to the wedding. But what frightened you?"

"You don't know what we've been through. The bishop called, just about the time we were getting ready to go with him, and said the mother had changed her mind and wouldn't give up the baby."

"Oh, Eric, how hard."

"I thought it would kill Alta. It was almost like we'd had her and she died. But I was proud of Alta. She rallied; you know, she's getting used to taking it. And then the bishop called again and said he'd be by, that it was all settled. And Sig, we've got her ... the papers are all signed, and she is ours—or as much as she can be for a year. Then we'll take her to the temple and have her sealed to us, and she will always be ours."

"Eric ... I'm so happy for you. I've got to go now; the groom is at the front door. Tell Alta I will call her later and get the details."

Signee hung up. "Mother, Eric and Alta are the parents of a new baby girl."

262

"Yes, I know."

"Well, they thought they weren't, but they are ... tell you later."

Signee hurried to the door and ran into Kolby's arms. Turning, they ran down the steps together and into his waiting car.

"Shall we check on the pictures for framing first?"

"Fine," said Signee, settling down in the seat beside Kolby. She was thoughtful, but smiling.

"All right, what are you thinking?"

"I was thinking how blessed I am."

"I told you that."

"I know ... but I have a few side orders of happiness, too. First Minta settling her life, and now Eric and Alta."

"What about Eric and Alta?"

"They have a new daughter."

"I know, you told me."

"No, they thought they'd lost her. The mother had changed her mind, you know, just like Minta did. But then they got her back. Yes, I've had a lot of blessing."

"Just like Minta ... ?" The usually noisy Kolby was suddenly quiet. Signee caught his thinking and sat up.

"Just like Minta? You don't think...."

"I don't know. It's quite a coincidence, isn't it?"

"It really is," said Signee, her mind racing. Then she shook her head. "No, it's too fantastic."

"But possible ... even though they are so far away."

"I wonder if they do that."

"What?"

"Place a baby quite a few miles away."

"Sounds logical."

"Oh, Kolby, you are an incurable romantic."

"We'll never know, will we?"

"I guess we won't. I only saw Minta's baby once and her head was still swollen from birth. I'd never recognize her after it—"she stopped—"never mind, I'm just going to be grateful that everything has worked out for everybody."

"I have to admit, Sig, that when you save a life you do a good job."

"Yes. And if you were going to add," she cuddled even closer under his arm, "that the life I've saved has been my own, you are absolutely right." She smiled up at him and wrapped both her arms around his one. He looked down at her out of the corner of his eye.

"Hey, what are you doing so far away? Come closer."

She laughed and pushed herself away. The car swerved, then recovered.

"Look what you did, bride ... you almost caused a wreck."

"I almost did ... but I don't have to worry. I've got a strong groom ... he recovers quickly."

"Lucky for you, I do," he smiled and pulled her head down on his shoulder, as he touched the bright light switch with his foot and flooded the road with a beam of light to guide them home through the night.